Sudhindra Nath Ghose (1899–1965)—best known as Sudhin Ghose—was born in Bardhaman in Bengal. He moved to Europe as a student in the 1920s where he first studied science and art history before completing a doctorate in literature. Though he spent his entire writing career in the West, Sudhin Ghose, like his contemporaries Mulk Raj Anand, R.K. Narayan and Raja Rao, based his work on India, drawing material from the villages and towns of Bengal. An impeccable prose stylist and a master of sprawling narratives which draw inspiration from myths, fables, legends and epics, Sudhin Ghose is among the greatest writers in Indian English literature.

Sudhin Ghose wrote journalistic pieces, a scholarly tract, and three volumes of Indian folktales apart from the work for which he is best remembered: a quartet of novels comprising *And Gazelles Leaping* (1949), *Cradle of the Clouds* (1951), *The Vermilion Boat* (1953) and *The Flame of the Forest* (1955).

THE FLAME OF THE FOREST

SUDHIN N. GHOSE

SPEAKING TIGER

SPEAKING TIGER PUBLISHING PVT. LTD
4381/4 Ansari Road, Daryaganj,
New Delhi–110002, India

First published by Michael Joseph, London 1955

ISBN: 978-93-86338-54-9
e-ISBN: 978-93-86338-55-6

10 9 8 7 6 5 4 3 2 1

Typeset in Adobe Jenson Pro by Jojy Philip
Printed at Thomson Press India Ltd.

PART ONE

Cave Canem

I

'One good turn, you know.' He grinned slyly as he plucked a few chords of his lute. He then sermonized, 'One good turn deserves another.'

I did not like his looks, while the sight of his partner was positively frightening: a nautch-girl in gaudy tinsels, loaded with cheap jewellery and decked with jingling bells; she was veiled like a bride ready for the wedding ceremony.

'Mr Scholar!' The street-musician went on, 'You don't mind my telling you the truth. You are young, and you have many things to learn.'

I loathed his addressing me in a familiar fashion. But what could I do? I did not see an easy way of escape. The crowd formed a circular wall round me, or rather round the three of us. So I had to listen to his palaver. Finally, profiting from a pause, I mumbled something about my being in a hurry. I had an important appointment for a job.

'I understand,' he said, and nudged at the nautch-girl.

'Of course, we understand,' she repeated like a trained talking bird, and curtsied. 'Great men are always busy. They have little time for poor folks like us. But, Mr Scholar, it would do you no harm to listen to a song. You don't care for dancing, you say. But what about singing? Certainly you are not in such a hurry as to refuse to hear a song.'

'I always tell her,' the other broke in, 'Myna, it is good to do a good turn at all times.'

'Even when one is in a hurry,' Myna commented.

'She has a good voice,' the musician declared. 'She dances divinely. It would delight anyone's heart to watch her pirouette. She is straight as a deodar and supple like a wand of willow.'

Myna made a deep reverence to express her full approval of what was said. The bells of her armlets and anklets tinkled. She parted her veil to wink at me. I noticed she was heavily painted—her eyes and eyebrows ornamented with kohl.

'That's very nice of you,' I stammered.

'You are a Rajah,' Myna warbled. 'A prince should not refuse a poor woman's plea. You should come with us to hear me sing.'

Evidently they want to be tipped, I thought. I cursed Calcutta's traffic for getting me into such a scrape. Reluctantly I dug my hand into my pocket: there was just enough money for the return to my hostel. 'What must I do,' I asked myself, 'to get rid of this wretched couple? That woman is certainly a tart.'

'Mr Scholar! Never refuse the invitation of a friend,' the fellow kept on. His voice sounded more oleaginous than ever. 'I am your friend.'

'If I were you,' someone counselled from the crowd, 'I should make the most of a bad bargain.'

'So should I,' cooed Myna. 'So would any reasonable person, Mr Scholar.'

'Thank you,' I mumbled, withdrawing my hand from my pocket. 'Thank you. I do appreciate what you say. But I have an urgent appointment. Moreover, I fear I haven't much money with me. You are wasting your time on me.'

'Money!' The street-musician manifested his indignation with a theatrical gesture by throwing out his arms and swinging his lute: the instrument almost grazed my face. I stepped back just in time. The lute, or whatever else it was, seemed to be a formidable weapon. Its stem was short, bent at the top, and its body looked like a large melon, strengthened with bands of wood—several layers thick. 'Money!' He cried, 'Heavens! Who wants money from a well-wisher? It would be a crime to accept any money from you.'

'It would be mortal sin,' Myna chimed in. 'You are more than a friend. You are like a brother. For services to a brother does a sister expect any money?' To emphasize her argument she made another impressive reverence, bending her body double and almost touching the ground with her forehead; she got up without the least effort and stood immobile on the tips of her toes. I could judge she was lithe, and in spite of her buxomness, her limbs were remarkably supple. She was sinuous, like a serpent. 'For you,' she continued, 'everything is gratis. On the house, as they say. You have a heart of gold, and that's wealth enough for us. We are at your service.'

'Always,' he said, coming closer to me. 'We are at your disposal, any time, any day. One good turn, let me repeat, deserves another.'

'I am not out for a ride,' I muttered half-audibly.

'The moment Uncle saw you,' Myna began, without heeding my imprecations, 'he nudged me. And I said, "That's an honest face." "He must be an up-country man," he replied. "Someone from the hills," I remarked. "A hillbilly, if you will. A simpleton, if you prefer. But he has an honest face. I will sing for him, I will dance for him, I will do anything for him." Didn't I say so, Uncle?'

'Of course, you did,' the musician replied. 'And I told Myna,

"An honest face is often a rogue's asset. It is a mask to cover his devilry." I never judge a man by his mask.'

'A tree should be judged by its fruits,' Myna responded like a schoolgirl repeating her lesson. 'And a man by his deeds.'

'That's it,' he declared triumphantly. 'That's what I tell Myna every day: Judge a man by his deeds. Mr Scholar, you are an honest man with an honest face.'

'We were sure you would let your purse be pinched in no time.'

'That's exactly what happened. The man who patted you on the back took away your purse.'

'I told Myna your story. You have helped me more than once. You are more than a friend to me.'

They kept on this sort of patter without paying any attention to my pompous remark in English, 'Who steals my purse, steals trash.'

Though I was no townee I did not like the idea of being labelled 'an up-country man,' 'a plain yokel,' by a bazaar musician and his tart of a nautch-girl. I had half a mind to tell them frankly what I thought of them. But as I did not know my bearings in that strange quarter of Calcutta, I let them do their spouting and salaaming. After all, they were willing to show me the way.

'Who steals my purse,' I repeated, 'steals trash.' The thing was not worth much. It was an empty wallet the pickpocket stole from me. It contained my expired pass to the Indian Museum Reading Room, the notice of my prospective expulsion from the ASA—the Alipore Swimmers' Association—for non-payment of membership dues and a few odd cuttings from newspapers, advertisements of vacancies: these, as I have said, were of no great value.

Though hailing from the backwoods, I was not quite a

greenhorn. Or perhaps because I was relatively green, I was more cautious than most true-born sons of Calcutta.

The city's reputation of harbouring thousands of light-fingered pickpockets and bold cut-purses is, I believe, universally established. It is, of course, well known in the Penhari village I come from. 'Calcutta,' they say in the Penhari Parganas, 'boasts of at least a million certified kleptomaniacs, without counting its lawyers, doctors, and professional patriots. They are defter than the habitual thieves, and certainly more nefarious.'

'No action,' it was generally held by my villagers, 'can be taken against Calcutta's maniacs because they carry medical certificates testifying to their congenital weakness. The city fathers are charitable to them, and so are the lawyers and jurors. "Our poor brethren," the authorities sigh, "they are mentally feeble." Therefore they are allowed to roam about the streets and to pocket surreptitiously anything they fancy. Apart from the kleptomaniacs, there are in Calcutta many dangerous lunatics and uncertified eccentrics.'

'It must be pretty risky to live in Calcutta.'

'Risky is not the word,' the wise men of the village enunciated. 'Living in any city is risky, whereas in Calcutta it is positively dangerous. Even a stroll down a so-called quiet street in that megalopolis is full of hazards. Be careful. Don't allow yourself to be fleeced. Never carry more than the bare minimum with you. Just your tram fare and no more. A few annas at most, and these too in loose coins—copper cents. Otherwise you will have to fight with the tram and bus conductors.'

'Fight! Whatever for?'

'If you give him a ten-rupee note, the conductor will give you your ticket and the change for five rupees. "Where's the rest?" you may ask, and he will snarl back, "What more do you want?

You gave me a five-rupee note, and I have given you your change." Give him a five-rupee note you will get the change for a rupee. It's no use arguing with a conductor in Calcutta.'

'Why?'

'The Law is always on his side. A passenger is expected to tender the exact fare. And that's that.'

Will not a policeman help?'

'Great God! A policeman is not paid to help you. If you are knocked down by a taxi you will find a score of them rushing towards you—not to help, but to handcuff you—for careless walking and causing obstruction. Remember, the more people a policeman arrests the quicker his promotion. That's the Law in Calcutta.'

'Are there no friendly conductors and policemen?'

'Friendliness in Calcutta! That's rare, very rare indeed. The laws of the Penhari hills are unknown in that inferno. If in Calcutta, a stranger pats you on the back, you should turn round and hit him on the jaw. Such a fellow is sure to be a professional pickpocket or a cut-throat. Or, maybe, he is a receiver of stolen goods. Don't forget the Penhari saying:

> Foisted friendship
> Leads to hardship.'

'Are there no Penhari people in Calcutta?'

'Ah! There are a few. Some of them are good and others are not so good. And if you come across them, don't forget to embrace them. They will pat you on the back as true friends, and you will take their patting as a decent young scholar. That's the Law.'

One day, shortly after my installation in Calcutta, I was standing at the corner of Dhuramtollah gaping at the stream of traffic and marvelling at the way the taxis were managing to avoid collision, when someone patted me on the back in a most friendly fashion. It was, I thought, the manager of the Ultra-Modern Hindu Hotel and Extra-Chic Dhuramtollah Eating-House. His niece attended some of my cramming, that is to say, coaching classes; as I gave her some extra help—gratis lessons—he occasionally entertained me to free meals in his restaurant. Fancy, therefore, my surprise when on turning round I was confronted with a strange face: a man with a stubbly chin, carrying a beard of a few days' growth, stood in front of me. He seemed to be out of breath.

'Sir!' He panted, 'Sir! May I borrow a drink from you? My throat is as sticky as the neck of a gum-bottle.'

I was astonished. In fact, too amazed to utter a single word. It was the first time in my life anyone had addressed me as 'Sir.' Moreover, the nature of his request was astounding even in a wonder city of perpetual surprises like Calcutta. I do not recall exactly what I murmured in my embarrassment: I might have told him the time of the day, and referred to its being inauspicious for drinks.

'Sir,' he persisted, 'if I can't borrow, let me at least beg a drink from you. Won't you join me at the bar of this hotel?'

Then, without waiting for a reply, he disappeared through the swivel door of the Ultra-Modern Hindu Hotel and Extra-Chic Dhuramtollah Eating-House.

Had he gone to any other place I should not have bothered about him and allowed him to enjoy his drink all by himself. Unfortunately, as I have said before, the manager of the Ultra-Modern Hindu Hotel was known to me, and his niece—a fairly attractive girl, in whom I was more than somewhat interested—occasionally served at the bar. Therefore, I had no choice but to follow in the steps of my strange accoster. 'There is no knowing,' I reasoned, 'what he will say when it comes to paying. He may easily claim to be my friend, and I may be held responsible for his bills.'

When I came to the counter I found him gulping down a drink and holding in his hand my wallet, my own wallet bearing the heraldic sign of the Penhari Parganas.

'I can swear,' I cried, 'that wallet is mine.'

The man seemed to be nonplussed. Instead of looking at me, he silently stared at the design.

'The coat of arms of the Penhari Princes,' I kept on. 'Marine conch shells, surrounded by seven concentric zig-zags to represent waves.'

'All right,' he interrupted. 'Certainly this is yours. But it is empty.'

'Empty! It contains my cards.'

'Of course, it does. But nothing else. Why do you carry it about in your breast pocket?'

'To create a good impression.'

'That's all right for you, I presume. But how are we to pay for our drinks? Really, I have jumped from the frying pan into the fire.'

The man's story in brief was simply this: he was an amateur prestidigitator—in plain language, a juggler who was extraordinarily skilful with his fingers. Unfortunately, he had strolled far out of his 'beat' and was being hotly pursued by a number of rivals. He had to throw them off the scent. Hence he had to take cover somewhere. 'Dog does not eat dog,' he philosophized, 'but in Calcutta pickpockets eat one another.'

This did not make much sense for me. However, just then the tough fellow who looked after the bar when it got rowdy came in, and I took pity on the thirsty juggler.

'You must have a heart of gold,' he mumbled when I settled the bill.

Of course, it was not my goodness that led me to be generous. It was the wink I received from Bina, the niece of the manager of the Ultra-Modern Hindu Hotel and Extra-Chic Dhuramtollah Eating-House: she was ready to go out and I was at liberty to accompany her. Her smile put me in an expansive mood, and I went to the extent of offering the man a rupee to get back home.

'Where do you hide your money,' he asked. 'In the soles of your shoes?'

I did not bother to answer him as Bina was already at the service-exit of the bar.

'Wish you luck,' he said, 'if you ever come to Boita-khana district you may look me up.'

He made some further comments about how to hide a wad of banknotes inside the body, but I did not pay much attention to that.

I remembered, however, his parting remark: 'If all men were like you, poor pickpockets would have a thin time.'

Therefore I smiled at the words of commiseration of the nautch-girl and her uncle.

'You will get your money back,' Myna vouched. 'We know everyone here. We will make the man who stole your purse bring it back to you.'

'I swear that in the name of Devi,' the street-musician repeated. 'Mr Scholar! You have nothing to worry about. Leave the matter to us.'

The turn of events was most unexpected. It took me some time to realize that the rather disreputable-looking couple, Myna and her uncle, really wanted to help me. It was almost unbelievable, nevertheless true. I was mystified by their behaviour. Instead of wishing to be rewarded for having saved me from a pack of importuning hawkers and vendors, they wanted to do me a good turn.

The bother with the hucksters, pedlars, and their entire brotherhood of Bow Bazaar Street was due entirely to my stupidity. I ought to have been more careful. 'The careful alone,' they say in my village, 'get no blows.'

I believe a long-established code was inadvertently broken by me.

'Every city has its conventions,' I was told by Kolej Huzoor ages ago, long before I dreamt of leaving my Penhari village. 'These are inviolable. No one can break them with impunity.'

Kolej Huzoor was an important figure in the Statistical Department of the Government: the Bureau of Weights and Measures, A Fellow of the Royal Society, and a Doctor of Science. I had a high regard for him. He was much travelled and well read: a real mine of unusual—and often useless—information on many abstruse subjects. 'If the street traffic,' he said, 'can keep to the left in London, and to the right in Paris, why cannot Calcutta's traffic keep to the middle of the road, with equal justification?' I did not know what to say on the spur of the moment. 'We don't want,' he continued, 'to impose our tradition on London or Paris. Nor do we wish slavishly to accept theirs.'—'What about traffic jams and accidents?'—'These form an integral part of Calcutta's life,' he propounded. 'To change our traffic system would mean robbing our city of one of its peculiarities. Now, please bear in mind, a city's peculiarities make a city's life. To deprive it of its most striking feature is to sap it of its vitality—its very soul. And that is criminal. Imagine London without its pubs and dogs! It would become as dull as Kumbhakonam without its holy Brahmins and Brahmany bulls or Paris purged of its cafes and cabarets. I tell you, street accidents add to the zest of life in Calcutta.'—'What about the taxis? Why can't they slow down at bus and tram stops for the passengers?'—'Why should they? Calcutta is no city for sissies and sluggards. Taxi-drivers are entitled to run you down. It's your job to save your skin by running faster than a taxi.'

This salutary advice—'It is your business to save your skin'—was completely forgotten by me, because I was worried.

I was on my way to the Boitakhana district, to see an advertiser about a job. I did not know that part of Calcutta. All that I was told was that I should get off at the tram stop for the Mahratta Ditch Culvert, and there ask someone for Diwan Nishi Kama's House in Hargila Lane. If I had been alert I would have kept my eyes open for my tram stop. But I did the contrary: I fixed my gaze on an advertisement panel behind the conductor.

'Not yet,' the conductor repeated to me from time to time. 'Not yet.'

He thought I was staring at him, whereas I was reading and re-reading the advertisement. It was about the products of the 'celebrated Bonko Brothers of Benares.' The announcement read somewhat as follows:

> *In order to help you do the right, economical, and fruitful planning for the coming year, we have decided to effect heavy reductions in all our articles so that you may make use of them without any great financial burden.*
>
> *The reduced rates will be closed on December 21th, after which our usual prices will again come into force.*
>
> *The Bonko Bottle of Liquid Moonshine for transforming the user into a handsome being: usual price Rs. 30: reduced price Rs. 20.*
>
> *The Bonko Super-magnetised Ring Number One: for becoming a good player in any game: usual price Rs. 45; reduced price Rs. 15.*

Ditto. Ring Number Two: for financial gains from speculative enterprises and law suits: usual price Rs. 350: *reduced price Rs.* 150.

Ditto. Ring Number Three: for business success: usual price Rs. 150: reduced price Rs.100.

Ditto. Ring Number Eight: for winning a beautiful bride with a handsome dowry: usual price Rs. 100: *reduced price Rs.* 10.

Ditto. Number Nine: for obtaining a desirable scholarship for studying abroad (exclusively for University Graduates]: usual price Rs. 150: *reduced price Rs. 145.*

Ditto. Number Ten: for securing employment in these days of slump: usual price Rs. 65: reduced price Rs. 60.

The last two items fascinated me.

'There is no harm,' I said to myself, 'in jotting down the address of Bonko Brothers. Maybe, one day when I revisit Benares I shall call on them. They must be thriving magnificently on the worries of fellows like me.'

The conductor, I noticed, was not quite happy about my fixed gaze in his direction. He must have thought there was something wrong with his uniform, or some such thing. More than once he adjusted and readjusted the incongruous pill-box cap on his head; he felt his fly to be assured there was nothing amiss. However, when he saw me take out my pencil to scribble down the address of Bonko Brothers he guessed what had attracted my attention and gave a sympathetic smile.

'Ever been to Benares?' he asked, after he had read out aloud the address for my benefit. 'They say it is a wonderful place.'

'Certainly it is,' I replied proudly. 'I have been there more than once.'

'With your college football team, I believe. You are lucky. Benares is a place I should love to know.'

'Are you not happy in Calcutta?' I asked, hopefully expecting to hear some original comments on the bewildering metropolis which at once fascinated and frightened me. 'Do you not like Calcutta?'

'Of course I do,' was his immediate answer. 'Who doesn't? I should hate to live anywhere else. Once you have grown to like Calcutta you can't leave it easily for any place in the world.'

'That's what they all say.'

'However,' he remarked in a meditative mood, as though talking to himself, 'Calcutta is all right to live in. But there is no city in the universe like Benares to die in.'

I sighed as I thought of my brief sojourns there in the house of Pundit Malaviya. It was in Benares I had my first contacts with some extraordinarily stimulating strangers: Patrick Geddes, Josiah Wedgwood, Sylvian Levi, James Hackin, and others. The conductor was right: my very first visit to the holy city was connected with an inter-university football match.

'Benares is a most sacred spot,' the conductor continued. 'It is the very heart of Mother India.'

I told him that my much-travelled friend Kolej Huzoor was of the same opinion.

'New York is not America,' Kolej Huzoor often propounded in emphatic terms. 'London is not England. But Benares, make no mistake about it, is India.' On other occasions he declared with considerable warmth, 'Whoever fails to understand Benares will not understand India. Sanskrit literature will remain meaningless to him, and the Hindu mind a sealed book.'

I remember telling him about my first impressions of the sacredmost city of the Hindus, and he listened (apart from interrupting me just once) with unfeigned interest. That was something contrary to his usual habit. For he rarely allowed anyone to finish a sentence without breaking in with his absurd ejaculations and strident asides.

The first glimpse I had of the ancient city of Benares remains graven for good on my memory. It was obtained one early dawn from a crowded railway coach after a most uncomfortable night journey. My train was then standing immobile on the ugly iron bridge spanning the Ganges and a sudden clamour of many voices had broken my fitful sleep. '*Joy! Visva Nath! Joy!*' the passengers chanted in ecstasy—men, women, and children—with their outstretched palms joined together and their heads bent in deep reverence. 'Glory! Glory to the Lord of the Universe!' they repeated in unison. In a rather irritated mood, trying to gather the threads of an unfinished dream, I thrust my head out of the window. My eyes were still heavy with sleep. However, the sight before me acted as an electric shock: it made me immediately jump to my feet. In an instant I was wide awake, and staring with dilated eyes to take in all that was before me.

I held my breath as I gazed in wonder at the panorama of the stupendous crescent sweep of the river and the many-templed city, half-hidden in a pearly haze, standing on a cliff by the Ganges' bank—with its monumental *ghats*—stone-encased terraces and stairs—flight after flight, descending the broken precipitous cliff—a couple of hundred feet—right to the water's edge, and the cliff itself heaped high with tall houses, balconied structures, immense caravanserais, rose-tinted palaces pierced with deep archways leading to mysterious winding streets thronged with early worshippers, while in the background the crowning cupola of the Golden Temple flashed fire and in the foreground loomed the domineering Aurangzeb mosque with its austere silhouette, white domes, and twin minarets impaling the tourmaline sky. Seen from the distance, the multicoloured crowds on the *ghats*, scattered over the league of the waterfront, looked like swarms of exotically-tinted, microscopic ladybirds.

Benares lay all on one shore of the silver-and-blue river while the other shore—the concave side—was just a waste of white sand and glistening mud, heightening by its desolation the majestic effect of the cyclopean bastions on which the city's structures stood.

'Most picturesque,' I murmured. 'Once seen, never forgotten. Once loved, ever prized.'

'A fig for your picturesqueness!' was Kolej Huzoor's impatient outburst at my outpourings. 'Repeat all that nonsense to the *manes* of Malaviya or to the ghost of Pierre Loti. But not to me.'

'But,' I protested, 'Kolej Huzoor, say what you will, Benares is picturesque.'

'Picturesqueness be hanged,' he rapped out. 'Paeans in praise of picturesqueness may be raised in the whores' quarters of old Marseilles and in the smelly slums of Edinburgh. As for your flights of steps, my dear fellow, I can assure you that those in Genoa or in Lausanne are equally exhausting.'

'Don't you, then, like Benares?' I interrupted. Though no globe-trotter, I refused to be brow-beaten by a man who praised Benares one moment and ran it down the next.

'Most certainly, I do,' he replied. 'But for a different reason.'

'What's that?'

'Benares is the heart of India,' he declared. There was almost a note of triumph in his voice. 'Nowhere else will you find real holiness and rank hypocrisy rubbing shoulders to the same degree as in Benares. Not even in Jerusalem which, by the way, is an extremely picturesque city. Please note, Benares is the sanctified seat where Buddha elected to preach his first public sermon on universal charity and compassion. And it is also the centre the first thuggees chose for the discussion of the best means for strangling innocent people and getting rid of their corpses.'

'Why, then, do you call it the heart of India?'

'I have given you my reason. Mother India's chariot is drawn by strange pairs: high intelligence and utter stupidity, generosity and cupidity, the desire to serve and the urge to thwart, self-abnegation and exhibitionism.'

I felt bewildered.

'Friendship goes by pairs,' he went on. 'Our virtues are always accompanied by vices of equal intensity. Benares is the place to probe into them. The holy city is the epitome of Hindustan. It is the very mirror of the country's soul.'

~

I was still musing over Benares and the advertisement of the celebrated Bonko Brothers of that city when the conductor tapped me on the shoulder. 'The last stop was yours,' he said. 'Did you not hear me call out Mahratta Ditch Culvert?'

I jumped up from my seat.

'Be careful,' he shouted. 'Mind the death-traps.'

'Mind what?' I asked as I got off the moving tram.

The answer came the very next moment in the shape of a yellow taxi juggernauting down the street at a breakneck speed. I ran for my life. It missed me by a fraction of an inch, and I do not know how I found myself safe but on all fours, sprawling on the pavement of Bow Bazaar Street at the feet of a street-vendor sedately squatting on the ground beside his huge pyramid of printed chintzes and rolls of cloth.

'Calcutta is no sissy city,' the street-vendor philosophized. 'It isn't meant for those who do not know how to sprint. You are an up-country man, I suppose.'

I admitted my home was in the country.

'Your good luck has saved you,' commented another street-vendor, who was selling soft drinks bearing impressive American names: Hollywood Pineapple Syrup, Palm Beach Tomato Juice, Texan Thirst-Killer, Hay Rita Pick-Me-Up, and other labels of this sort. 'Country folk are generally lucky.'

Slowly I got to my feet and began dusting myself. 'No bones broken!' the chintz-seller exclaimed. 'You are a marvel. Another fellow in your place would have been killed outright.'

'The up-country people are remarkably tough,' the soft-drink seller declared. 'They are big-boned and thick-skulled. Just look at him. He is already on his feet. Any other man would have allowed himself to be run over by the taxi. But not he! He must be from the hill country.'

'All the same,' the chintz-seller said, 'he will perhaps need an American drink to put his nerves straight. Have a glass on me. Are you feeling all right? Do you need first aid? An ambulance?'

'I am quite all right,' I murmured, still marvelling at my own narrow escape. 'Thank you. I don't want any drink. I am looking for Diwan Nishi Kanta's house in Hargila Lane.'

'That's not far,' the chintz-seller assured me. 'Only a minute's walk. Near Omichund's Tower. You have no need to hurry. Just have a drink on me and tell me where you come from.'

'From the Penhari Parganas,' I replied rather reluctantly. To get involved in an interrogation would mean, I was quite sure, 'staying put' for one solid hour.

'Never heard of such a place. What sort of folk live over there?'

I told him that the more common name of the Penhari Parganas was the Santal Parganas.

'Santals! Great God! They are said to be head-hunters.'

I regretted being dragged into conversation with him, but could not help telling him that the Santals were hunters, at least some of them, but they were no cannibals.

'What are their women like?'

'Pretty.'

'Do those pretty women care for pretty pieces of cloth? They do! Then why not have a look at my things?'

I reminded him that I was expected at Diwan Nishi Kanta's house, but he ignored my excuse.

'I have marvellous American things,' he went on. 'All machine-made. Not like your coarse country stuffs. Look at the patterns. The latest Hollywood fashions. Designs made to suit pretty women.'

I did not say anything, waited for a pause to ask him once again the way to Hargila Lane.

'Ever been to a cinema? Have you seen *Sirens sans Sarongs* at the BIKINO—the Boitakhana Imperial Kino? Well, my patterns are guaranteed up-to-date, exactly like those in the film. I tell you, they are all machine-made. Thousands of yards made in an hour. Not like your Santal homespun loin-cloths, a month's hard labour to produce a yard. What do you say?'

'I like home-spun materials,' I said.

'Do you? You surprise me. Let me tell you in confidence no one in Calcutta cares for coarse stuffs. Never ask for crude things in Calcutta. Calcutta is like Hollywood. Here everyone is for progress. Americans are not clodhoppers. Neither are Calcuttans.'

I blurted out something about the attractiveness of our country designs.

'You hurt me, Babu,' he replied. 'I am pained to hear such things from you. A man wearing a college blazer and scoffing at American patterns! This is really too bad. Let me tell you the truth: you are an up-country man, and that's why your taste is poor. Here in Calcutta we are all for progress and refinement. But the Santals prefer to stick in the mud, and that is bad: it's simply wicked. Do you know how chintzes are made in the Santal country?'

Without any encouragement on my part he began an elaborate explanation condemning the slowness of our traditional methods and home industries. Five different dyes, I was told, went to the making of hand-spun chintzes, each dyeing was done separately: the process was time-consuming. The colouring matters were 'sprinkled,' and that wasted a lot of time. The patterns were either hand printed or hand impressed, and this procedure too was extremely sluggish.

'It takes ages and ages,' he concluded, 'to finish a roll of cloth in your up-country fashion. But in Calcutta, all refined people prefer things done rapidly. We are for progress, for things made by machine. Do you understand? Everyone loves American stuffs. Look at my things. Are they not fine?'

A piece of rather attractive checked material caught my eye in his stupendous pile. 'Looks like something familiar to me,' I said to myself. '*Fleurs de lis* and diamonds on blue checks! The colours of Dupleix College of Chandernagore!' Being an ex-student of Dupleix College I felt almost hypnotized, and pulled out a corner of the fringe to examine the pattern better, cursing under my breath the rogue who was trifling with Chandernagore's tradition by manufacturing a thousand yards of college colours every hour. Involuntarily, I caressed that roll of cloth.

That was, of course, very wrong on my part. I should have

known better. One simply cannot finger the outer folds of a piece of cloth tucked away in the midst of a mountain-high pyramid and then try to escape from a crusty street-vendor of Bow Bazaar Street as though the gesture meant nothing.

In a split second the man had forestalled my move: swiftly burrowing into his pile and drawing from its midst a length of the stuff I had the misfortune to caress, he stood, grinning at his own dexterity, and barring my path with outstretched arms that automatically unrolled the cloth. He held it right before my nose. The folds were shaken out with exaggerated affectedness, and the piece spread out for me to admire.

And that was the signal for other cloth-sellers to crowd round me with shawls, saris, sashes, scarves, cummerbunds, turban-cloths, bed-spreads, tablecloths, napkins, veils, priests' counterpanes, printed cotton, and silk stuffs. I was surrounded by a hedge of people, all proclaiming the virtues of their wares and guaranteeing the authenticity of their American origin.

'Have a look at this,' one of the fellows cried, nudging at me. 'Meant only for adults.'

'I don't want any of these.' The hubbub round me nearly drowned my voice. 'I am looking for Diwan Nishi Kanta's house.'

'Never mind,' the man persisted. 'Babu, have a look all the same. Real French pictures printed on fine linen handkerchiefs.'

A dozen large scarves were spread out on all sides for my delectation. They carried horrid technicolor reproductions of thirty-two Kamasutra poses.

'From real photographs,' a dozen strident voices assured me. 'True to life!' 'Correct to the smallest detail.' 'Meant for adults only,' 'The police won't let us sell these to the public. But for you we are taking the risk. How much will you offer?'

'I don't want anything,' I shouted. 'Don't tug at me. Let me go.'

'You make me turn the whole stock upside down, and now you don't want anything. What sort of a college Babu are you?'

'Babu!' someone patted me on the back as he shouted in my ear, 'I have something very attractive. Extra special. Name your price and take it. A pair of Hollywood starlets making love to each other. Life-like pictures on a bed sheet. Meant for college students. For Bachelors of Arts.'

'No,' I cried at the top of my voice. 'I don't want anything.'

'All right, Babu,' responded a particularly greasy fellow on my left. 'It's quite right. Why should you buy a thing you don't fancy? But look at my thing. It is lovely. This is a real love charm. Won't it make a fine bedspread? It has life-size pictures. A hula-hula baby embracing a strong negro. Have a look at it and feel its sheen. It comes straight from Honolulu. A real hand-made American curiosity. A smuggled article.'

'Listen! You are wasting your time.'

'Why, Babu,' the man kept on, 'I am at your service. My time is at your disposal. Just examine the bedspread and tell me what you think of it. It feels like the *mamo* cloak of Hawaii's chief rajah.' He then began extolling the beauty of the Hawaiian girls, the splendour of their thighs, their adroitness in cajoling men into amorous extravagances. It took, according to him, ages to prepare a *mamo* cloak—three generations of ceaseless labour by a host of skilful craftsmen, especially trained, and assisted by a regiment of adept bird-catchers who spent their days as well as their nights in the most inaccessible glens of volcanic islands luring the almost extinct *mamo* bird—as elusive as our more gorgeous kingfishers—to rob the poor thing of its finest down growing on the delicate under-part of its tail. 'My *mamo* bedspread is a real love charm. It will give you the strength of a negro in love-making. Show it to any woman and, I swear, she will immediately fall for you.'

I felt like hitting him, instead I trod deliberately on his toes.

He howled with pain. And a pandemonium ensued.

The soft-drink man came to the fellow's aid, brandishing an empty ice-cream container and wailing that I was trying to escape without settling his dues—the price of his most expensive cordial. Several vendors simultaneously supported his allegation, accusing me of emptying a bottle that I had not even touched. Some tugged at me while others pushed. My blazer was nearly ripped off my back.

It looked as though I should have to fight my way through that noisy throng. I began rolling up my sleeves.

'You are in for it,' my inner voice reprimanded me. 'You can't break a convention in Calcutta with impunity.'

~

At this juncture, when I was on the point of hitting out blindly with my fists and making a bigger ass of myself, the street-musician and Myna made their appearance. A new clamour rose; a shout of rejoicing to greet the couple.

'Oh! Our Bahurupi!' they burst out. 'Our Bahurupi is here!' Some clapped their hands, some whistled, some shouted, '*Sabash!*' as they thronged round the new arrivals.

I ceased to be the centre of attraction. No one—not even the soft-drink seller—minded my crossing over to the other side of the street. Indeed, I could have slunk away from the scene completely unnoticed had not the street-musician called out for me when he found me engaged in conversation with an elderly man with a pince-nez on his nose and a grandson by his side.

~

'A fool at forty is a fool indeed,' the grandfather responded enigmatically when I asked him the way to Hargila Lane. 'I am more than forty, and I don't know that Bahurupi. I presume I am a fool.'

'I beg your pardon,' I said apologetically as I repeated my question and added, 'I am a stranger here. Hargila Lane must be somewhere near Mahratta Ditch Culvert. That's all that I know.'

'It is indeed. It is just a stone's throw from Mahratta Ditch Culvert.' Slowly he adjusted his pince-nez, only to put it at a more precarious angle. 'But first you must tell me what is a Bahurupi?'

The conundrum of the grey-haired man staggered me. Even a toddler in the country would not have put such a question, because the answer is so obvious.

'The other day,' he continued, pointing his finger in the direction of the street-musician and his partner, 'the Bahurupi came here all by himself: his body wrapped in a striped tiger skin, his face hidden in a tiger's mask, and his behind decorated with an imposing tail.'

'The Bahurupi was then a Malayan tiger, Grandpa,' the grandson lisped. 'He was a Malayan tiger. Because his tail had a twist.'

'Now, now,' the grandfather growled. 'Don't interrupt me when I am talking. Where are your manners? Who tells you that the Malayan tiger has a twist in its tail?'

'The Bahurupi told us the other day,' the child replied with alacrity. 'The Malayan tiger has a twist at the very end of its tail, and the Malayan bear has no tail at all.'

'Stuff and nonsense,' the grandfather grumbled. 'Arrant nonsense. Don't repeat cock-and-bull stories.'

The child looked crestfallen.

'Bad luck,' my inner voice reproached me. 'From the fire you have managed to climb into the frying pan, and no further. The old man must be crazy. The child has more sense than he.'

'Now, sir, what do you say? What do you think of that Bahurupi?'

His persistence was annoying. To rid myself of him I made the matter-of-fact observation that though Bahurupis were rare in Calcutta they were as numerous as raree-shows in the country.

'Does that mean,' he broke in, 'they are as plentiful as black-beetles in your village?'

'If you wish to put it that way,' I said. 'They entertain children by dressing themselves in different disguises. They tell amusing stories.'

'Are you quite sure? Do they not belong to some secret society? Some political party?'

'Not that I know of.' I added, as a second thought, that the chameleon is also called Bahurupi in some parts of the country because it changes its colours every few minutes.

My inadvertent remark about the chameleon upset the old man. He began mumbling about the country going to the dogs and no one doing anything about it: 'The chameleons ought to be exterminated.'

'What's wrong with the chameleon?' I asked, becoming more and more mystified.

'Hush! Not so loud! The Bahurupi on the other side of the street may overhear us. We must be careful. Let me whisper something to you. Please remember in Calcutta a chameleon is called a *tik-tiki*, and a detective is also known as a *tik-tiki*. It makes you think. Doesn't it?'

I felt like laughing, and told him that in Dacca a horse is called *goora*, so, too, a redcoat. 'Not only that, *goora* is also *powder!* No one worries over such conundrums. Only children and philologists get some fun out of them. And that's that.'

'No.' The old man shook his head meditatively. He looked unhappy. 'You don't follow me. It is not a conundrum.' He shook his head once again and his pince-nez nearly dropped off his nose. 'My eyesight is bad,' he murmured as he readjusted his pince-nez and straightened the ribbon attached to the frame. 'I am no longer forty. Please have a good look at that *tik-tiki*—that chameleon—that street-musician with his lute and his nautch-girl. And tell me if he does not look like a real detective. He must be a police spy. A snooper. An eavesdropper.'

I did not know what to say. I looked in the direction of the Bahurupi and Myna: they were regaling a large knot of people with their stories.

'I tell you,' he went on, getting more and more excited, 'that woman is an agent-provocateur and that man is a detective in disguise.'

'What makes you think so?'

'Plain common sense, young man! My plain common sense tells me that the nautch-girl is pretty enough to cause a riot. That's why she is thickly veiled. My eyesight may be bad, but I have noticed her feet: they are tiny: as tiny as those of my grandson. And her waist! Why, it can be spanned by my thumb and forefinger. Have you noticed the swing of her hips? She walks like a film star. Frankly, I can swear she is no ordinary nautch-girl. Have you seen her fingers?—they are so sinuous that they could be bent backwards to touch her wrist. She has the voice of a siren. She must be an agent-provocateur. And her man is a police spy.'

'Grandpa!' the child whimpered, 'I want to hear the Bahurupi's stories. I want to hear the story of the tiger.'

The old man fell once again into a thoughtful mood. He ignored the child's pleadings.

'Profit from his meditative trance,' my inner voice counselled.

And I decided to make a move. Immediately he became alert and clutched at me, whispering like his own grandson, 'You are not going to leave me in the lurch.'

'What would you like me to do?'

'I am no longer forty, and I cannot bear perpetual suspense. Tell me the truth. Is that Bahurupi a detective or not? He has shifty eyes. And all his tales have twists in them.'

I confessed I could not grasp his point, especially as I had never heard any of the stories. I had almost blurted out something rude, but checked myself in time: the old man seemed so worried that I decided to do the good deed of the day by listening to his inanities.

~

The Malayan Tiger has a twist in its tail. Do you know why?

'You look rather thin, Brother Goat,' said the Monkey. 'What has happened to you?'

'I am starved to death,' replied the Goat. 'I can't graze any more on the river bank on account of the striped Tiger. The brute has come there recently, but he has already broken all the laws of the jungle. He kills whom he likes and when he likes. I dare not graze in the open any more.'

'Is that so?' The Monkey thought for a while and said, 'Don't worry, Brother Goat. I shall settle him. Get me a nice striped melon, and carry me on your back to the Tiger. And you will see what I shall do to him.'

The Goat did as he was asked, much against his will; he was terribly frightened, but the Monkey convinced him that the bully of a Tiger was a coward and could be easily driven out of the country.

The Tiger licked his lips when he saw the Goat from a distance. When he noticed the Monkey on the Goat's back he became curious. Finally he became somewhat apprehensive as he discovered the Monkey munching away at what looked like a Tiger's head and urging the Goat to hurry on.

'You Goat! You wicked Goat!' The Tiger heard the Monkey shouting, 'You wicked Goat! You promised me a dozen tigers. And now I see only one over there. Hurry on, otherwise the Tiger may escape, I must bring at least a dozen tigers' heads for supper tonight. Hurry on. Don't be a sluggard.'

This was more than enough to make the Tiger turn tail; he dashed through the jungle to return to China where he came from.

'Brother Tiger! Brother Tiger!' The Bear called out, 'Why are you running so fast?'

'To escape the Devil that feeds on tigers' heads. He is coming after me on the Goat's back.'

'Nonsense,' said the Bear. 'Don't make a fool of yourself. Devil or no Devil, the world belongs to us: we two are lords over the jungles and the plains. What business has anyone to drive you or me out? Come, show me your Devil and his Goat. I will settle them both.'

'No, I dare not. I am afraid of the Devil that feeds on tigers.'

'Don't be silly,' the Bear jeered. 'I shall be with you. And if you think I am going to be frightened you are mistaken.'

The Tiger was not to be easily persuaded. The Bear, however, found a means of giving his friend courage: by tying his stumpy tail to the Tiger's. 'You see,' he said, 'I want to be with you through thick and thin. Two fighting together means more than two fighting separately.'

'Union is strength,' the Tiger admitted.

At the river's bank they found the Goat and the Monkey.

'What are we to do now, Brother Bear?' asked the Tiger. 'There is the Devil on the Goat's back.'

'Leave it to me,' replied the Bear, nearly choking with laughter. 'I am not crazy enough to tremble before the Monkey.' He had not, however, foreseen that the Monkey was quick-witted.

'You, wicked Bear!' the Monkey shouted, waving his half-eaten melon. 'You promised to bring me a dozen tigers for my supper. And now you are back with only one! What does this mean? Did I not spare your life on condition you brought me a dozen—?'

The Tiger did not hear the whole of the Monkey's speech. He turned round and fled, dragging his friend along with him. The Bear struggled hard to get himself free. He tugged at his tail. So did the Tiger. They pulled hard: the Bear in one direction and the Tiger in the other. Finally, the Bear's tail being stumpy was wrenched completely off his body; it went with the Tiger's tail.

Since that day the bear has no tail and the tiger carries a twist at the tip of his.

~

The child clapped his hands with delight. 'The Bahurupi says,' he prattled, 'this tale of tails has no moral.'

I smiled.

The grandpa, however, was not so happy. He wondered if the story of the Malayan tiger bore any analogy with Krylov's *Fables*. Had I any comments to make? I had none. I disclaimed all acquaintance with the Russian author called Krylov, and indeed with anything remotely connected with Russia. This made him still more unhappy. He shook his head as though protesting against my keeping something back from him.

'The blind bat eats many a fly,' he maundered gloomily. 'I may be over forty, but I am not as blind as that. I do see through things, though it takes time. Frankly, I refuse to swallow the street-musician's poisoned bait. His stories are tricks to find out his listener's politics. Do you now see my point?'

Unfortunately, I did not. However, to cut his ramblings short I said, 'Are you not making an elephant out of a fly? What's wrong with the story? Isn't it just a fable to amuse children like your grandson?'

'Babu!' He expostulated, 'The story may sound innocent. You may laugh with the youngster. But I tell you it is not quite so simple. The tale has its own twists. Why? It is charged with dynamite. It is packed with political implications, slanderous innuendos, international complications.'

'What are the complications?' I asked impatiently. The old man was getting on my nerves.

'They are legion,' he started to ramble off an almost interminable list of enigmas raised by the Bahurupi's fable.

Did I realize that the word 'monkey' was an anagram of the initials of the Finance Minister? Everything hinged on that keynote. Was it not clear that the gift of a melon to the monkey implied that the Finance Minister was ready to have his fingers buttered? In other words, he was corrupt! Was this not a very serious charge? There was the possibility of a different interpretation: the monkey might symbolically represent India; in that case the Bahurupi was condemning India's policy—the favourite technique of using others to pull chestnuts out of the fire for India's benefit. What about the bear? Was it not obvious that the shaggy, treacherous beast symbolized Russia? And the striped tiger the U.S.A.? Were not these two powers anxious to share out the world among themselves? About the tiger, there were, however, perplexities. China could be represented by a tiger, while Bengal, too, could claim that nasty beast for its own symbol. What did the goat imply?

'Babu!' the grandson interrupted, tugging at my sleeves. 'Babu! The Bahurupi is salaaming you from the other side of the street.'

I turned round.

'Grandpa!' the child shouted, 'The Bahurupi is coming this way.'

The child was right. The street-musician was waving his lute to attract my attention. He was calling out to me as though I were his long-lost brother. Myna, too, was making signs. They wanted to have a word with me, Could I wait for a second?

'Birds of a feather!' the old man muttered. 'Birds of a feather! Now I know, sir, why you didn't want to believe that the Bahurupi is a spy. He is your friend. He wants to talk to you.'

'I don't know him.'

'You don't know that strapping wench either!' the old man's whole frame shook in sudden rage. 'Let me tell you frankly, I don't believe you. Certainly you belong to their fraternity. They will help you to find Hargila Lane: It is full of skinflints and capitalists.'

The old man hurried away, dragging his reluctant grandson with him, muttering imprecations against the spies, detectives, plain-clothes policemen, and all inhabitants of 14 Elysium Row, headquarters of the political police. His parting shot, however, was, 'Mind you, young man, I have said nothing. I have never uttered in my life a single seditious word against Ek Nambur.'

~

'Scholar!' The street-musician greeted me, 'You come from my Pargana. You are as my brother.'

I demurred. I knew most of the Bahurupis of the Penhari Parganas: the street-musician was surely not one of them. What was the objective of his striking up an acquaintance with me? Perhaps he was making a mistake, confusing me with someone he knew.

'Forgetfulness of past favours,' according to the street-musician, 'is the greatest of sins. How can I forget your favours?'

'We may be poor,' Myna chimed in, 'but we are not sinners.'

'Look here,' I protested, 'you have brought a crowd along with you. They want to hear your stories. You shouldn't disappoint them. Just now I am in a hurry.'

'They can wait,' the street-musician declared grandly. All my excuses were brushed aside: I was deemed to be more important than all the children, street-vendors, shopkeepers, busybodies, and loafers lumped into one. 'Moreover,' Myna broke in, 'one does not come across one's benefactor every day.' 'If only I knew your address,' the other continued, 'Mr Scholar! I should have called on you to write my petition for me. I wasted good money on a rogue of a scribe, all for nothing.'

'His handwriting is not bad,' Myna condescended to explain. 'But he does not know how to make a petition touching.'

There was no reason for them to take me into their confidence. And in ordinary circumstances I should not have hesitated to tell them so: I hate people who carry their hearts on their sleeves. But just then, as I have explained before, my situation was awkward. It was the intervention of the street-musician and Myna that saved me from the mob of street-vendors. I had to express my gratitude in some tangible way. As I had nothing to offer them as *baksheesh*, I could not evade the bother of listening to the story of the petition: it was a proposal that instead of using tear gas the authorities should employ Bahurupis and buffoons for quelling riots and dispersing street-fighters.

'Certainly,' I said, 'a most original scheme.'

'I assure you,' the street-musician proudly declared, 'they love my stories. I am famous all over Bow Bazaar.'

'Why not all over Calcutta?' I asked ironically.

'Ah! Mr Scholar!' he regretted, 'That's impossible. In Calcutta everything goes by the district.' Every policeman, I was told, stuck to his beat, and every bus to its route; every gambler to his own haunt, and every tout to his particular hunting ground. To go beyond one's own district would be breaking the unwritten law of the metropolis.

'I understand,' I admitted: for I recalled the plight of the pickpocket who had to save his skin by rushing into the Ultra-Modern Hindu Hotel.

'A saint in Kalighat,' Myna added, 'is a rogue in Tolly-gunge. And an intriguer in Ballygunge is a statesman in Burra Bazaar. That's the law in Calcutta. We are known only in Bow Bazaar and in Kalighat.'

'Even a beggar must stick to his district,' the street-musician began again. 'And I stick to Bow Bazaar. Myna is a *kirtani*. She can go anywhere. But Bow Bazaar is the quarter she prefers.'

'So you know Bow Bazaar well?' I asked.

'Of course,' they both replied at the same time. 'Every inch of it.'

'In that case you will have to take me to the house of the Diwan Nishi Kanta.'

The street-musician readily agreed. Myna, however, laid down one condition: I must listen to her songs one evening, preferably after midnight!

'If I get a suitable job,' I replied, 'I shall be only too happy to hear you sing every night.'

'You flatter me, Mr Scholar, The Penhari men are great in paying compliments to womenfolk.'

I assured her that I meant what I said.

'Then please note where to find me: at the Kala Bhairab shrine.'

II

The Diwan's house was surrounded by a solidly built high wall crowned with a glittering layer of jagged, sharp-edged bits of broken glass embedded in cement, and surmounted by heavy rolls of rusting barbed wire. The appearance was anything but inviting. Had I not been assured that the structure behind this formidable barrier was the residence of the man I was expecting to see, I should have concluded that the walled enclosure was a depot for high explosives: for the nondescript, straight parapeted and flat-roofed brick house, on account of its huge size and small windows with iron bars, gave the impression of a government factory run with prison labour. True, it had no chimney—the inevitable adjunct to all factories in Calcutta—but in its stead a number of high shafts resembling radio-transmitter masts.

I was inclined to retrace my steps without further ado. But my companions insisted that I should try my luck.

'You knock at the back door,' Myna counselled. 'That's the best way of getting into the house. And when you get in you will talk to his wife.'

I wondered what was wrong with the main entrance. Why could I not tell the gate-keeper that I had an engagement with the Diwan? Was he not expecting me? 'I have a horror of back stairs,' I declared. 'After all, it is the Diwan who wants a secretary. Not his wife.'

'Poor Scholar!' Myna laughed. 'Don't you know the saying, "As the master is, so is the servant"?' 'Like master, like man,' the Bahurupi added.

They claimed to know everything about the people who lived there. I was told that the Diwan was erratic, and so were the servants. The door-keeper was sure to ask for a *baksheesh*, and after pocketing my money he was likely to turn me away with a curt announcement that the Diwan was out.

'What will you do then?'

This was, of course, something I had not foreseen. But what about the maid-servants? Was there any likelihood of their being any different?

'Poor Scholar!' Myna twittered. 'When will you grow to be a man? Are you still a village boy? It is time that you picked up the ABC of life in Calcutta. Learn the simple truth:

> Such mistress, such Nan;
> Such master, such man.

'The mistress is not the same as the master. Neither the maids the same as the men. She is his second wife, and he dotes on her. You talk to her and win her over before you see him.'

But what could I possibly tell the Diwan's wife to justify my intrusion?

I felt nervous. I was no good at *viva voces*. Interviews were my bugbear. At the Civil Service Selection Board I made an ass of myself at the final, all-important oral examination. 'It seems,' the Chairman of the Board declared morosely, 'you have done well in your written papers. You have the gift of memorizing, I must admit. But have you initiative? Tact?'—'Now,' the Psychologist of the Board struck in, 'will you give a verbal description of yourself in as few words as possible.' I stared at him, wondering what he was driving at. 'Give a self-portrait of yourself,' the Psychologist explained, 'in one single sentence.' He emphasized the word 'single.' I thought for a second and stammered, 'My body is perfectly equal to the limited demands I make on it.' 'That will do,' the Psychologist grinned to the Chairman, and I was shown out, only to learn within a few minutes from the smirking ushers (whom I had not tipped on principle) that I was declared unworthy of admission to the fraternity of higher civil servants: the Sons of Belial, as a distinguished Government official has named them. I made a bigger ass of myself at the University Selection Board of Teachers: there the interview began with a shower of bouquets: I was complimented on my record of examination results, my sports results, and what not. But I was thrown out when I gave my frank answer to their question on 'Progressive Educational Systems of America.' Kolej Huzoor tore his hair when he heard what I had said. He was genuinely sorry for me.

'Look here, Curly Locks!' he said, 'I look upon you as my disciple. It is no credit to me—your *guru*—to see you loafing round, doing nothing but giving private lessons and attending law classes in the evening. Did I not promise your aunt that I would do everything to find you a suitable job? The Diwan Nishi Kanta is looking for a private secretary. I have written to him. You should go and see him at once. He may be of great help to you later on. You may talk to him frankly. He is not a Government official.'

'To talk frankly to a man is easy,' I confessed to Myna. 'But to a woman, that's a different affair.'

'Why?' she asked. 'Are you not talking to me? Why can't you talk to the Diwan's wife?'

'You come from the Penhari Parganas,' I murmured. 'That makes things easy. And then, you spoke to me first.'

'I will tell you,' the Bahurupi interrupted, 'what you should do. Get into the house by the back door: it is a grated iron gate. And when you see her you will tell her, "Mother, I have come to pay my respects to you." Don't forget to address her as *Mataji*—Mother. Is that clear?'

'And I will tell you something more,' Myna whispered some further counsels. The Diwan, I was told again, apart from being elderly, was erratic: it was not improbable that he would be found prowling about in the back garden of the zenana with an impossibly fat bulldog: I could safely ignore the master and his dog, and walk straight into the inner quadrangle and ask for *Mataji*. *Mataji* was given to intermittent ablutions in the quadrangle from morning till sunset—all on account of the Diwan's dog! For whenever the wretched beast came within a sniffing distance of her she made it a point to divest herself of her clothes and rush straight to a tap in the courtyard to wash herself. She did not mind interviewing her callers when engaged in this occupation of ridding herself of canine contamination. I was to ignore her state of nudity or semi-nudity, as the case might be, and address her as though her wriggling under a running tap was nothing untoward, on the contrary, something most natural. 'Remember,' she added, 'this is Calcutta. Here in every household women spend most of their time in dressing and in undressing and washing their bodies. They are terribly afraid of contamination.'

I thanked them for their useful tips, and wanted to know what I should do after paying my respects. Was I to withdraw immediately?

'You must offer her a *nuzzar*—a token gift. Give her a tiny present and receive a big one in exchange. That's the universal law. She will see to it that you become the Diwan's secretary.'

'But,' I remonstrated, 'I haven't brought anything with me. What can I offer her?'

'What about one of these?' Myna produced a handful of country-made necklaces and strings of beads. 'Are they not pretty? Take the *tulasi* beads. Prayer beads of the sacred basil plant are good enough for any lady, even for the first lady of the land.'

'That's extremely kind of you,' I protested. 'But how can I accept the gift? I have nothing to offer you in return.'

'Nonsense! Why should you tempt the Devil with your pride? Never refuse a gift coming from the heart.'

'That is very kind of you.'

'Now, don't waste any further time. Get in by the back door. You will know it by its two carved pillars on either side. Just knock and go into the back garden. The rest will be quite simple.' Myna further explained that the back door was an iron grille, and that the carved pillars represented the guardian deities: Anadi the Everlasting and Ananta the Never-ending. 'Don't forget to salute them before you knock. And think of Krishna playing on his flute.'

~

Left to myself I decided to explore the lie of the land before knocking.

Through the forged-iron grating one could see the back garden. A deathly calm reigned there: nothing moved; there was no sound; it was the hour of the mid-day hush. The aspect was the usual one of the forgotten ornamental grounds of the decaying patrician houses of Calcutta. 'To call it a garden in its present state,' I said to myself, 'is a euphemism.' However, it still bore traces of being well planned. No doubt, in some remote age it had been well looked after, and then, for financial stringency or some other reason, abandoned to the care of Mother Nature.

Dwarf areca palms flanked the tiled pathway leading from the forged-iron gate to the zenana of the house. On one side of the garden there was a *chabootra*—raised dais of brickwork—round the trunk of an aged *kadamba* tree bearing globular composite blossoms. The tree looked bedraggled—the gardener was evidently not anxious to remove the dead branches—while the circular platform at its base was bulging with cracks, and strange weeds were sprouting through every fissure. To set off the dais there was, on the opposite side, a round basin for a fountain; though better preserved because it was of stone, it was waterless and covered over with nondescript runners. The pergolas—probably at one time the glory of the place—were leaning at precarious angles; they were overrun with wild climbing plants, which were trying to smother the attractive *aparajitas* renowned for their trumpet-shaped flowers and the much-prized climbing jasmines whose heavily-scented red florets symbolize for us hope and faith. Originally, these flower-bearing creepers must have made the trellised arbors lovely. However, the unwanted, nefarious weeds were gaining ground everywhere. Only a clump of florescent oleanders still vigorously held their own against all intruders; they therefore looked all the more gorgeous.

An ideal retreat, I mused, for poets addicted to melancholic reflections and green thoughts.

A pair of palm squirrels sped across the tiled pathway. They were tiny like newborn kittens, though their bushy tails—three times the size of their bodies—gave them a bigger appearance. They raced after each other, making fantastic zigzags and extraordinary curves; they rolled themselves up into balls of fur one instant and the next they exhibited their full length while turning somersaults. They gave demonstrations of their climbing feats, running up the tree-trunks to tumble down from the topmost branch and then to climb again at a greater speed. 'A palm squirrel is born,' they say, 'to do nothing but play all day. And its frolics make the drongo bird laugh.'

Whatever may be the truth of this country adage, a *jantri* bird started its rattling call as though to announce to the palm squirrels that it was enjoying their gambols and antics from its cover. The playful little things refused to accept the *jantri's* trilling as a worthy substitute for the drongo's laughter, and scampered away to hide themselves underneath a bush. The *jantri* went on trilling. I searched in all directions to locate it. As I did not see it anywhere I wondered if it was not, after all, a drongo imitating the call of the *jantri*. The drongo possesses the gift of imitating any sound, even human laughter and children's wailings. And at times it finds pleasure in hiding itself in most impossible places.

While looking for the drongo I made the discovery that in spite of the apparent neglect by the gardener, the plot of ground was not devoid of charm. Its air was perfumed with pleasant aromas: occasionally whiffs of the heavy scent of the Bussorah rose reached me, though no specimens of this exotic flower met my gaze as I stood peering through the grating.

I was no longer prepared to surrender the back garden to poetasters who penned mediocre verses. The palm squirrels—the playful furry things with tufted ears and dark stripes on their backs—and the bird that raised the trilling sound made a world of difference. I revised my earlier judgment and concluded that the apparently neglected ornamental ground was not a picture of nature unadorned; on the contrary, it was like a pretty woman, looking all the prettier because she was arrayed with artful carelessness.

Before knocking I had been advised by Myna to salute the images of Anadi the Everlasting and Ananta the Never-ending. I examined carefully the two pillars: they represented the divine child Krishna subduing two *nagas*—half-human and half-serpentine semi-divinities—not unlike the mythical denizens of the Greek nether world, children of Aether and Earth. They were of dark blue stone—of chlorite, I presumed—highly polished, distinctly different from the mass-produced articles of Calcutta bazaars. They were undoubtedly works of art, prize pieces for any museum. As there were some flowers strewn at their base I guessed they were treated as sacred images and worshipped.

On the whole, it was a most unusual back door.

As a rule, in Calcutta the entrance to a private house, however palatial, was extremely mean—just a gap or an opening in the bare wall—or frightfully ugly and so vulgarly ornate as to be atrocious. Here, however, was a remarkable exception. To be frank, it was the attractiveness of the so-called back door that made me ignore a notice-board of plain deal inconspicuously hooked across a corner of the beautiful grating of forged iron: it was in English, inadvertently hung upside down: 'Private: Female Entrance. Beware of the Dog.'

I took hold of the two enormous twisted iron rings—looking like a pair of interlocked, flattened torques—serving the purpose of a knocker, and shook them vigorously. The jangling noise made a street-cur prick up its ears and stop sniffing at a garbage bin. It looked at me for a while, baring its teeth, and then all of a sudden ran away with its tail between its legs, yapping as though chased by a pack of its brethren. Evidently, I deduced, the wretched beast did not belong to the district and it was conscious of its intrusion into strange quarters.

Apart from the dog's barking no other sound responded to my call: '*Koi hai?* Hi, who is there?'

I called out again, and this time someone hissed, 'Hush! Don't disturb the doves.'

I looked round me to see where the voice came from. Strangely enough though it sounded quite close to me, yet I failed to locate its source. At first I thought one of the servants was trying out a practical joke. Perhaps he was hiding behind one of the bushes of the back garden.

Once more I tried out the knocker and immediately heard someone curse.

'In God's name,' the voice expostulated, 'can't you leave those knockers alone? Why can't you walk in without raising a din? And don't frighten the birds with your cat.'

~

A rather bulky man on stilts was admonishing me without even looking in my direction. In a corner of the garden he was engaged in watching with uplifted face the inmates of a dovecot, poking at them from time to time with a long pole that also served to support him. Near him sat a bulldog, equally engrossed in the movements of the birds in the cot. Neither the dog nor his master took the slightest notice of me: they did not even condescend to cast a casual glance at me. Their whole attention was concentrated upon the doves.

It was a strange dovecot. I had never seen one like it before. It resembled a miniature built-up mast of a sailing ship: its lower mast bore the topmast surmounted by the topgallant mast and the royal mast, which carried a bright pennant; but, instead of the yards, or cross-beams, the mast had at the appropriate heights a number of trellised platforms for the birds to roost on, and its crow's nest was replaced by a beehive structure for their nocturnal repose. It then dawned upon me that the shafts adorning the roof terrace of the Diwan's residence were nothing other than similar dovecots.

'It is getting late,' the man with the perch said to his dog. 'The doves must have their exercise, otherwise they will become fat like you, and equally lazy.'

The dog wagged his twisted tail without shifting his position or his intent skyward gaze. Evidently he enjoyed watching his master toil with his pole to tease the doves. For he began drumming the earth with his tail to manifest his feelings.

'Piram! You are fat,' the man repeated. 'You are lazy. You do nothing but eat and sleep and watch the birds.'

The dog Piram seemed to be highly amused. He wagged his tail with greater vigour.

Fat certainly Piram was, and perhaps lazy as well. But he was by no means an abnormal member of the canine species. Whereas his master was a sight: a real monstrosity of obesity. The stilts must have been of hardened steel to bear the weight of a man of his volume. For such a man-mountain to accuse his dog of excessive plumpness sounded like a circus clown's joke. His bald pate, sleek appearance, and ridiculous manipulations with a perch reminded me of the giant performing seal known as Mambo the Marine Mammoth—the chief attraction of Professor Probhat's Animal-Parade—a celebrity in Calcutta on account of its huge bulk, walrus moustache, and fantastic dexterity in balancing a barge-pole while precariously standing on a seesaw. 'A spectacle,' Professor Probhat's posters announced, 'deserving the patronage and admiration of our national leaders and nation-builders.'

The human seal on stilts groaned, 'The doves have not yet had their first outing.'

This time the dog elected to ignore the master's comment.

'It's getting late.' The man went on mumbling to himself as he poked at the doves with his pole: it was an extensible fishing rod.

The birds did not relish being prodded at. They were not interested just then in an outing. For they clung to their roost, avoiding their tormentor's thrusts by shifting their position: they moved from one platform to another—the one immediately above. They were, however, goaded on to a still higher one. Finally, in their desperation they sought safety on the topmost perch: it was beyond the reach of the fishing rod. However, it had one great inconvenience: it was not large enough for the entire flock. The birds jostled and pushed at one another. A couple of them lost their footing and began flapping their wings frantically, and thus dislodged a few more of their brethren from the platform.

The ousted birds fluttered round the mast a few times, looking for a suitable resting-place; and finding none, they rose petulantly in the air, challenging their friends to do likewise. Their example was almost immediately followed by a few more. They flew out, one behind the other, forming a chain of quivering wings. The chain became a lengthening festoon as the remainder of the flock dashed out in quest of the errant ones. They rose higher and higher in widening spirals with the dovecot as the centre, so to say, of a reversed cone—an aerial one—of immense dimensions formed by the ellipses they made. As they reached the region beyond the pall of factory smoke, their wings caught the sun and reflected back the light like scintillating gems—now they looked like a bright chaplet of sparkling sapphires, soon changing into a circlet of translucent moonstones, finally transforming into a shimmering string of argent seed-pearls.

Soon the air throbbed with many, many more wings. For all the doves of all the dovecots were astir. They wanted to outbid those winging on high. A thousand flocks shot out in the air from every quarter: each flock flew in a single file, in the wake of its leader: each determined to give a display of graceful flight surpassing all the rivals.

Tremulous streams of jewelled garlands adorned the heavens. A feast to the eye, an angelic vision to delight and bless every beholder. 'A miracle,' I murmured. 'A miracle to be witnessed only by those dwelling under Calcutta's sky.'

The bulldog Piram was endowed with an aesthetic sense. He wagged his tail uninterruptedly as he watched the birds in flight. And the master, now lying on his back by his pet's side, waggled his walrus moustache in profound satisfaction. His labours, he reckoned, had received their reward. An expression of beatitude spread gradually over his countenance. He drummed his paunch with his chubby fingers, while his dog, Piram, beat time with his tail.

After about ten minutes' flight the birds returned to the dovecot. They dropped down, a few at a time, on to their perch; they alighted, at irregular intervals, with closed wings, and stuck fast like well-aimed lumps of clod to where they descended. Soon the whole flock was back home.

'That will do for today,' the man said to his dog, and the animal stopped wagging his tail and reluctantly raised himself from his crouching posture.

It was time, I thought, to make my presence felt. I moved forward to help the dog-owner to get back to his feet.

'No, no,' Piram's master protested, 'I should not let anyone rob me of my only exercise.'

I felt somewhat ashamed to stand there doing nothing and watching an elderly man panting and puffing to get up from the ground. He struggled like a blind buffalo caught in a quagmire. However, after many floundering movements he did manage to get to his feet unaided. This cost him so much effort that he became completely breathless. 'Ready to drop,' I said to myself, and feared for the worst. Fortunately he sat down of his own accord to regain his breath on the edge of the raised dais round the kadamba tree, and signed to me to do likewise. The dog, Piram, did the same without being asked.

'Don't think,' he panted, 'I am too proud. But I do need some exercise every day. Take, for example, the Aga Khan. On wet days when he can't play golf he refuses help for putting on his coat. "That," he says, "is my only exercise till it becomes fine." It's pretty much the same with me.'

I wondered how he came to know the Aga Khan. Was he bluffing? Could a man like him ever play golf? He was very simply clothed: a sleeveless shirt and a *dhoti* coming to his knees. A dog boy or a stable help in a rich man's house would be more amply dressed.

'Where's your cat?' he asked. 'You may now show it to me.'

His question astonished me. Who was this odd fellow harping on a non-existent cat? Was he the Diwan's dog boy? Certainly Piram was the bulldog with whose exploits Myna was familiar. She had, however, told me nothing about the dog boy.

'Just a second,' the man said as he turned his face towards the dovecot. 'Before we examine the cat let me ask you something. Did you notice how the doves returned to the cot? I mean the last ones of the flock.'

I stared at him, not knowing what to say.

'Please try to think,' he went on. 'Did they come from the right hand side? Or from the left?'

'I think,' I replied, 'they dropped from the zenith.'

'Are you sure?' He became thoughtful, began counting his fingers and mumbling to himself. The dog, as though guessing his perplexity, snuggled closer to him.

I assured him that as far as I could make out most of the birds—and particularly the last ones of the flock—dropped like stones from overhead.

This assuaged his fears. He smiled. 'Our augurs,' he said, 'will tell you that the result of this afternoon's flight of birds and their homecoming forebodes neither good nor evil for the household. You can't call this a forecast. It is just fifty-fifty.'

'Taking all things into account I would be inclined to give a different interpretation.' Neither good nor evil, according to me, gave the guarantee that there were no immediate prospects of a riot in Hargila Lane, of a conflagration, of a flood, nor of other troubles of this kind. 'So long,' I concluded, 'as things remain as they are why should you worry? Why not come to my conclusion? The weather forecast is "Fine". No immediate worry—'

'Ha! Ha!' He laughed and tapped his paunch with his fingers. The dog wagged his tail and uttered a friendly bark; the first sound to come from him since my intrusion into the garden. 'You are a clever fellow! So you define pleasure as mere absence of pain, joy absence of sorrow. Not bad! Ha! Ha! You are a real expert in ornithomancy. I have been spared the trouble of issuing a bulletin.'

I wondered if he really believed that the future could be foretold from the flights of birds. He was a strange man. Perhaps he could help me to meet the Diwan's wife. Evidently he belonged to the household. How was I to tackle him? I made some general remarks about the more expensive varieties of pigeons. 'The silken-tailed pigeons,' I said, 'cost three thousand rupees a pair. The Talukdar of Pagulpur breeds them. I believe he calls them *Rishmis*.'

The man went off again in a strange mood, and asked me brusquely if I wanted a similar sum for my cats!

I confessed his question puzzled me.

'Look here, young man,' he began in a serious tone. 'It's no use playing hide-and-seek with me. I know everything that's passing in this house. Only I have no time to bother about small matters, and I can't put my foot down on zenana affairs. But if it is a kitten that you have brought, you had better take it back. Piram will gobble it up at a single go. And you will have to bring another kitten tomorrow. That one, too, would go inside Piram. I can't be after that dog night and day. I have other things to do than to look after Piram.'

He rattled on in this way for quite some time. I did not get the chance of putting a word in edgeways. I heard to my surprise that the dog was not usually friendly. He was quite a terror in the absence of his master. Several dog boys had been badly mauled. As a rule he did not budge from the chair of his master in the 'smaller drawing-room'. But it was not the dog's fault if people came there to tease him and to lure him to other parts of the house. 'I have to look after a thousand things,' the human seal complained. 'Do you know what time I left my bed? At four in the morning. And do you know when I shall retire? After twelve at night. And even then half of my work will remain unfinished. I have no time to relax, no time for physical exercise, no time for meditation.'

The fellow was certainly crazy. 'Humour a madman,' they say in my village. 'Don't contradict him. Don't argue with him. And part company with him as soon as you can.' Therefore I told him as sweetly as I could that I was terribly sorry to know that he was so overworked, though, judging from his looks one would have thought otherwise. As for the poor dog, it must be hard for him to spend long hours without his master. I recounted to him the story of a dog I never had, and how the poor thing died of a broken heart when I left my village to discover a gold mine in Calcutta.

'I am sorry for the dog,' he interrupted. 'Now, I presume, you have taken to cats.'

I shook my head. I did not mind cats, but they were certainly not my favourites.

'Then why are you foisting cats on the mistress of the house?' he asked angrily. 'Why have you told her that she should keep a cat? "A cat will undo the evil of a dog," she says, and you are behind that stupidity. And you have been fleecing her, charging fantastic prices for your wretched kittens. How much have you charged her? Three thousand rupees for a pair? Why? That's the salary of a Cabinet Minister. So you have discovered your gold mine in Calcutta!'

I protested vigorously, forgetting all about the wise adages concerning the art of handling madmen, and confessed frankly that my objective was simply to pay my respects to the mistress of the house before calling on the Diwan with a letter of introduction from the Director of the Bureau of Weights and Measures. I told him also about my bother with the pickpockets of Bow Bazaar, and that that was why I was unable to show him the letter of Kolej Huzoor: it was folded inside my lost pocket-book.

'I don't believe a word of what you say,' he remarked gruffly. 'Not a word. You are a clever rascal. You wanted to know if I was interested in the silken-tailed pigeons. They cost three thousand rupees a pair! The same price as your Siamese kittens! Fantastic! Anyway, let me have a look at your kitten.'

Reluctantly I produced my *tulasi* prayer beads and told him once again that I was not interested in cats, and being in the financial doldrums I could offer only the string of prayer beads as a *nuzzar* to the Diwan's wife. 'I know it is worth nothing,' I added. 'But prayer beads are prayer beads. She might perhaps deign to accept them, and say a few words in my favour to the Diwan.'

The man was on his feet now, chewing the corners of his moustaches. He stretched out his hand to examine the *tulasi* beads. He took them, cupping his hands, and bent his head with his eyes closed: he held them like an oblation before an altar: suddenly he was in a meditative mood, and began praying in silence.

I respected his silence and stood to a sort of moral attention, waiting for him to address me again.

'Part company with a madman as soon as you can,' my inner-voice, however, counselled. 'Go while the going is good.' And I slowly took a couple of steps backwards, making as little noise as possible lest the madman's trance be broken.

I could easily have made my escape unnoticed but for that wretched dog. While slowly moving backwards with my eyes fixed on the madman I tripped over the beast, and my fall broke his keeper's meditative catalepsy.

III

'I would have strangled that dog, if I had been you,' said Gama, one of my hostel mates, when he heard my story.

As Gama was a champion wrestler I listened to him in silence. The wrestlers enjoyed the same prestige among sportsmen as the cows among Calcutta's fauna. Tradition accorded them parity with Brahmin pundits. Being a traditionalist I granted him his due. Moreover, he was the honorary secretary of my hostel, which was run on a co-operative basis; in other words, he gladly did the odd jobs that fell to my lot on account of the exasperating rota-system. Therefore it was highly impolitic to enter into any argument with him over the tenacity of the Diwan's overfed bulldog, Piram.

I shook my head meditatively, and he mistook my gesture for a demonstration of my love for dogs.

'All right,' he went on, 'I would not have killed him. But I would have grabbed him by the scruff of the neck and given him a sound thrashing. What's the use of your being a champion footballer if you can't administer a sound kick to a brute of a dog? You are becoming a softy. That's the trouble with you.'

I reminded him that Piram was waiting at the door of the hostel, and perhaps he would oblige me by chasing him away: he had already driven away the local pi-dogs and bitten a score of human beings. 'Gama,' I said, with all the sincerity I could command, 'I promise you a splendid dinner if you manage to drive Piram away.'

'Do you really mean it? I am fed up with our hostel grub.'

'Of course I do. I am sick of the sight of that dog. He has been on my track ever since I escaped from the Diwan's house.'

'Give me five minutes, and no more. I shall discuss the menu when I come back.' Gama went out of the room whistling. In less than a minute's time he rushed back, yelling at the top of his voice, closely followed by Piram. The brute was growling and chewing one of Gama's shoes. The wrestling champion's clothes were in shreds and it looked as though he himself was going to be torn into shreds soon. 'For heaven's sake,' he cried, 'do something about that dog.'

In spite of Gama's discomfiture I burst out laughing. Piram immediately dropped the half-eaten shoe and made a dash at me. I was nearly knocked over. The brute wanted to lick my face. I had difficulty in restraining his manifestations of profound affection. He wagged his powerful tail with such violence that my rickety table was knocked over. The noise of the crash induced Piram to make joyous bounds. It seemed as though he was determined to make mincemeat of the rest of my furniture. He nosed round the room baying his delight to the consternation of Gama. Finally he hit upon the plan of dragging my pillows from my bed to use them as cushions for his repose at my feet. Trembling, Gama profited from the dog's preoccupation with the pillows and made his escape on tiptoe.

No sooner had the dog installed himself comfortably than he fell fast asleep. It may break the heart of a dog-lover, but I have no hesitation in confessing that my own thoughts at that time were concentrated on the best means of throwing Piram out of the window.

~

Just then a man in a moth-eaten uniform stepped in through the door. Sleeping Piram did not stir: the intruder's noisy entry did not disturb him in the least. He lay quietly on my pillows as though he were a hibernating creature determined to pass a whole season in a state of coma.

The man in the moth-eaten uniform bearing the insignia of three fish-devouring storks introduced himself as an Inspector of the Corporation of Calcutta; he then handed me a piece of paper to sign. 'Your temporary dog licence,' he declared laconically.

I was too surprised to say anything.

He fumbled in his satchel and produced another piece of paper, which strangely enough did not require my signature. 'Your fine,' he muttered, 'for keeping a dog without a licence.'

'What?' I exclaimed. 'This is going too far.'

The Inspector did not bother to utter a word of explanation. The expression on my face must have convinced him that I was not going to give in easily. He looked into his satchel once again and presented me with an ink-pencil and a receipt book. 'Signature,' he demanded. 'On the dotted line, please.'

'What's all this?' I asked, and added that it was against my principles to sign anything without consulting a lawyer.

'All right. Just give your thumb impression here. This is only to confirm that I have called on you. Article 39BB of the Corporation of Calcutta Act of 1869 as modified by the Act of 1922 demands that you should acknowledge my visit—'

'That dog isn't mine.'

'The question does not concern me,' was all that he had to say.

I explained to him that the owner of the dog was the Diwan Nishi Kanta. 'He has been,' I said, 'following me about the whole day on his own accord. It's not my fault.'

'You might as well say that the dog belongs to the Prime Minister! The whole quarter has been complaining about your dog at the Corporation Office. I may tell you in confidence that the police have been informed as well. And I am going to report you to the Society for the Prevention of Cruelty to Animals.'

'Listen,' I interrupted. 'Can that huge brute be lodged in a tiny room like this?' Then I recounted to him my adventures with Piram.

~

After leaving the Diwan's house I boarded a bus. There was nothing for me to do but to return home: I felt too depressed to call on the semi-dumb niece of the Manager of the Ultra-Modern Hindu Hotel; she had only one idea about 'entertainment'—the cinema—and I did not feel like watching simpering faces and listening to nasal intonations for three unbroken hours. I tendered my exact fare to the conductor and he snapped, 'What about that dog?'

'Which dog?' I asked. 'I haven't one with me.'

'Babu!' he barked arrogantly, 'Now, don't try to cheat the Company. That dog is certainly yours.'

'Certainly not,' I protested. But hardly had the words escaped from my lips when Piram came to my side with a single bound, wagging his twisted tail and making funny noises. He decided to take his seat by my side, to make himself comfortable, and upset by his clumsy movements a fellow passenger's marketing basket. The owner of the basket was a portly lady allergic to dogs, and she went into a fit. Her companion, a grim female in nurse's uniform, raised her umbrella to hit Piram: she would have done better had she thought of administering first-aid to the allergic lady; for the threat put the dog's back up: he became so infuriated that he snapped the offending umbrella in two, and then began tearing at other umbrellas. Needless to say, this caused a general commotion among the passengers. They became as excited as if they were in a street-fight.

As in any fight, two parties were formed almost automatically. Half of the passengers were convinced that the dog belonged to me and that I was egging him on with code signs to cause havoc among them. The other half were equally convinced that Piram's owner was an American capitalist. 'Otherwise,' they argued, 'the brute would not behave with such arrogance.' Some thought of killing the beast on the spot, while the others wanted to hand him over to the police. Meanwhile the enraged dog upset every marketing basket in the bus, totally impervious to the blows showered on him. A couple of Kabulis sacrificed the seats of their baggy trousers to Piram's whim.

At first I felt sorry for Piram, but by and by my sympathy evaporated. 'After all,' I reasoned, 'he is not my dog. I must not get involved in this fight. Self-preservation, they say, is a man's first duty.'

I jumped off the moving bus with only one thought in mind: 'How am I to rid myself of that animal?' He was certainly most friendly towards me, but I did not care for the friendship of an ill-bred dog, nor for his company. I gave one backward glance to see how the bus-passengers were faring: they were engrossed in tackling Piram. Evidently the dog was unaware of the fact that I was trying to make good my escape while he was tearing away at the marketing bags and baskets. Suddenly he uttered a heart-rending howl and leapt out into the street through one of the windows. I began running as fast as I could.

I ran, and the terror of a dog ran after me, profusely salivating and uttering strange sounds that could be interpreted as, 'Why are you making your lazy pet run so fast?' Within a short time Piram disproved all the theories I had ever had about dogs in general and about bulldogs in particular. He ran faster than a greyhound across open spaces and public squares; he nosed his way through jostling crowds with the unerring assurance of a bloodhound on his victim's track; sniffing the ground like a terrier in quest of a ferret, he caught me up whenever I slowed down for breath; he boarded moving buses and running trams with the agility of a monkey; he avoided racing taxis with the facility of a true-born son of Calcutta; and whenever he caught me up he rolled over with delight at my feet, baying like a mastiff. Not only that, while pursuing me, he gave demonstrations of his temper by snapping at anything or anybody that happened to be in his way.

'Go home, Piram!' I shouted as I ran. This only urged him to amble faster to have the joy of licking my face. 'Go home and watch the birds.'

In my mad flight I managed to get in a taxi. 'Drive me fast,' I implored the chauffeur. 'Drive me anywhere. I have had enough of that dog following me for no reason.' The driver thought I was mad. He shrugged his shoulders and started the motor. But by the time I had banged the door, Piram was inside through the window. I had to jump out and run again.

In my desperation I hit upon the idea of climbing Omichund's Tower in the Boitakhana district. Its spiral staircase, I knew, was extremely narrow: too narrow, and the steps were too high, to allow a dog of Piram's size to climb right to the top. With one bound I cleared the high platform on which the Tower stood, and the next moment I almost fell on my knees to express my gratitude to the Almighty. My conjecture about the stairs was correct. Piram was unable to keep up the pursuit when I negotiated the high steps—some two hundred of them.

How thankful was I when I reached the top of the Tower! Omichund might have been a double-crosser, a swindler, and a rogue, but at that moment—having succeeded in putting a couple of hundred feet between myself and Piram—I blessed him. I leant over the parapet to see if Piram was waiting for me at the entrance to the Tower, and heaved a sigh of relief when I noticed him moving towards Hargila Lane in the wake of a pack of yelping pi-dogs. He soon disappeared from my view and I felt a heavy burden lifted off my shoulder. And I allowed myself the luxury of meditating on the strange career of the most remarkable crook in Calcutta's history.

'Eight-cornered columns are loved by the god Vishnu,' Omichund was told by the soothsayers. He sought their advice as to the best means of appeasing the dread deity *Ati*—Nemesis. 'A worshipper of Vishnu has nothing to fear from Ati. Vishnu protects his adorers and repentant sinners.' Omichund was at that time—the middle of the eighteenth century—concerned about a dirty deal. He had in the preceding year succeeded in cornering the grain market and in ousting his former employers, Boistab Sett and Manick Sett; this success was followed by still greater successes with forged documents: he was now the richest merchant in Hindustan, the biggest property-owner in Calcutta, and the principal black-marketeer in Chandernagore. 'An easy success,' the soothsayers warned him, 'leads to an easy fall. The goddess Ati is a jealous goddess. She should be appeased.' 'Blast her!' Omichund swore, 'Blast that bitch! I am not a Hindu. Why should a pious Sikh bow before the idol of Ati? I am not superstitious.'

'Superstition or no superstition, you would do well to take no chances.'

'What must I do to appease that bitch Ati? You don't expect me to shave my head?' He was told there was no need for him to go through the *puja* ceremony as he did not believe in prayers, but he could put up an eight-cornered column in honour of Vishnu and practise the three Rs: Restraint, Rectitude, and Righteousness. 'Leave your three Rs aside,' Omichund remarked. 'But a high tower has publicity value. I shall get this tower put up. It will be higher than any tower in the land, taller than the pillar of Asoka in Benares.' 'Even if you drink of the water of life unwittingly,' the soothsayers held, 'you will be endowed with eternal life.' 'But,' Omichund's favourite nautch-girl murmured, 'it is a sin to do the right thing for the wrong cause. Performing a rite without reverence provokes Ati.' No one paid any heed to her fears, and in due course the Tower was erected.

Its erection, however, did not save Omichund from disaster: in due course he received the visitation of Nemesis. All the same, I thanked my stars for having thought of Omichund's Tower as a safe retreat. Its windy parapeted gallery was as good a place to hide as the vault of a bank. I was, however, too optimistic in judging the movements of Piram: as soon as I was back on solid earth he turned up from nowhere to keep me company. He reminded me of the dread goddess Ati, and I made no further attempts to evade his attention. He followed me faithfully to my hostel, and only by a clever manoeuvre did I manage to shut the door in his face.

'Alas!' I sighed, 'Now Piram is there under my table, sleeping on my pillows.'

~

The stone-faced fellow of the Corporation of Calcutta remained unmoved. He insisted on my giving the fingerprint as an acknowledgment of his visitation of my hostel. His badgering got on my nerves and gradually I began raising my voice. Instead of throwing the dog out of the window I felt like throwing the Inspector out.

My problem was, however, settled by Piram. He woke up all of a sudden and without any encouragement on my part decided to tackle the gentleman wearing the insignia of three fish-devouring storks. I regretted that Gama was not there to laugh with me when the Inspector bounded away with the seat of his trousers missing and the contents of his satchel scattered on the floor.

With equal firmness Piram dealt with my other unexpected callers. They were numerous; the chauffeur of a car with punctured tyres, accusing Piram of making the holes; a missionary lady from the Highlands of Scotland, interested in animal welfare and anxious to know if Piram was well treated by me; a Salvation Army Sister wearing a strange costume—half-Indian and half-European. I failed to gather the precise nature of her complaint; a number of murderous-looking Kabulis armed with brass-bound cudgels—I did not give them the chance of explaining the object of their visit; two anaemic half-idiots of the Dumb Friends' League—they wanted to take Piram away; half a dozen members of the Emenroy Comradeship and Combined Bands of Brothers, accusing me and Piram of anti-Trotskyist views because one of their colporteurs had been attacked by a stray dog; the cook from a neighbouring eating-house, charging Piram with the crime of spoiling a whole week's meat ration; a vegetable-seller equally anxious to accuse Piram of filching a cart-load of bananas; the man from the Gas Corporation, he had nothing to do with Piram, but he wanted to take the readings of my meter; a zealot of the Anti-corruption League canvassing for new members...

I expected any moment the police to turn up with submachine guns to deal with Piram and me. Fortunately, nothing of the sort happened.

~

By the time I was getting ready for the evening meal, Piram was declared to be an ideal dog by all the inmates of my hostel.

He had made peace with them. Even Gama, with his wounds cauterized, patted his head.

'I think,' our champion wrestler pronounced gingerly, 'I must have frightened poor Piram when I wanted to shoo him away.'

I did not contradict him.

'A frightened dog, you know,' Gama spoke with growing self-confidence. 'A frightened dog of that size can do desperate things. Piram and I have wrestled together, and we have become friends.'

Piram wagged his tail approvingly.

'From now on,' they all declared, 'Piram will be our dog. It is good to have a real fighter to protect our hostel in these troublesome days.'

'We must build a nice kennel for him,' Gama suggested.

They all became enthusiastic over this proposal. I did not utter a word: I was sick of that wretched beast snorting at my feet and using my pillows as his cushion. A committee was immediately formed to discuss the details. Gama with Balaban, a student of architecture, and Cowry, held a three-cornered debate over the size and shape and colour of the proposed kennel. The debate lasted for a disgustingly long time. A fourth fellow, whose cousin worked in a furniture shop at Ballygunge, was invited from a neighbouring hostel to give his expert opinion. He made the issue more complicated. Before any agreement could be reached he proposed that the committee should know the exact measurements of Piram and his precise weight. A couple of measuring tapes and foot-rules were brought.

But Piram was nowhere to be found in my room. He had gone! The damage he had wrought was the only sign of his visit to our hostel. I sighed with relief.

Gama and the others searched for him everywhere: even in most unlikely places, like my chest of drawers, locked cupboards and book-cases, the water tank on the roof of the house, and the junk-room in the basement. There was no Piram anywhere.

'He has left us,' Gama sighed.

'He's gone for good,' Balaban moaned.

'A nervous dog can sulk,' Cowry commented. 'Intelligent dogs are generally nervous. Piram was highly intelligent.'

The furniture expert wondered what made them think that Piram was gone for good. But they paid no attention to his remarks.

'Perhaps,' Gama lamented, 'I frightened him without my knowing it. Poor Piram! I hope he won't get lost. Calcutta, you know, is full of dog-thieves.'

They all regretted Piram's departure. I didn't, though I pulled a long face out of consideration for their feelings.

IV

It was nearly midnight when Gama woke me up to abuse me. I was accused of being brutal and heartless: a callous materialist and a soulless atheist.

'How can you sleep on a night like this?' he asked. 'Perhaps at this very moment poor Piram is being murdered by those bloodthirsty Kabulis. Can't we two do something about it?'

I heard with indifference that all the members of the hostel were out in quest of the lost Piram.

'I am sure,' Gama propounded, 'Piram was lured away with fried sausages.'

I hate being disturbed from my slumbers. That was the reason why I occupied a most inconvenient room for the sole advantage of its being single-bedded. Just then, however, I did not mind being awakened: I was in the midst of a nightmare, reliving all the calamities of the day. The worst part of my dream was that Piram had learned the art of climbing the high steps of Omichund's Tower.

'Fried sausages,' Gama repeated. 'Do you understand? Dogs can never resist the temptation of nicely grilled meat. The Kabulis must have been parading our street carrying basketfuls of *sish-kabab* or fried sausages. And while we were talking about the kennel the poor dog must have jumped out of the window to run after those rogues.'

'Were those sausages poisoned by any chance?' I asked as I yawned. I felt like telling him, 'Good riddance,' but somehow my argumentative mood got the upper hand and I demanded what made him think that sausages were the best bait for oversize bulldogs.

'Don't pretend to be a bigger fool than you are!' Gama gritted his teeth. 'Haven't you read Jaroslav Hasek's book—*The Good Soldier Schweik?* How did the dog-stealers work in Prague?'

I reminded Gama that it was my principle not to discuss the contents of any work by a Slav, and it was most unfair to make use of Piram's disappearance to make me violate one of my principles. 'Today,' I added, 'an old fogey in Bow Bazaar wanted my opinion on Krylov. I told him frankly that Slav authors and Marx were outside my orbit.'

'You are an imbecile!' Gama hissed. 'A prize lunatic! None but an idiot would refuse to enjoy the Marx Brothers on principle. You are a stiff-necked buffalo.'

'There you have it,' I said as I rolled round to make myself comfortable. 'Leave that bulldog to his fate. He has eaten up one of your shoes and badly mauled you. Is that not enough? He has torn up my pillows, broken my table, ruined my bed. I have had more than enough of him.'

'All right,' Gama said after a pause. 'But remember, I have my principles, too. If you don't come out with me I won't do your chores any more. Nor take any messages from that skinny girl at the Ultra-Modern Hindu Hotel. You will have to look after your own affairs yourself.'

'What?' I was now up and trying my best to calm him. But he was obdurate and insisted on my accompanying him to Kalighat. 'At this hour of the night!' I pleaded, 'Kali's temple is closed till six in the morning. Do you want me to believe that the Kabulis intend offering Piram as a sacrifice to the goddess?'

'Don't try to be sarcastic,' he rated. 'I know an astrologer in Kalighat. He makes forecasts only after midnight. He will certainly tell us where we may find Piram.'

I argued that it was one of my principles not to consult astrologers, not even those thriving in Kalighat. But my argument was set aside.

'You need not come into the astrologer's house. After all, I am going to consult him, and not you. You will wait for me in the porch of the temple of Kala Bhairab—the Dread Lord of Time Eternal. Look here, man, you must show some interest in Piram's fate. We are all so upset.'

I yawned noisily to gain time to think out excuses for not going out with him. I told him that in the days before the Mahratta Ditch was dug the Kala Bhairab temple was the meeting-place of Calcutta's professional thugs. Now it was likely to be thronged with dangerous characters.

'Do you take me for a booby?' Gama burst out. 'No further excuses. I give you exactly five minutes to get ready, and no more. If you don't come out with me now I won't do your chores in future. And that's that!'

I was ready in less than two minutes: for it suddenly dawned upon me that Myna had promised to secure my stolen pocket-book. 'If you come to the temple of Kala Bhairab—the Dread Lord of Time Eternal,' I remembered her telling me, 'you will find me in the Pavilion of Dancing Women. Usually I sing there after midnight.' I decided to kill more than one bird with the same stone: going out with Gama meant keeping the promise to hear Myna sing, calming Gama himself and other hostel mates, and exploring the possibility of retrieving my pocket-book.

I did not divulge to Gama the real motive of my following him so meekly. Certainly I hated doing chores, but the hope of recovering the letter of introduction to the Diwan was uppermost in my thoughts. The pocket-book itself, as I have said before, was of little worth: it contained absolutely nothing except some unpaid bills and that all-important letter that Kolej Huzoor had written for me.

~

'Have you any idea when the dog was born?' Gama asked gloomily as the tram carrying us to Kalighat rattled along the Chowringhee. 'The astrologer may ask for his horoscope.'

'He isn't a puppy. That's all that I can tell you. Neither is he very old.'

'That's no good,' he grumbled. 'What's wrong with you? You are not in the least helpful.'

I looked out of the window and pretended not to hear him.

In spite of the lateness of the hour, the Chowringhee was crowded. The cinemas were closing and the more expensive night-clubs were opening. Midnight, I thought, is perhaps the only time when the Chowringhee presents its most agreeable aspect. 'It is then,' in Kolej Huzoor's words, 'a sight comparable with the

Corso by the Pincio Gardens of Rome. Mind you, without the *maidan*—the grazing fields with their trees—the Chowringhee would be nothing. Manohar Dass's *maidan*, right in the heart of the city, covers an area larger than London's Richmond Park.'

I did not know the relative sizes of the Pincio Gardens and of Richmond Park. But that did not prevent my enjoying the pleasant vista across the *maidan*, looking all the more enchanting on account of the bordering trees and bronze statues being floodlit. A glorious moon made a magic carpet of that immense area with the Lady Bagan, the Esplanade, and the Ochterlony Monument at one end and the Racecourse and the Victoria Memorial at the other and, in between, the playing fields, parks, football grounds, golf courses, pasturages, and pleasure gardens. The vast plain was dotted with groves of plants and adorned with pools of water; it was criss-crossed with winding paths, segmented by broad drives and traversed by the immaculate Red Road with its flanking balustrades of pure white and rows of gaunt effigies of alien administrators and warriors who made India's history, but did not make India their home; westwards it stretched right across to the strand of the mighty Hooghly river, and I fancied I saw beyond the glacis of the octagonal eighteenth-century Fort the ocean-going ships with red and green lanterns on their masts, and I thought I heard the lapping of tidal waters against their barnacle-covered sides telling the tale of many voyages across the seven seas. One glance in the direction of the *maidan* was ample compensation for the misery and squalor of the unswept pavements of the Chowringhee.

Gama, however, preferred to direct his gaze the wrong way. He was, I saw, annoyed with me. Therefore he decided to admire morosely the neon-light signs, the gigantic advertisement posters, the peeling facades of the pseudo-Georgian buildings, and the garish fronts of the modern structures lining the east side of the Chowringhee.

When the tram was passing between the Manohar Dass tank and the Indian Museum, his face suddenly lit up. 'Do you know,' he said, 'Kala Bhairab's image is now housed in the Museum?' He was happy to tell me something about Calcutta that I did not know: we often had our friendly feuds over historical monuments and sites. 'Half of the Kala Bhairab temple has been washed away by the Adi Ganga. The image was found in the river's bed. They think it dates from the time of Singha-Bahu.'

'That means at least some six hundred years before the Nativity.'

'Yes. More than two thousand five hundred years ago.'

Now that the ice was broken I decided to tackle him about a matter that had been worrying me from the day I came to Gama's much-loved Calcutta. It was about the Chowringhee.

~

The Chowringhee was Calcutta's pride and joy. It was the city's main artery. In fact, its principal avenue, boulevard, parkway, high road, shopping centre, necking parade, and pilgrimage route: all combined in one. 'Let Rome boast of her Via Sacra, and London of Rotten Row,' so the saying ran, 'Calcutta's Chowringhee beats them both.'

Maybe, those who lauded the Chowringhee did not know anything better. 'No one can blame them,' was Kolej Huzoor's argument. 'I know a lady of Nottingham who nearly fainted away when I told her that Nottingham was a filthy hole compared with Zurich. And I have met Chicagoans claiming Chicago to be a greater marvel than Paris. So you must not blame the true-born sons of Calcutta if they break into ecstasies over the Chowringhee. After all, you must concede that the road leading to the shrine of Kala Bhairab is older than the Via Sacra. And it would be idle to deny that the Chowringhee accumulates in a day more horse-dung than Rotten Row in a week. Facts are facts. They are sacred. And ignorance is bliss. A son of Calcutta would rather die than praise any other city in the world.' In this respect, I believe, the conductor who queried me about Benares was a typical son of Calcutta. However that may be, I did not deny that the Chowringhee *with* the *maidan* deserved commendation. 'But,' I often asked, 'why, in the name of God, do the authorities permit the city's principal sight to degenerate into a vast open-air lazaretto?' Walking along the Chowringhee meant fighting one's way through a throng of importuning touts and disgusting beggars. It would be an understatement to say that they infested the thoroughfare from dawn till dusk: for many of them—they numbered thousands—did make it a habit to live actually in the street for twenty-four hours of every day of the week. At night they slept on the pavements and in the day-time they plied their obnoxious trade of badgering the passers-by. With the unerring instinct of born hunters tracking down their prey, they selected as their victims for persecution strangers like me.

'Could nothing be done,' I asked Gama, 'to rid the Chowringhee of this pestilence of beggars and touts?'

'My dear fellow!' he chuckled, 'You have been caught napping. Study Calcutta's history, and everything will be clear.'

'Why not let me have the answer now?'

'The answer is two-fold: Jungal Giri Chowringhee and our lack of *matra*—the sense of measure.' Jungal Giri Chowringhee was the man who cleared the jungles through which the ancient pilgrim route to the shrines of Kala Bhairab and Kalighat passed. Originally this path was called the Deadman's Gully on account of the ruthless bands of armed men who lived in the surrounding thickets and attacked all passers-by. Once Jungal Giri Chowringhee was victimized by these robbers and he had his revenge by widening the Deadman's Gully, clearing the jungles, draining the marshes, and instituting a system of *chowkidars*—watchmen—to protect all wayfarers. The only wayfarers in those days were the pilgrims. 'And they were anxious,' Gama held, 'to acquire greater merit by bestowing alms on the deserving. Unfortunately, or fortunately, whichever you will, there were no beggars in this area a couple of centuries ago. Therefore Jungal Giri Chowringhee took the novel measure of announcing throughout the land that those seeking succour should come to his newly built avenue. And there you have the answer. Are you satisfied?'

'No. Certainly not.'

'You claim to be a traditionalist, don't you? Then why should you object to the continuation of an old custom?'

'I do. Because it goes beyond the bounds of *matra*—all measure. The fakir Jungal Giri died more than two hundred years ago, and men of Calcutta do not any more believe in the virtue of alms-giving. Therefore visitors and strangers have to be victimized! That does not make sense. Your city fathers have no knowledge of *matra*.'

Gama laughed when I reminded him that according to our ancient tradition men without *matra* would receive Ati's visitation—the curse of Nemesis.

At the end of Russa Pugla's Road we parted company. He went to his astrologer's house and I started my hunt for the walled enclosure of the shrine of Kala Bhairab—the Dread Lord of Time Eternal.

~

'Just a moment, sir.' A man six feet high stopped me. 'Will you please help us?'

Such a demand at that late hour would certainly have been ignored by me in normal circumstances. I would have told him to stop a walkie-talkie police car and seek what he needed. But the circumstances were abnormal, or, at least, his appearance was abnormal: he was accompanied by two women. (The mere presence of a pretty woman has always intensified my enjoyment of things—good or bad.)

'Will you please help us to find a few large bricks to hurl through that window? We have thrown a pebble or two. But we need bricks.'

The strangeness of the demand would have made any Haroun-al-Raschid rub his hands with delight. I have had many requests in my life: some of them were singularly odd, but not one of them could be compared with that of this six-foot-tall man demanding bricks while standing on Calcutta's macadamized streets at twelve o'clock at night.

I looked round about me. The bright moon and the street lamps lit up the pavements, which, freshly washed and swept, looked exceptionally clean. I knew that from midnight till six in the morning there was not a ghost's chance of picking up any debris from the streets, let alone a brick.

'Do you hear?' he asked. 'No,' one of the women remarked. 'They have stopped.' 'Only for a minute,' the man corrected her. 'They are probably winding the gramophone. Sir, you will hear them in a second. They are playing obscene songs on a night like this. You will have to help us.'

I asked him for further details about his complaint.

The man, as I have just said, was an altogether striking figure. He reminded me of Gagan Thakur in his younger days. A gaunt figure garbed in an unusual costume: a bright short-sleeved silk *punjabi*—collarless shirt—and a sleeveless short-coat, and a pair of immense many-pleated *pajamas*—Gagan Thakur's 'Mamamouchi Turkish trousers'—flounced at the bottom and held in position by a wide cummerbund, while a pair of what we call Grecian slippers garnished with enormous curly toes as huge as rams' horns adorned his feet; on his head he carried an embroidered black velvet cap, not unlike in shape a surgeon's cap, and in his right hand he held a silver-mounted ebony staff that might have been a sword-stick. His companions were equally dressed—or undressed, if you will—*à l'outrance*, in the style of the painted ladies of Ajanta.

Evidently they were not of Calcutta, where fashion for men demanded off-white *dhoti* or reach-me-down White-chapel western suits. Moreover, their accent made it clear—unless they were professionals from the stage—that they did not belong to Calcutta. This last factor made the rebel in me turn a sympathetic ear to their demand for bricks. What did they want the bricks for?

'Listen to the music coming out through that window. This must be stopped on a night like this.'

I heard snatches of a popular melody: one of those ephemeral favourites patronized by the lovers of western music in Calcutta, 'The Cat of the Tin-pan Alley.'

> O Ma! Mao! Ma!
> There goes the tom-cat of the alley.
> O Ma! Mao! Ma!
> There goes the cat that's naughty,
> The cat that licks tiny chicks to ease its belly.
> O Cat, you're nasty!
> But you're the cat for me, Lili, and Hali.

O Ma! Mao! Ma!
There's mummi after the cat of the alley.
O Ma! Mao! Ma!
Mummi's after the cat that's naughty,
The cat that licks tiny chicks to ease its belly.
O Ma! You're nasty!
That cat's only for me, Lili, and Hali.

'What do you say to that?' The man was trembling with indignation. 'Such profane songs on a night like this!'

I commiserated with him.

'Curse the *topiwallahs* of Delhi! They are burning money to Americanize India! They will ruin the country.'

'Hush! Hush!' said one of his companions, and the other one drew his attention to the full moon. He looked up, and raised his hands above his head, his straight staff carefully tucked under his armpit. Reverentially he joined the outstretched palms of his hands and brought the tips of the thumbs to the middle of his forehead: the *anjali* salutation to the midnight moon of the month of Ashwin.

It was, I recalled, the night of the Kojagar Lakshmi: the most propitious time for honouring Lakshmi—the Goddess of Grace and Plenitude.

Under such a moon, the man declared, his forefathers, after performing the traditional ceremony of feeding a white owl, went out into the meadows with the inmates of their harems for picnicking: the only lanterns they carried were wire lanthorns filled with fireflies. 'Not that they needed any earthly light,' he added. 'But these were placed inside the bushes of the *sephalikas*—the entwining jasmines—and by the sides of lotus-pools. These were parts of our religious ceremony. They fasted till midnight and then went out to feast under the full moon. And what are the fellows of today doing? Rejoicing in imported music from America!'

Fortunately, the song about the cat was at an end. The lover of western music was now regaling himself with snatches from a talkie called *Love Parade,* which apparently did not produce the same irritating effect on the company.

Like the elderly man who was interested in Krylov's *Fables,* my present interlocutor, too, complained that the country was going to the dogs. 'Hand over hand, I tell you. Because parents have no time to educate their children. Mothers have no time to sing lullabies to their babies. And the hundred-per-cent-patriots and the *topiwallahs* are shouting, "Produce brats and hand them over to us. We shall look after them—from the cradle to the crematorium or to the cemetery, whichever you like. We shall educate them. Meanwhile, give us your votes. We shall soak the rich, and make the masses happy." What do you say to all this?'

I made some banal remarks about the Age of Quality coming to an end with the Age of Quantity—the Age of Gold overthrown by the Age of Iron.

'Is that necessary? If only parents would look after their children. Why on earth do people have children if they are not prepared to bring them up decently? Do you know the fellow who was playing the cat's music is the son of our Cabinet Minister the Diwan Nishi Kanta? What a recommendation to have such a son! I feel like breaking my stick over his head.'

'Not that one, I hope,' one of his companions said. 'It will break your heart,' the other bantered, 'if anything happens to it.'

'Perhaps not this one,' the gaunt fellow admitted. 'This one is too good for the Diwan and his Americanized son. It is a century old.'

I told them that once I had handled a divining rod that had a name of its own: Mahendra Chandal; it was used for bringing down rain.

'Mine is not quite as useful, but it is handy. It tells me the time during the day.'

'Does it?' I asked, somewhat incredulously.

'It is my *fakir's rod* when the sun is shining. Haven't you ever seen one like it?' He held out his staff by its strap, suspending it like a plumb-line, for me to admire: it looked like the tall rod of the tipstaff; its round knob was of silver with enamelled designs. I wondered if it was a sword-stick. On closer scrutiny, I noticed that the stick itself was not round, but hexagonal, and bore a number of notches; near the strap, round the knob, there were a number of holes, one of which carried a tiny peg.

How did the rod help him to tell the time? What were the tiny holes for?

'These are for putting in the peg,' he explained. 'I can easily remove the peg from its present hole and put it into another. The shifting depends on the season.'

'I see,' I murmured, still mystified about the technique of using the time-measuring rod. 'Our year is, of course, divided into six seasons, of two months each. That's why there are six holes.'

'That's it. With the two-monthly seasons my peg is shifted from one hole to another. And the shadow cast upon the body of the rod gives the hour. The notches—the longer ones—are the hours, from sunrise to sunset.' The sun's path, I was reminded, is not at the same height throughout the year: the midday shadow in summer is shorter than in winter. 'Now you see why I have as many sides as seasons.'

I agreed with him that his rod was a wonder, and it deserved to be copied.

'There is no need for you to copy it,' he said. 'You come to see me at Luktam. And there you will find one waiting for you. My address? That's easy. You ask for the Rajah's residence. It's near the Kalinjar temple. There are some fine things to see at Luktam.'

V

I had no difficulty in spotting Myna at the Kala Bhairab shrine. She seemed to be well known to the temple attendants.

'My poor Balaram,' Myna sighed when she heard my story. But gradually she became cheeky, and interrupted the recital of my misadventures with murmurs of 'Poor Scholar!' 'Bad luck!' These were uttered not so much in sympathy as in a spirit of irony. Finally she had fits of laughter: 'Puppy-love for Roma has been followed by doggy-worry over Piram. Isn't that too bad?'

That was more than enough for me, and I brought my tale to an abrupt end.

'Have you forgotten, my dear cousin,' she asked as she fondled my hands and played with my fingers, 'our Penhari sayings?

> A mare by bridles restrain, and an elephant by a bar,
> A damsel fair by her heart: otherwise the answer's
> "Depart!"

What's the use of reading loads of books and teaching students to pass their examinations if you cannot remember our saws and maxims? They contain more wisdom than trucks of printed books.'

There were, I admitted, worse evils than being abandoned by the girl one admired or being pursued by the dog one hated.

The wretched Piram evoked Myna's sympathy; she lectured

to me about the legendary King Yudhistir who refused to enter the portals of heaven unless the stray cur accompanying him was also allowed the same privilege. She quoted a couplet from the *Great Epic* for my edification:

> The gate of heaven opens to none alone:
> Save thou *one* soul, and it shall save thine own.

She overlooked the fact that just then my concern was not with the other world but with this mundane earth. I was jobless. Odd lectures and coaching could not be called a regular occupation.

'Call it silly, if you will,' I confessed to Gama on more than one occasion, 'but I can't help it. I have a great weakness for the people of my Penhari Parganas. I may be taciturn with others when it comes to my personal affairs, but with my own people I am only too ready to exchange confidences.' 'Blood is thicker than water,' was his invariable response. Perhaps it was this call of blood that led me to tell Myna all about myself since my arrival in Calcutta. She was not only from the Penhari Parganas but almost from my own native village: from a hamlet within hailing distance. Moreover, she had seen me—at a semi-religious ploughing ceremony—when I had not as much as a stitch of clothing on my back, and she herself was no better dressed. It was she who had handed over to me the brass-bound divining rod known as Mahendra Chandal at a most critical moment when the success of a rain-bringing ritual was in grave jeopardy. It was on that occasion they had given me the name of Balaram: for I impersonated the Promethean deity Balaram who taught the first Hindu the art of ploughing. Hence Myna called me at times 'Balaram,' at times 'Scholar,' and finally, 'thou.'

'My memory for faces has never been good,' I told Myna. 'I ought to have recognized you the moment you parted your veil to give me the glad eye.' I did not dare tell her that I had thought her then to be a plain nautch-girl of Bow Bazaar, garbed as a painted bride for the Bahurupi's benefit. To make up for my initial mistake I admired her present costume, and asked what she was supposed to impersonate on the night of the full moon of Ashwin. Was she, by any chance, in the guise of Lakshmi, the deity of Grace and Plenitude?

She shook her head and said that a scholar ought to recognize her identity from her costume!

'What are you, after all? You seem to know everyone in Calcutta, even the pickpockets and the Cabinet Ministers. You must be a roaring success. The man you prefer may well hoist the flag of fortune.'

'I am only a *kirtani*,' Myna answered with a smile. 'Singing *kirtans* is my profession. What am I? A plain woman who sings plain songs in the praise of the Lord. A *kirtani* is a companion of Radha the divine shepherdess. And what is she? Less than the red dust of Braja that Radha trod.'

One of the strange oddities of our women lies in their art of shifting from the comic to the serious mood. 'The Penhari people are all crazy,' Kolej Huzoor propounded. 'Schizophrenics. Not one demon but a dozen devils dwell in every one of them. Once I had to collect some statistics from a lunatic asylum in Hazaribag. And what did I discover there? Some of the inmates had escaped and they had been replaced by a number of your so-called sane people! Even the psychiatrist I brought with me failed to find out who were the real loonies and who were posing as loonies for the benefit of the careless keeper of the asylum. Can you imagine such a thing anywhere else? I can't, and I have seen a good bit of the world. This is impossible even in Hamlet's England. Your Penhari men are the limit.' 'What about our women?' 'The less said the better,' Kolej Huzoor replied in a bitter tone. 'They change their minds and their moods in a split second.' There is, I must admit, some truth in what Kolej Huzoor said. And at that moment I did not know whether Myna was talking seriously or not about her being a very plain itinerant singer unworthy of the confidence of a university graduate.

I told her that in her own estimate she might be anything. But it was her turn to be reminded of a Penhari saying about all women all over the world:

> Nature herself gives women wit;
> Men may learn from books a bit.

'So says the scholar!' she said ironically. 'What next?'

As regards her alleged plainness, I emphasized, she was not quite as plain as to be a nonentity. Her form, which evoked the spontaneous admiration—and profound suspicion!—of the grandpa addicted to Krylov's *Fables*, her suppleness with which she bewitched the rascally vendors of Bow Bazaar, her oval face with the dainty chin, her lustrous eyes with long lashes, these and her other virtues entitled her to be counted a beauty even in a bevy of film stars and deepy-heart-throbs. I did not tell her—though it was uppermost in my mind—that she had the bosom of a goddess and that her skin was like ivory polished with the attar of Nur Jahan roses.

I am doubtful if she paid much attention to my compliments: for she began humming something to herself as though trying to recall the melody of a forgotten song.

I scrutinized her colourful costume. Her many-pleated bell-shaped skirt of heavy material came almost to her ankles: its colour was a pleasure to the eye, scarlet with a touch of warm orange; it bore patterns of tiny dots of flame-tinge surrounded by white circlets. This variety of scarlet is traditionally known as the dye of the soil of Braja. Her tight, sleeveless bodice was of the country style, in other words, extremely short, exposing the neck, part of the bosom and midriff and the entire back; it was flame-coloured, and its pattern was the reverse of that on her skirt, white dots with scarlet centres. Over her head she wore, like a hood, a semi-transparent tasselled stole of azure blue—the blue of the sari of the divine shepherdess Radha. And then her jewellery! Her old-fashioned ornaments if displayed in a museum showcase would have drawn a crowd. They were the choicest achievements of the master craftsmen of the Penhari Parganas. Each piece merited close scrutiny and admiration. I noticed that her anklets, girdle, bracelets, bangles, armlets, armbands, necklaces, carcanets, and even her ear-rings bore minute clusters of berry-shaped bells. Radha's companions were, I understood, adorned in this way for dancing to the music of Krishna's flute.

I was not exaggerating when I told her that she looked far prettier in her Braja-bashi costume than when I had seen her in the company of the Bahurupi.

'That is as it should be,' she replied in a matter-of-fact way, and went on humming.

I found it rather strange that she should be swallowing my choicest compliments without any murmurs of mock protest. Only a minute ago she was referring to herself as a simple *kirtani* unworthy of sitting beside a scholar! Therefore I asked her if she did not feel a bit weighed down by her splendour.

'No,' was her ready reply. 'Why should I? Certainly not tonight. Am I not Radha's handmaiden?'

What was passing in her mind just then I did not know. However, I surmised that the full moon of Ashwin meant the anniversary of Radha's first tryst with Krishna, therefore Myna—a self-elected handmaiden of Radha—deemed it to be her night of tryst as well: she was decked to be worthy of the goddess she adored.

~

Strange thoughts raced through my mind. They were sheer blasphemy. But it was always like that with me. A chance-heard remark has often caused me a series of headaches, a casual word intense cerebration.

'Is she a good-looker, this Myna of yours?' Gama had asked me, I recalled, at the tramway terminus before we parted company. 'If she is a good-looker and if she really means to do you a good turn I would give you a piece of practical advice. Take her in a taxi to the New Hurrah Club, and try your luck. The dope may work.'

'What do you mean?'

'Look here, old chap,' he spoke sharply, 'I don't mind, but our accountant is getting sick of you. He won't let you run up any further bills. It's high time you got into some steady job.'

The long and short of Gama's admonition was simply this: I was to take a pretty-looking girl to the New Hurrah Club or to the '99 Gay-Necks Roost' and spend there a few minutes looking for someone not likely to be among the all-night carousers, for example, Ek Nambur or his Chief Assistant, and then walk out. The rest, according to him, would be simple: My future would be settled for good.

'How?'

'You may leave the matter to me. But I promise you one thing.

If you do as I tell you there will be a well-paid job waiting for you with the sunrise.'

'It doesn't make much sense,' I said. 'The Chief Assistant is now away lecturing, and surely Ek Nambur is confabulating with Sheik Agah Ali in Kashmir. Only a lunatic would look for them in the night-clubs of Calcutta.'

'You are a prize lunatic yourself,' Gama raved. 'You are the limit! Now let us not waste time quarrelling over your idiocy. Listen to me and learn.'

I listened and learned that the number of fast ladies in Calcutta, though appallingly large, was not large enough for the black-marketeers, tax-evaders, and professional patriots of the city. They were anxious to make new discoveries, and once a man acquired the reputation of being some sort of a ladies' man he was bound to be courted by the new-rich and the after-us-the-deluge gang—our new masters.

'They will all run after you,' Gama propounded. 'The lecherous dogs will lick your feet and beg you to introduce them to the beauty destined for, say, the flourishing Baniahs. Do you understand? I will talk for you, and tell those dogs, "Give my friend a job and you will get what you want. But you must give him a job with a contract. Preferably a job outside Calcutta." Do you see what I mean? If Myna returns you your purse, ask her for a further favour.'

'But, Gama, you have forgotten one of my principles. I refuse to exhibit any one as a bait to the rogues.'

'Go and hang yourself,' Gama hissed as he trotted away in the direction of the astrologer's house.

Though I was not interested in Gama's suggestion, it occurred to me that if I could ever induce Myna to accompany me to a floor-show in any of the more expensive night haunts there would be a general commotion: some of the professional beauties would faint off, and most of the favourite singers would get attacks of sore-throat. Thanks to Haren Ghosh—the only cabaret agent I knew in Calcutta—I had had occasional engagements as a flautist in some of the clubs, and knew for myself that there was considerable truth in what Gama said. Moreover, I was not quite immune from offering bribes. At times I did offer tips for services yet to be rendered. But to use Myna as a pawn for securing a job was revolting.

However, the idea of causing a sensation with Myna as my partner tickled my fancy. And when she started singing I felt almost mesmerized.

~

Myna's soprano voice was like that of a song-bird in ecstasy, pouring its heart out in melodious notes. And the words of her chant! They were as exquisite as her voice. She recounted Radha's story in songs and dances to the enthralled listeners: they sat cross-legged in serried circles round her on the stone-paved courtyard of the Kala Bhairab sanctuary. The glorious full moon of Ashwin was overhead. Its resplendence obliterated the stars from the sky, and inundated the earth with unearthly beauty, transforming the weather-worn cobblestones of the yard into ravishing moonstones of rare quality; the crawling Adi Ganga was metamorphosed into a silver stream sparkling with precious pearls and scintillating sapphires.

The listeners sat in respectful silence, carefully attending to every word that came from Myna's lips, to the minutest modulation of her voice, and to her slightest gesture. They heard what every one of them knew by heart: a tale told so often that it had no novelty whatsoever. Yet they listened with such rapt attention that a stranger, were he there, would have thought that a new mystery was being revealed by a sibyl to a hypnotized throng. And had the stranger been acquainted with the language in which the twice-told tale was being recounted he would, in all probability, have been deeply shocked. He would have found nothing edifying in it. For it was, in Kolej Huzoor's terms, 'plainly erotic—the story of an illicit love-affair'—Radha's amorous longings for the fickle cowherd, Krishna.

~

'I want him,' Radha whispered to her companions. 'I am love-lorn. I am dying for him. Yet I want him not if he does not desire me. Therefore I have hidden myself in this secret grove. Let him seek and find me.'

Radha's cheeks were wet with tears.

'But,' Radha sobbed, 'I am unhappy. What shall I do should he try to find me and fail to discover my hiding-place? What would you do if that were the case? Tell me, my *kirtanis,* what should I do? I cannot live without him. Yet how can I humble myself? Do you think he wants to spurn me?'

Radha's tongue uttered what her heart desired but her reason disavowed:

> 'Go to him—win him hither—whisper low
> How he may find me if he searches well;
> Say, if he will, joys past his hopes to know
> Await him here; go now to him and tell
> Where Radha is, and that hence she charms
> His spirit to her arms.'

Meanwhile, Krishna himself was in quest of Radha. However, he, too, did not know if his beloved Radha wanted him or not. Where was she? Not in her usual arbour? Where was she hiding herself? And why? Was it because he was unworthy of her love? Perhaps she was ashamed of his profession of a cowherd?

Krishna talks to his flute, and receives the response, 'Breathe into me, Lord! Caress me with your lips.' At the touch of his lips the reed instrument sings.

Its sad strains complain of Radha's absence and Krishna's sad plight.

> If I were a bulbul, a trilling bulbul, my Radha!
> I would stray where'er you pray
> to chant your sacred echo.
>
> If I were a bee, a humming bee, my Radha!
> I would fly where'er you hie
> to chase your scented shadow.
>
> If I were a coral, a burning coral, my Radha!
> I would hide where'er you bide
> to steal on your sweet lips' bow.

The trials of Radha and Krishna moved everyone to tears. And I was no exception.

VI

When the recital came to an end and I was getting ready to rejoin Myna, someone whispered to me that I ought to be more careful as there might be some plain-clothes policemen and detectives about.

'What's all this nonsense?' I growled. 'I can look after myself.'

'Forgive me, sir, but your jemmy is showing.'

I sprang to my feet instantly as though stung by a dozen wasps. It was, I knew, the invariable practice among Calcutta's cut-throats, when likely to be apprehended by the police, to shove their lethal weapons into the pockets or bags of unsuspecting people, and then to join in the general hue and cry. How did a jemmy get into my pocket?

'Please hide your jemmy,' the man repeated. 'Its handle is showing.'

I felt for my breast pocket. Thank God, it was not a jemmy but my own fountain pen: the gift of Dinesh Sen: an object of mammoth proportions; it was like a piccolo in length and diameter. 'I have written several million words with it,' Dinesh Sen told me when he bestowed this monumental pen on me. '*My History of Bengali Literature* would never have been finished but for it. From now on it is yours. Keep it always with you. And write one day with it the History of Bengali Religious Literature in Bali, Laos, and Champa.' I felt like giving the profferer of good advice a sound kick. He was still sitting cross-legged on the ground: a thin, half-starved creature with an expensive all-chromium camera in his hand. I glowered at him. His miserable physique spared him the privilege of enjoying a kick from a champion footballer.

Moreover, I became interested in his camera: it was one of those newly imported things that took splendid pictures even in the dark without any flares or flashlights. A magnificent camera like that was enough to soften my heart. But what was he?

'I am a punk,' he stammered as he got to his feet. 'I mean a photographer's punk.'

'And what is that?'

The fellow mumbled that until recently he was devilling for a press-photographer as a mere punk. But he was not on his way to become a fully-fledged photo-reporter himself. 'If you would only help me,' he stuttered. 'You seem to know the *kirtani* well. With your help I may perhaps get a good illustrated interview out of her. I work for *Life-in-Technikolor*.'

'Why don't you talk to her yourself?'

'The trouble is,' the photographer grinned, 'the *kirtani* seems to be uneducated. You know what I mean. She does not realize the publicity value of being photographed for my weekly. And then she seems to have no knowledge of Shakespeare.'

'Is that a great handicap for a simple interview?' I was genuinely surprised: for the weekly *Life-in-Technikolor* was destined, as far as I knew, for the illiterates and semi-literates. It had an enormous sale on account of its pictures, crossword puzzles, and prizes. It hardly carried any reading matter except explanations or captions of its lurid technicolor photographs. So I told him, 'You are speaking to me in plain Bengali, not in Shakespeare's English. Why can't you do the same to her?'

He began maundering in a way that made me impatient. He had, I understood, tried to tackle Myna on his own, but with no success. Perhaps with my aid he could get her response to a Shakespearian quotation:

> What's Hecuba to him, or he to Hecuba,
> That he should weep for her?

I was too amazed to interrupt him.

He told me that his 'American boss' had consulted some Shakespearian authorities and hit upon that question as the most suitable for gauging the reactions of India's 'indigenous actors' to the aim and purpose of drama in general!

Among others figuring on the 'American boss's remarkable list of Shakespearian scholars there was the name of Foni Dhar: a man I detested. During his thirty years of professorship of English literature this fathead had not written a single essay on any subject remotely connected with Shakespeare or English literature. He had one pet theory: that Shakespeare's plays were meant to be read and not acted. Had he propounded this thesis in writing, it would have been something. But this lazy pedant's academic activity consisted of being particularly nasty to those candidates I coached. I was anathema to him because I owned some early editions of Shakespeare's works, and I had not asked him to open an exhibition entitled 'Shakespeare and Calcutta,' organized by me. This exhibition consisted mainly of the printed programmes and handbills of Shakespeare's plays given in Calcutta during the eighteenth century and the first half of the nineteenth. Much to Professor Dhar's chagrin it was a Javanese artist passing through Calcutta whom I invited to give the inaugural talk.

'Do you think,' the fellow repeated, 'the *kirtani* will answer the question, *What's Hecuba to him, or he to Hecuba?*'

'That's something for the B.A. candidates,' I replied dryly. 'And they generally spout out the answers their professors have dictated to them.'

The fellow muttered something about Professor Dhar.

At the mention of that fathead my temper rose, and I gave vent to my feelings by calling Professor Foni Dhar the Master Bluffer, the perfect nincompoop, an ignoramus who knew as little of Hecuba's trials as of Radha's. 'He does not care two hoots for

Shakespeare and still less for Greek theatre. It is unfair to put a question to Myna which your great authority Foni Dhar himself cannot answer.'

'You may be right,' the photographer whined. 'But I have to think of my job.' I was told that *Life-in-Technikolor* was partially owned by an American concern, and the representative of the American shareholders was just then in Calcutta. He was a Chicagoan with progressive views and was very keen about promoting mass-culture through pictures. 'Up till now I have been only a punk. Now, thanks to him, I have got my new assignment as a press photographer. I must get a series of shots on the "Indigenous Actors' Reactions to Shakespeare's Query". I have to cover this evening somehow. My pictures are ready. But I want the captions. Otherwise I shall lose my job. So you see my dilemma? My boss—Sol Mischkon—is known as Hard-Shell.'

I saw his point and congratulated him on having secured a culture-loving, progressive Chicagoan as his boss. I regretted, however, that I could do nothing to secure any answers from Myna for the benefit of Shakespeare-lovers like Foni Dhar the Fool and Sol Mischkon the Chicagoan.

The half-starved photographer clung to me as I turned my back. He murmured something about his rice bowl being cracked and a man in affluent circumstances like myself having an obligation to the needy.

'Look here, my dear man,' I barked angrily. 'I try to make both ends meet by coaching students. What makes you think that I am wealthy? Because I am not dressed in the off-white costume of Calcutta people? And even if I were wealthy there is no reason why I should waste my time on a man with a camera worth fifteen hundred rupees.'

I had a few words with Myna before I left the sanctuary. She asked me to call on her again with my flute. I promised to do so.

In the street the photographer kept on whining by my side. Could I not tell him something that might do for the captions of his pictures? How was he to make Radha's story comprehensible to the American from Chicago?

'You may,' I said, just to get rid of him, 'do that in a single sentence: Radha is supposed to represent the human soul's longing for reunion with the Divine, symbolized by Krishna.'

'You are so helpful,' he murmured as he produced his notebook. 'It is very kind of you.'

'Radha's story is similar to that in the biblical Song of Songs. Yes! The exact title is *The Song of Songs* or *The Canticle of Canticles,* if you will. The Chicago University version is by Theophile Meek. It is excellent except that the word "navel" in it should be "woman's sex". Is that clear?'

'Most certainly. But one word more. Do you think Radha ever lived?'

'Of course she did. She does even now. Every woman in love is Radha, and her lover is Krishna.'

The fellow went on scribbling in his notebook as I boarded a bus going in the direction of the Hooghly: I wanted to bathe in the river before returning home.

Did he understand, I wondered, why Myna had chosen the Kala Bhairab temple for singing her songs? The throne of the deity was flanked by a monstrous stone tiger –'The symbol,' in Myna's words, 'of Love's fierceness.'

PART TWO

Life-in-Technikolor

I

I had to smile in spite of myself as I thought of the vague promise wrung out of me by Myna. 'Give me your word of honour,' was her demand, 'you wouldn't ill-treat Piram if he came back to your hostel.' Her solicitude for that wretched beast surprised me, and the promise was given.

I grinned because there was a general rejoicing in the hostel: Piram was back! He was quietly reposing under my table. Gama was out. So was Balaban. They had to go out early to their office. But they had left a message for me extolling the virtues of the astrologer of Kalighat: for a small consideration the expert on stellar influence had prophesied that if Gama searched for the animal in the proper quarters he would find him safe and sound!

Piram was certainly safe and sound under my table, and my homecoming was welcomed by the beast with manifestations of unfeigned joy. Myna, too, foretold this eventuality without consulting the stars. 'It may seem trifling or trivial to you, my Balaram,' were her words, 'but it is good to know that an animal like Piram trusts you implicitly. Sometimes it is not unimportant to feel that someone needs you badly, be it even an insignificant creature like a dog. If King Yudhistir could bear with a stray cur you can certainly put up with the Diwan's pedigree dog.' I was further exhorted to manifest some affection for Piram so that he could gradually gain faith in himself and a growing kindness towards the world.

'Babu,' the trembling cook reported from behind the safe barrier of a wall, 'Piram would have killed the photographer who came to take pictures. The poor man managed to escape in time. He has left a card for you.'

It was a message from the *Life-in-Technikolor* fellow. How did Piram guess that the reporter was not an inmate of the hostel? The cook did not know. Neither did I. Piram had a twinkle in his eyes. His facial expression was rather stupid, somewhat lethargic, but his eyes revealed that he had a sense of humour. So what could I do except pat Piram on the head? I counselled him again not to harm any inmate of the hostel except the accountant fellow who was getting annoyed about my unpaid bills. Piram wagged his tail to assure me that he understood what I meant.

II

With Piram to protect me from all intruders, I enjoyed my midday siestas and thought over many things, particularly Myna's comments. I was now a regular visitor to the nightly gatherings in the Kala Bhairab shrine, and acting as Myna's flautist.

III

The presence of Piram under my table was the occult confirmation of Myna's thesis that all was not well in the many-roomed mansion of the Diwan. Was the old boy not getting on with his second wife? Perhaps the bickerings in the household got on the dog's nerves. The poor thing needed peace and affection: this was perfectly comprehensible.

'Most likely,' Myna held, 'Piram will spend the days with you and the nights with his master. The Diwan is rarely at home in the day-time. He may love his dog and his pigeons, but is too busy to look after them. He is much worried over his son.'

Perhaps Myna was right.

'A son is not a blessing you can buy. And the Diwan's America-returned son is certainly no blessing to him. They say he is the error of the Diwan's first wife. The poor woman—she wanted to buy a blessing and got a curse instead.'

'Can one ever buy a blessing?' I asked myself.

Immediately Myna's emphatic affirmation came to my mind: 'Of course one can *secure* a blessing if one wants to.'

'Nonsense! Arrant nonsense!'

'Don't be too sure of your views,' was Myna's rejoinder. 'Did you not help your village to secure the end of a drought with the divining rod, Mahendra Chandal? Was that not a blessing?'

'Perhaps that was a coincidence.'

'Poor Balaram! Was it a coincidence that you went through a forest fire unscathed? Why did not the falling trees crush you to death? Have you forgotten the yogini who rode a tame nilgai? Were you not blessed by her? Was that, too, a coincidence?'

'I was then a mere child. I can't recall the details.'

'Don't try to deceive yourself. You recall perfectly well that the yogini made you walk through fire. Now Calcutta has changed you, and you don't want to believe in miracles. Isn't that the case? Balaram! Be truthful. Give me your answer. Look into my eyes. What have you to hide from me?'

'All right. Have it your own way. I am simply afraid of things I can't explain.'

It was no use arguing with Myna. She knew all about my miraculous escape from the forest fire. But how did one secure a blessing? It depended, Myna held, on the person who sought the blessing and the blessing itself. 'A mite may do for a poor widow who has faith, and a million may not help a faithless monarch. Take the basket-maker's widow at Luktam. She got what she needed; while the Diwan's wife received the wrong thing. The Rajah of Luktam will gladly tell you whether I am right or not. You have met him, haven't you?'

It was true the Rajah was there with his two wives in the courtyard of the Kala Bhairab temple, squatting on the ground amidst other listeners. He was, I came to know, a cognate of the Diwan. It was silly of Myna to suggest that I should ask him to recount the folly of the Diwan's wife, or even to talk about the basket-maker's widow; it was hardly the place to discuss it. 'Myna!' I said. 'Call me an atheist, if you will. But I am not mad. There is such a thing as *matra*. Can any reasonable man bother the Rajah—or anyone else—just now?' 'There you have it,' she said. 'The man who knows his *matra* will easily secure what he wants: he will not be denied the blessings he deserves. He can buy it for a song.'

In other words, the basket-maker's wife knew her *matra*, and the Diwan's wife did not: the one received a blessing, and the other a curse instead.

~

The basket-maker's widow plied her dead husband's craft. She was hard-working. She never gave herself any rest. Nevertheless, all that she earned simply went to make both ends meet. She could never save a cent. This worried her, not so much for herself as for her child. 'What will he do when he grows up?' she wondered. Though simple and unlettered she had enough sense to see that hand-made baskets were fast going out of fashion. 'In ten years' time,' she said to herself, 'perhaps no one will want any baskets. Therefore there's no point in teaching my son the art of basket-making.' However, what could she teach him instead? 'If only I had a hundred rupees,' she told her neighbours, 'I should then buy my son a plot of land, and train him to be a market-gardener. But where am I to find the hundred rupees?'

'You should try to secure a blessing,' they said. 'That would end your worries.'

'Where does one secure a blessing?'

'Why! In every place of pilgrimage, as a matter of course. Even in our temple of Barga-Bhima, which is only a mile away.'

The poor widow thanked her neighbours and thought over the matter till she reached a strange conclusion. 'The more inaccessible a place of pilgrimage,' she reasoned, 'the greater its potency for conferring blessings.' She did not want too much: just one hundred rupees and no more. Now Ganga Sagar was one hundred miles from the place where she lived. Therefore, as far as she was concerned, Ganga Sagar was the predestined holy spot for securing a blessing.

A few days later she talked to one of the boatmen carrying coal to Ganga Sagar and Calcutta. She had with her the handsomest basket she had ever made. The boatman was amazed at her request to exchange her handiwork for a blessing.

'I have never heard of anyone buying or selling blessings in any port of the world,' he laughed. 'Dear Mother! Someone must have been pulling your leg. Whoever could have given you this crazy piece of advice to exchange your best basket for a simple blessing at Ganga Sagar?'

'Never mind who gave it,' the widow replied. 'I am a poor woman. I have to think of my son's future. What harm would it do to you to exchange this basket for a blessing at Ganga Sagar on your return journey? Please take it with you and see what can be done.'

'What does a blessing look like?' the boatman asked in a mock serious tone.

The woman said she did not know. A blessing could be in any form, even as immaterial as a dream, or a song. The boatman, though reluctant, was eventually persuaded to take the wickerwork basket with him. But very soon he forgot all about it.

At Ganga Sagar the boat was loaded with its usual cargo for the return journey and was on the point of setting sail for Luktam when the boatman heard someone crying, 'Who will buy a blessing? The last blessing of the season. Who will buy my blessing?' This reminded him of the widow's request.

'Hey! Crier! What's a blessing?' the boatman demanded.

'How much do you want for it?'

'A blessing is a kind of porpoise,' the seller explained. 'I will take anything you would care to offer. It's the last one of the season. And no one wants it.'

'Will you exchange it for this basket?'

The transaction was readily concluded.

When the boatman cut open the porpoise for salting he found a large oyster-shell inside the animal's stomach. 'This is very handy,' he said to himself. 'The basket-maker is such a simpleton she does not know what a porpoise looks like. So I shall give her this oyster-shell and tell her that this is what they call a blessing at Ganga Sagar.'

And that was what he did when his boat returned to Luktam.

The poor widow did not know what to do with her oyster-shell. Her neighbours laughed when they saw it was all she had received in exchange for her best wicker basket. 'The boatman has cheated you,' they said. 'He must have made a few rupees, and picked up that oyster-shell for nothing at Ganga Sagar.'

'If this comes from Ganga Sagar,' the widow replied, 'then it must be a blessing. Ganga Sagar is a holy spot, a renowned place of pilgrimage.'

'Then split it open. Keep one half for yourself and give the other half to your son. A blessing is to be shared alike by those living under the same roof.'

When the oyster-shell was split open it was found to contain two of the richest pearls ever seen. 'My pearl,' the widow said, 'I shall offer to the goddess Barga-Bhima. My son's will buy him a plot of land.'

'The basket-maker's widow received a blessing, but the Diwan's wife received a curse. And a curse, too is shared by all living under the same roof.'

Why a curse, and not a boon? She, too, had faith. Did she not worship the goddess Lakshmi? Did she not make the Diwan keep with her the vigil of the full moon of Ashwin every year as long as she lived? What sin had she committed to merit the punishment of having an unworthy son?

'She did not know her *matra*. She wanted a miracle: she wanted to revive the dead with the *Nishir Dak*.'

Well, what exactly was her full story?

'Have you never heard of the *Nishir Dak*? The weird call at dead of night?'

'Apart from the noisy wailings of Fakir Cheraguddin for alms and the howlings of the pi-dogs, I don't think any other noise has disturbed me in my slumbers.' The fakir in question was trying to raise a big sum for a mausoleum dignified enough to contain his holiness. Each night at about eleven he passed in front of our hostel carrying a bowl in one hand and a lighted lamp in the other—his insignia of office—and announcing the amount he had collected during the last twenty-four hours and the balance still required for the completion of his tomb. The niggardliness of the almsgivers was denounced by the pious man in loud and bitter terms. His chief complaint was that though he was most anxious to leave this world of sin for the abode of the celestial houris, the projected fine mausoleum was still unfinished: the sooner it was erected the better it would be for all concerned! Therefore, all men of goodwill were urged to fill his begging-bowl to the brim with silver and gold. This holy fakir's call was certainly most weird. But was it what Myna called the *Nishir Dak?*

'The cry of the *Nishir Dak* is raised by a woman on a dark night. If you ever hear it, don't answer it. Just ignore it, or, if you care, watch in silence the woman who calls out your name or somebody else's name. But don't respond to her summons. She may yell right into your ears, but you must not say "Yes" to her invitation.'

'Must every cry for succour at night-time be ignored?'

'No, not necessarily. The outcry of the *Nishir Dak* can be raised only by a woman after midnight, and not every night, either; exclusively on the dark nights of the new moon. And then, it is out of the question during the months of the monsoon. Heavy downpours would never permit a lighted coconut to be carried far.'

'With a lighted coconut! Is it used as a torch? How does one change a coconut into a torch?'

'Not into a torch, you silly. But into a rushlight, and this is easily done with a burning wick floating on a layer of vegetable oil inside the nut.'

My sluggish brain demanded further details.

'The top of a green coconut is hacked off with the single blow of a sharp billhook anointed with vermilion, and some oil is poured inside, on top of the milk of the coconut. Naturally, the oil comes to the surface and feeds the flame of the burning wick.'

'Why is the lighted coconut the most sinister thing about the *Nishir Dak?*'

'Because it is her witches' cauldron. Not only that, it is her armour and weapon, and garment as well—though not much of a garment. It is carried aloft on the crown of her head, and kept in position by the left hand, while the hacked-off top is carried in the right hand. She goes about calling out different names, and whenever a person responds she puts out the light by replacing the severed top in position. Then her mission is done.'

The lighted coconut, I understood, is of great help in judging the errand of a naked woman out and about towards midnight, walking as though in a trance, with her hair undone and wearing nothing save wreaths of red hibiscus flowers.

'Give such a woman a wide berth,' was Myna's counsel. 'Never, never answer her call. She may ask for charity: she may say her son is in great distress and a man of good will ought to help a poor distracted mother: her only child is dying and would no one part with his life to prolong her son's? Give her a wide berth, Balaram. Don't be misled by her meanings. She may stretch out her hands to grasp yours. Don't touch her and don't let her touch you. If you touch her or answer her call you will fall in a swoon, and by the time you regain your senses you will cease to be your usual self. You will not die, but when your eyes reopen you will find yourself lodged in someone else's body, and your own changed into a lifeless corpse.'

'If I ask her from the top of my balcony, "Hello! Who are you? What has happened to your clothes?" What will happen then?'

'Nothing. She will not hear you unless your remark is made in response to hers.

'However, the moment one acknowledges her call his spirit will be attracted by her as though by magic, like iron filings to a magnet; it will go inside the coconut, and the woman will keep it imprisoned by replacing the top of the nut. She will then rush back to the house from which she has emerged. Her trance will come to an end, and the people who commissioned her to go out on her errand will pour out the milk of the coconut on the dying person whose life they wish to prolong.

'The dying person will be revived with your spirit. From then onwards you will continue to live your natural term of life inside his body.'

'So that is the *Nishir Dak*. But what did the Diwan's wife do?'

'She prolonged her son's life with the help of such a *Nishir Dak*, otherwise her son's body would have rotted away ages ago. That's why I say the Diwan's son is not his son, but his first wife's error.'

~

'May I have only one son,' was the prayer of the Diwan's first wife. 'Give me, O Lord, as many daughters as you may care to bestow. But let me have just one son.'

This was contrary to the time-honoured demand of all Hindu wives. Who cared for daughters? None. But the Diwan's wife was an exceptionally intelligent woman: she did not want more than one son because she had seen the tragedy of the patrician homes blessed with more than one male scion; they were rarely on speaking terms during the life-time of their parents, and when the paterfamilias departed this earth the sons started their battle royal over their inheritance. They fought like the monstrous sabre-toothed dogs of prehistoric days. Though they did not tussle with their own teeth and claws—only with paid retainers, hired thugs, and shady lawyers—they carried on their struggle till they destroyed each other. The daughters, however, did not show any such bellicosity.

True to the tradition of all Hindu households, the Diwan's wife—then aged thirteen—kept her night-long vigil on her wedding night; she was shown the Pole Star and counselled to refer to it as the Star of Constancy, and she was further told that whatever one prayed for—with sufficient earnestness—on the morning following the wedding night was invariably accorded to a believing bride.

With the end of her vigil she undertook, as all Hindu brides did, the pilgrimage to the temple at Kalighat. On her way back she stopped with her companions in the middle of the Chowringhee to visit the Indian Museum. This ceremony, too, was part of a religious rite, though neither she nor any of her companions knew of this fact.

Ages ago, when Jungal Giri Chowringhee built the highway to the shrines at Kalighat, an image was excavated near the Manohar Dass reservoir: it was a standing figure in the round of the Buddha with his right hand raised in blessing. The facial expression of this Buddha was the same as that of the seated statue on the altar of the Kala Bhairab shrine on the Govindapur Creek. The image of the blessing Buddha was placed in a temporary structure opposite the Manohar Dass pool, the present site of the Indian Museum. Since then all pious people returning from their pilgrimage to Kalighat have deemed it their duty to perform the rite of circumbulation of the area sanctified by the image of the standing Buddha with a raised hand.

The Diwan's newly wedded wife did not, as has just been said, know anything about the reason why all pilgrims made it a point on their way back from Kalighat to visit the Museum and to scurry through it. Like others she was hustled round the never-ending galleries and corridors of that vast building in the same way as the worshippers were hurried round the altars of deities: the quicker the circumambulation the better for the guides. When passing through the hall of the Siwalik Fossil Remains the sight of clay models of a number of prehistoric beasts made her tremble with fright: she became panic-stricken by the Amphicyon, a doglike animal as large as a polar bear, and the Machairodus or sabre-toothed tiger, with its canine fangs about a foot long with a body in proportion to its teeth.

'My God!' the thirteen-year-old bride gasped, 'How did these monsters come to be killed off? In those days men had no guns.'

A short-sighted man in an off-white dhoti and a buttoned-up coat, none too clean, was wiping his glasses with a stained handkerchief. He thought the question was addressed to him. He gave a sour grin.

The spectacle of a girl-bride surrounded by companions not much older than herself gave the short-sighted man the inspiration to deliver an address. He was a confirmed bachelor—and what was more, a misogynist, a corresponding member of an American religious body called the Shakers. His hortation was not on fossils but on the evils of conjugal existence and the sin of begetting children: it ended with the remark that the sabre-tooth tigers destroyed themselves in brotherly embraces. 'The same was the story of the dinosaurs. Each pair fought with each other till they both perished. Each died of the wounds inflicted by its brother.'

'How horrible.'

'No more horrible, I can assure you, than the end of the Hindu rajahs, Pathan conquerors, Mogul emperors, and their successors. They all destroyed themselves in fratricidal fights. Our present rulers, too, will destroy themselves in the same way.'

'Is that possible?'

'Read this pamphlet, and you will understand better. If I were you I would not dream of bringing any children on to this earth. Not in this world of sin and corruption. And certainly not in this period of human history.'

The bride was on the point of bursting into tears. She was hustled away by her companions. They had a glance at the pamphlet: it was entitled 'The Admirable Story of the Saintly Body of Men and Women commonly known as the Shakers with an Annexe disproving the Allegation that Edward the First was born when his Mother was aged Thirteen.' Its author was Sri Jiban Dhan Soonri, F.Z.S., F.R.A.S., Cabinet Maker. The cover of the pamphlet was decorated with the reproduction of a mythological monster: Minotaur by G. F. Watts.

The bride returned home and went straight into the family chapel of the Diwan Nishi Kanta. 'Give me, O Lord,' she prayed, 'one son and no more.' She wanted a son so that no evil tongue could accuse her of being barren. Moreover, she did not want the Diwan's line to become extinct. The family crest bore the audacious motto,

Ray Rayan
Chiradin Diwan.

This might be interpreted as the decision of the Diwan family to outlast the Doomsday. Therefore it behoved the new bride to make her due contribution towards the continuity of the race of Diwans. For this she needed divine succour.

~

Her prayer was answered, and in due course a child was born. As it was a male child the Diwan decided to sacrifice some of his time for its education. The wife protested, and during the first few years she had her say. But from the day the ceremony of writing the alphabet by the boy was conducted by the family priest, the father put his foot down: the zenana was henceforth out of bounds to the son.

The Diwan had his own view about education. It could be summed up in four lines:

> The youngsters nowadays run wild
> From petting; whipping makes them mild
> And therefore I would never pet
> But whip my child, that you may bet.

'Is it any wonder,' Myna asked, 'that the boy wanted to die? Only when he fell ill was he allowed to see his mother. Therefore he was generally unwell. Illness, after all, is the result of what one thinks. Life was a predicament to him, and he wanted to die.'

~

No one dies, according to Myna, save on his own choice and in his own time. When Pramatha, at the command of the Great God, moulded Man out of a clod and breathed life into him, the deities wondered whether the newly created being should be counted among the mortals or among the immortals. For Vishnu the Protector pronounced upon Man his benediction: 'No man shall perish unless he wants his own perdition. The messenger of death shall never steal into a man's abode unnoticed and uninvited. No man shall be scared into heaven or lured into hell against his own desire.'

Since that day this is the law that governs all mankind. Only when a man supplicates for death then alone does he receive the visitation of Death's messenger. And he must call out for his own dissolution not once, nor twice, but three times. And on each occasion he is given the warning, 'Think well before you receive the visitation! Think well before you take the irretrievable step! Have you fulfilled your obligations? Has life no further miracles for you?' If he still persists in his decision then only he will be brought before the judgment throne in the great hall of Yama, the Measurer of the Good and the Evil.

No man, however, dies whole at the time of his death. He moulders away over a protracted period. Bit by bit he casts his being—his personality—away. The messenger of Yama only dissolves the last miserable figments of manhood still clinging to him. Long before his physical dissolution he has elected to disintegrate himself mentally and spiritually: he has ceased to have any purpose in prolonging his own existence. Death, therefore, comes to him as a solace, a benediction to him and his relations.

The unresolved problems in the mind of the Diwan's son gradually affected his body. He became covered all over with sores: these were the outward expression of his inward conflicts. Diseases are not trials inflicted upon us by outside agencies, but they are our own nightmares made manifest. What physic could heal the boy?

'Will any draught cure the fakir who goes about begging for his monument when he falls ill? The day he has raised the sum needed he will most likely die. He may, however, perish even before then. The fear that the mausoleum might not be erected at all may act as a solvent upon him. Almost within the reach of his objective, he may fall down never to rise again.'

This was what Myna thought.

~

The boy's body began to wither, and the doctors gave up all hope. 'Nothing can be done to save him,' they said. The Diwan's wife wept; she then had a few words with her husband, and a *tantric* was invited to see what could be done.

The *tantric* was one of those red-robed priests adept in the art of black magic. He entered the house by the back door, the entrance reserved for the zenana. The Diwan's wife fell down at his feet sobbing, 'Please save the child! Save him with my own life! Make him live long.'

'Save him? How can I save one who doesn't want to be saved? All that he could do was to keep the boy's body from disintegrating. And for this purpose the rite of the *Nishir Dak* was the thing, but the dark night of the new moon was still a week ahead. The boy, however, was likely to die any moment. What did the horoscope say? He scrutinized the boy's clock of nativity for a long time and finally asked, 'Bring me your boy's best friend.'

The distracted mother said that her son did not have any friends. There were, of course, some twenty youngsters of his own age living under the same roof. They, however, happened to be the children of the poor relations of the Diwan, children of the cognates and agnates, and her son was never allowed to mix with them.

'What about his schoolmates?' asked the *tantric*.

He was told that the boy was not permitted to stray outside the compound of the house, and he was taught the usual school lessons by private tutors. Though he did not go to school he was not bad at his lessons. He knew as much, if not more, than most boys of his age. He could repeat by heart a large portion of the Ramayana and long passages from Plato's *Republic*. (The Diwan was an admirer of Plato's *Republic* and the Spartan virtues.)

The *tantric* was not concerned with the boy's intellectual capacities, but with his playmates.

'Alas!' The mother repeated tearfully, 'He has no playmates. He is not allowed to play. The Diwan does not like frivolities. My son used to do his P.T. alone before he fell ill. How am I to invent a playmate for him?'

The *tantric* had a few minutes' whispered conversation with the Diwan's wife, and then asked everyone to leave the room: he wanted to be alone with the boy; his objective was to find out if the dying boy cared for anyone in the world. Was he missing anyone through his confinement to bed? Was anyone missing him?

The boy gave a feeble smile and confessed that probably Dom the stable-boy was sighing for him. But no one ought to know anything about it. He admired Dom because he was so strong.

The *tantric* went to the stable yard and cornered Dom, a lusty boy four years senior to the Diwan's son.

The stable-yard was, of course, empty of horses and coaches. Before the days of the motor car a number of coaches and carriages and the appropriate number of horses were lodged in this quadrangle. Now it contained an ugly-looking antediluvian Rolls Royce for the Diwan's personal use and a slightly more modern, nevertheless ungainly, Packard for the Diwan's wife, and half a dozen streamlined, latest-model American cars for the poorer relations—the cognates and the agnates who did not know how to board the public vehicles of Calcutta. Dom, the so-called stable-boy, was in charge of the petrol pump in the yard.

The lusty stable-boy stopped whistling when the *tantric* told him, 'You are having a good time here. Aren't you? You have been tampering with the Diwan's son.'

'Why don't you mind your own business?' Dom replied sharply. 'Who has asked you to meddle in my affairs?'

The interview, which opened in this unpropitious fashion, ended very amicably. Dom, the stable-boy, declared that he would hate to be turned out of the house where he was having a good time; the idea of getting under the skin of the Diwan's son tickled his fancy. He even went to the length of offering the *tantric* a part of the sum the Diwan's wife proposed as his fee for saying 'Yes' to the *Nishir Dak*.

'Once I become the Diwan's son,' he swore, 'I shall make the Estate Manager lick my backside. Why don't you go ahead with your *mantram* right now? What sort of a *tantric* are you if you have to wait for the dark night of the new moon? I have heard of magicians who can turn day into night at will.'

Dom's elation was cut short by a swooning fit. When he regained his senses he found he was lying in a bed more uncomfortable than his usual one and his forehead was being sponged by the Diwan's wife.

'Lemme alone,' he yelled and had nearly a second fit as he discovered that his body was covered with suppurating sores and his voice sounded like that of the Diwan's son.

~

The *tantric* had done his job well. The Diwan's wife had no misgivings about it. Her boy recovered, but he was no longer the timid, shy creature of the days before his serious illness: he was Dom, the stable-boy, masquerading as her son; his manners were simply awful, and what was far more dangerous was that he manifested the aberrations of a mega-phallic satyr. The only consolation she could derive from her rite of the *Nishir Dak* was that there was no danger of the Diwan family becoming extinct through lack of progeny.

The household where peace had hitherto reigned became a den of cock-fights between the Diwan and his heir.

The Diwan blamed his wife for having listened to a *tantric*. Relatives of Dom, the orphan stable-boy—men and women about whose existence no one had any knowledge before—turned up in large numbers at the back entrance of the Diwan's mansion. They accused the Diwan's wife of having poisoned the apple of their eye, Dom, the stable-boy. She shed bitter tears in silence.

'How am I to expiate my sins?' she asked herself. 'What have I done to merit harsh words from everyone: I run a household where a hundred mouths are fed every day. I look after everyone and everything in this place. Yet no one says as much as one single word of kindness to me. I get only abuse and nothing but abuse for whatever I do.'

The worst culprit was the heir to the Diwan—the one for whom she was ready to lay down her life. He now badgered her to death. Had he decided to leave the parental home earlier to install himself with his merry men in Kalighat she might perhaps have been reconciled to her fate. But that was not to be. The sin of having tried to buy a blessing rankled deep in her. 'It is a transgression to resurrect the dead with magic rites,' according to Myna: she quoted the *Mahabharata:*

A calf can find its mother cow
Among a thousand kine:
So good and evil done returns
And whispers, 'I am thine.'

The Diwan's wife did not know her *matra*.

IV

'Babu! Do come out.'

Was I dreaming? Or did I really hear someone calling out for me? I hate being disturbed in my sleep. My ears caught some threats uttered against Piram.

'Babu! They want to take Piram away.'

'Curse the *Nishir Dak*,' I said to myself as I buried my head in my pillow. 'Curse the bitch. I won't have Piram's soul transferred to the body of a mangy mongrel.'

I do not know what made me think just then of a Japanese who gave an address in Sanskrit College. Pandit Bidhu Sastri apologized for the delay of the lecturer's arrival. The contretemps was due to the Japanese speaker's prolonged prayers over the departed soul of his favourite dog. 'The poor man!' Pandit Bidhu Sastri said, 'The dog accompanied him all the way from Nagasaki to Buddha Gaya. He was very fond of his pet. It is sad he will have to return home alone. I share his sorrow.' 'Palaver,' murmured some of the members of the audience: they were there for the sole purpose of heckling the Japanese visitor; as they were all Sinophils, their political conscience constrained them to be anti-Japanese. The poor Japanese pilgrim was, according to them, tainted with the sin of imperialism, and therefore he had to be taught a lesson—heckled and insulted. Pandit Bidhu Sastri was interested in Zen Buddhism and had written a number of books on this subject: so he, too, was suspected of imperialistic leanings! 'Palaver,' they grumbled. 'Mere palaver! Has a dog a soul?' The Pandit replied that the hecklers were probably Shylocks in disguise, and though he did not possess the forensic ability of Portia he would say, 'A dog has no soul for the Jews, Christians and Mohammedans. But for the Hindus and the Buddhists it is not a soulless creature.' His retort evoked applause from the more serious-minded section of the audience. 'If the Japanese pilgrim's dog possessed a soul,' something whispered in my ear, 'Piram, too, has a soul.'

'It would be wicked,' I murmured, 'to allow a bitch to steal Piram's soul. I won't have it.'

'Babu,' I heard the cook's voice. 'Please hurry! They want to take our Piram away.'

'Blast the *Nishir Dak*,' I cried as I jumped up: my siesta was over. I was not dreaming. The cook was actually shouting from the courtyard below that there were tipstaffs bent on removing Piram from our hostel.

Tipstaffs! That was enough to put me on my mettle. I was determined to give them a good time, and started hunting for my shoes. I mean my hobnailed, heavy football boots. Lawful or unlawful, I did not care! My blood was up: I was going to let them know how a champion footballer kicked.

'Piram,' I said, 'It may not be the *Nishir Dak*, but the rascal from the Corporation Office has returned with tipstaffs. We must put up a good show.'

Piram dashed out of the room even before I had opened the cupboard for my boots. There was a shout in the courtyard, followed by a confusion of wailings and howlings and cryings. Piram was fighting the tipstaffs unaided! The struggle was of a short duration; I heard the cook shout with joy, 'Bravo, Piram! They are running for their lives.'

A minute later I was presented with a trophy: the top of a silver-mounted stick. Piram brought it for me.

'What is it, Piram?' The object was dropped at my feet for my inspection. I picked it up. It bore imprints of Piram's powerful teeth, nevertheless, one could easily read the words engraved on the silver top:

Ray Rayan
Chiradin Diwan.

~

'The worm has turned into a dragon,' Gama shook his head disapprovingly as he examined the bitten-off end of the silver-mounted staff. 'What has happened to you?' He went on. 'You were never over-polite. But you were at least law-abiding. Now on account of your stupidity we may lose Piram.'

Balaban gave me a reproachful glance. Pulwan sighed noisily. The cook was in tears. All eyes were fixed on Piram, sleeping blissfully under my table.

'Yes,' Gama repeated. 'Your stupidity. Instead of playing the role of a gentleman-at-large, addicted to midday siestas and enjoying dreams of naked women carrying coconuts to spirit away Piram's soul, you ought to have done something to prevent the Diwan's *chobedars* getting into our hostel.'

The cook started to sob copiously. This made Gama all the more gloomy. He snarled at her to give greater vent to his feelings.

'Why didn't you use your head?' Balaban took up Gama's cue and began reprimanding the cook. 'Why on earth did you give away the secret? Who asked you to admit that Piram was in our Buffalo's room?' (Of course, the buffalo in question was no other than I.)

The cook went on shedding tears.

'The tiger has now turned into a pussy,' Pulwan commented sarcastically at my silence. 'Can't you suggest something? What's the use of your studying Roman Law and Ancient Law, and God knows what other laws if you can't find a way out of this difficulty?'

'What difficulty?' I asked finally. I must admit that I derived considerable pleasure at the sight of the whole hostel upset at the very thought of losing Piram.

'My God! Are you really as dumb as that skinny girl of yours at the Ultra-Modern Hindu Hotel? Can't you understand that the Diwan will now ask for the restitution of his dog? He knows now where Piram stays.'

Gama's knowledge of law was no better than Pulwan's and he expressed the fear that the Diwan would most likely get a writ issued by a high-court judge under 'the habeas corpus or some such act.' 'And if Piram is taken away from us,' he declared threateningly, 'I swear to God almighty, I will settle your bills and kick you out of the Hostel. You are a callous brute.'

'You need not settle my bills,' I said with an innocent smile as I produced a cheque. 'Look here! I have some money all on account of a culture-loving Chicagoan and his interest in Shakespeare.'

They all gasped with surprise when I told them about my talks with the camera-man of *Life-in-Technikolor,* the answer to the question, 'What's Hecuba to him, or he to Hecuba?' and my peroration on Foni Dhar's incompetence as a professor of English literature.

However, by the time I ended my story they were no longer

surprised, but fuming with rage. 'Now we know,' they shouted, 'how that rogue of a Diwan got the news about Piram. You are a headless buffalo. Why did you allow that press photographer to take pictures of your room?'

I expanded my chest and held out the cheque. I wanted to tantalize them with my silence, because just then no suitable retort came to mind. The cook, however, spoilt my game with loud wailings.

'It is my fault,' the fool whose cooking was ruining my digestion blubbered. 'It is all my fault. The man with the camera came here the other morning when no one was in. He wanted to take pictures of Piram.'

The cook's story might have been incoherent to the rest of the company; it was, however, perfectly clear to me. My thunder was stolen. Therefore I decided to bring the sitting to an end, and declared grandly, 'Let the Diwan try to take away Piram. I shall teach him a lesson. Meanwhile, I need a breath of fresh air. And in God's name, stop moping and moaning.'

V

Having failed to secure from Myna a suitable story for *Life-in-Technikolor*, the camera-man did the next best thing: he made the most of my biting remarks. His Chicagoan boss was delighted with my blunt comments. 'Culture-loving Americans,' he told the ex-punk, 'appreciate frankness. We are not like the British jingos. We love to hear the truth about ourselves. Try to get as much dope as you can out of this Penhari fellow. Track him down with your camera.'

'I believe,' the ex-punk told me, 'he is much impressed by your knowledge of Chicago.'

'But I have never been to the Earthly Paradise of the Frail Sisters.' Then, unwittingly, I committed the mistake of quoting some juicy remarks about Chicago from the Petrov Brothers' *Little Golden America.*

And the ex-punk dutifully reported my observations to his boss: Mischkon was much moved. He assumed I was in love with his native Chicago, otherwise there was no reason why I should know anything about that megalopolis. The fact that I was acquainted with the Chicago University version of the *Song of Songs* filled his heart with pride. That I was distantly related to Myna touched some tender spot in his soul: our relationship he found extremely original and entertaining—something with which to regale culture-lovers in America. The ex-punk was commissioned to take as many pictures as he could of my room during my absence: not only of my room, but of my books, cupboards and pets and friends as well.

The cook was either bribed or fooled to help him in his task. Piram, however, refused all co-operation, and after a couple of shots decided to show his teeth. The camera-man had a narrow escape. His rather unsatisfactory pictures did, however, find favour with the Chicagoan. And I was sent a cheque for the interviews and for the alleged permission to take pictures of my room and my belongings.

Unacquainted with the laws of libel in India, the Chicagoan rewrote in vigorous terms the camera-man's version of my off-the-record talks with him. When I saw in *Life-in-Technikolor* the article entitled, 'A Penhari Flautist's Views on Shakespeare and Shakespearian Authorities,' I murmured, 'Might as well be hanged for a sheep as a lamb,' and scribbled a line to the ex-punk: 'We must hang together, otherwise we are going to be hanged separately. Professor Foni Dhar is likely to bring a libel suit against your paper and me. And a few other people will most probably take up his cue.'

I was bumptious enough to treat my own praise as a due, but the article in question was flattery presented on a platter. So far as I was concerned it did not matter much that some of the details were incorrect or misleading. For example, I was credited with certain virtues I did not possess: such as fondness for dogs, admiration for Gandhi, love for plain living and high thinking, and similar eccentricities. I did not mind in the least the article's referring to my relationship with Myna: 'Cousin-brother-one-womb-removed.' Myna, too, might have forgiven the epithet, 'The living Venus of the Kala Bhairab shrine'; though it was doubtful if she would have appreciated the publicity given to her family: she was the niece of the Rajah of Luktam. However, even this was not so very shocking. But what came afterwards I feared would cause trouble.

The alleged Shakespearian authority from the backwoods of the Penhari Parganas was reported to be a man of the same stature as the Furnesses who issued the (American) Variorum edition of Shakespeare, Dr Leslie Hotson, and others of their kind! In the opinion of this man of the Penharis, namely, myself, Professor Saintsbury of Edinburgh was a perfect bore, devoid of any intuitive knowledge about Shakespeare's characters—a pedant of the same fold as Scaliger, whom no one read but everybody praised. The diatribe on Saintsbury was followed by some home truths about Professor Foni Dhar, Calcutta's favourite authority on Shakespeare and Western Drama: if Saintsbury merited the epithet of a Scaliger, Professor Foni Dhar deserved the title of Martin Tupper's lackey. 'One of Tupper's effusions,' I was reported to have said, 'the one entitled "The Ass" is Professor Dhar's favourite poem because of its autobiographical bearing.'

Undue modesty, I must admit, never figured on my list of desirable virtues. Kolej Huzoor, too, shared the same view. 'He that makes himself a sheep shall be eaten up by the wolves.' 'But mind you,' Kolej Huzoor counselled, 'it is no good changing oneself into a wolf. The status of a wolfhound ought to be enough. No amount of abuse from you or anybody in the world would improve the taste and judgment of fogies suffering from mental sclerosis.' Professor Foni Dhar was one such fogey, and being foolish I disregarded Kolej Huzoor's excellent advice and told the reporter of *Life-in-Technikolor* in plain terms what I thought of the pompous nincompoop Dhar. Dhar knew the ropes, and at a time of political complications managed to get himself a nomination for life! His second move was to get an anthology of his—*The Anna Nosegay*—prescribed as a text-book for all matriculation candidates: in other words, an assured annual sale of 100,000 copies, bringing him a royalty of one hundred thousand rupees a year. I did not mind his professorship for life or his making money on a scale which made Jain money-lenders turn green with envy. What I hated most was the contents of this anthology: Dhar's *Anna Nosegay*. (It was originally meant to be sold for one anna, hence its name. It was later priced at ten rupees. Its real worth was a cent or less.) Thanks to Dhar's *Anna Nosegay* about a million young people all over the country were made to learn by heart silly poems by Martin Tupper, Felicia Hemans, Thomas Moore, Robert Montgomery, Thomas Campbell, Samuel Rogers, and a number of other poets of similar standing. Dhar considered these poetasters to be the most representative of the British Parnassus—poets who had won popular admiration during their lifetime. His logic led him to proclaim that the mid-Victorian journalist Reynolds was the greatest novelist of his age because his books enjoyed huge sales!

In spite of my first shock I was not altogether displeased with my (alleged) interview with the editor of *Life-in-Technikolor.* It brought me some money, in fact much more than I usually made in a month. Secondly, I hoped and believed that it would make Professor Foni Dhar do some thinking. And finally, because it told something about my examination records, which were not at all bad, I hoped the Diwan would read the article and see for himself that I was the man for his purpose: a budding genius—a linguist, a dog-lover, an actor, a flautist, a relative of a rajah dethroned by the new rulers of Delhi, a voracious reader, one capable of unearthing obscure facts, a person who refused to believe that 'being fair' meant making concessions to the ignorant, an upholder of the Penhari principle:

> To fight the Devil
> It's never vile
> To take to tactics evil.

The article did, however, reveal my principal shortcoming: my incapacity for bearing fools gladly. But was that a grave sin? The Diwan wanted a secretary. Was I not eminently suitable for that post? Was William Lloyd Garrison's 'No Quarter' formula worthless? 'With reasonable men, I will reason; with humane men I will plead, but to tyrants I will give no quarter, nor waste arguments where they will certainly be lost.'

As *Life-in-Technikolor* had a wide circulation—it was issued in twenty different languages and in half a dozen scripts—I was more or less convinced that my indiscretions were bound to be brought to the notice of Professor Foni Dhar, and the picture of Piram reposing under my table to the scrutiny of the Diwan and his dog boy, the corpulent human seal who took hold of my tulasi beads in the back garden of the Diwan's house.

VI

It was therefore no surprise to me when I found the corpulent human seal trying to shadow me. He was accompanied by a number of *chobedars,* or silver-sticks, as they were commonly called.

This fat fellow had no sense of propriety, nor any sense of time. He tried to contact me in the precincts of the Kala Bhairab shrine after midnight; when I was whispering nice things to Myna and she was behaving like a cat repulsing caresses from a stranger. The sudden approach of a number of passers-by made her behave stiffly; I was on the point of gaining what I wanted when in the wake of the passers-by I noticed the human seal coming with a battalion of *chobedars.* Evidently he was in quest of me. It was fairly dark and I do not know how he recognized me, but he stood still the moment he saw me with my right arm round Myna's slender waist.

It is an unwritten law all over the world that an interlaced couple should not be disturbed. For harrying a pair of mating birds the sage Valmiki laid a heavy curse upon a thoughtless fowler; every schoolboy in India knows the anathema Valmiki pronounced: 'Thou shalt forever be joyless and homeless.' I was sure the fat fellow knew about it. Nevertheless, the fear of homelessness—that was Valmiki's imprecation—did not deter him from harassing me at a most critical moment. It was just like him.

Myna's situation was as awkward as mine, though I was responsible for compromising her.

It happened in this way. After prolonged arguments with

her and reminding her many times that I was the Balaram instrumental in ending the prolonged drought in the Penhari Parganas and that she had nothing to fear from me as I was her 'cousin-brother-one-womb-removed'—in the language of *Life-in-Technikolor*—or in plain terms, cousin-germane—I obtained from her the grudging permission to try the feel of her smooth skin—of her back—under the cover of her *chaddar,* which she wore as a stole. As it was no longer the full-moon night of Ashwin, there was no need for her to be too peevish, and then, the cover of a stole was as good as the barrier of a closed door. Nevertheless, she insisted that we should withdraw to the darkest nook before I could even touch her bare arms. 'Kiss!' She was horrified. 'Good God! What would people think? No, not here, at all events.' She wanted me to be discreet, and at the same time she herself threw discretion to the winds by telling the attendants the precise spot to which we withdrew: the corner known as the Reredos of the Bhairavs and Bhairavis. A high wall covered with low reliefs of dog-headed semi-divinities formed an angle with a stone platform bearing cavo-relievo representations of Rudrani, Unmatta, Kapalika, and other manifestations of Siva's consort, all readily identifiable because of their having the dog as their mount. This was the charming semi-hidden site where we went: it was reputed to be haunted and endowed with the gift of curing hysteria of the most obstinate type on certain new-moon nights.

However that might be, it was, let me repeat, most indiscreet of Myna to give away the secret of our hiding-place. Anyway, I could do nothing about it. The corner had, however, the advantage of being almost pitch dark, and it was a fairly safe place of retreat as people avoided it even in broad daylight on account of the terrifying reliefs of dog-headed Bhairavs and no less frightening Bhairavis astride canine mounts.

Well, there we were. Myna whispering every second like a mechanical time-keeper, 'It's getting late, I must get back to the Pavilion,' and I arguing with her in undertones that it was not the full-moon night of Ashwin and no one wanted her as much as I. As I have said before, Myna's skin was like the smoothest alabaster, polished and perfumed with sandalwood oil. My hand wanted to discover how her bodice was held in position, since it was absolutely without any back. Though I had promised her that I would not detain her for more than a minute, it was impossible for me to keep my word: my hand simply refused to withdraw once it was under her stole, and the cords that held her bodice in position got entangled in my fingers; they were on the point of snapping when the wretched human seal with his posse of *chobedars* turned up unceremoniously.

Just then I was having a fierce disputation—in whispers, of course—with Myna. Stray passers-by, as has already been stated, gave us a wide berth. This was as it should be. Even had she been recognized by any of them, it would have been natural for them to conclude that though not a *yogini* Myna was acting as mother-confessor to me. The less pious-minded but fairly reasonable ones among them assumed, no doubt, we were lovers, and therefore they considered it their duty to leave us alone. Calcutta's late birds were not heartless. In this respect even the taxi-drivers—a most frightening tribe as their epithet, 'Death's Outriders,' unequivocally indicated—were considerate: they followed the decent custom of dimming or dipping their lights as they invariably did when the fan of their headlamps' glare fell on lovers. However harsh and merciless during the day, Calcutta is soft-hearted at night. But that wicked human seal violated every convention and refused to leave me in peace. He was determined to hound me.

He stood stock still with his *chobedars* only a few yards away from us, and then noisily cleared his throat to make his presence more obvious. In a grating voice he demanded whether the *kirtani* Myna would be singing that night or not. To emphasize his importance he declared that he had come all the way from Hargila Lane to listen to her.

I thought of giving him a piece of my mind. 'He will hear,' I whispered to Myna, 'what I think of a cad like him.' But she forestalled me with a polite remark of abject humility: she did not know she was missed in the Pavilion! Her voice was honey. She breathed into my ears, 'Least said, soonest mended,' and gave me a pinch to keep my mouth shut: it was a pinch sharp enough to draw blood from a less thick-skinned animal than her cousin-brother-one-womb removed. As though that pinch was not enough she squeezed a portion of her *chaddar* inside my mouth and declared nonchalantly that as soon as she was through with her exorcism she would return to the Pavilion.

The fat fellow and his guard departed, making ceremonial obeisances. The human seal did not walk, he waddled; the rest of the company showed him such deference as to make me think he was their lord and master. He was now clad in a long coat, which hid his ample paunch, and a round cap on his bald pate disguised to a great extent the seal-like formation of his head: on the whole, he appeared much more human than when I first saw him. Only those who knew him well or were endowed with X-ray eyes could guess his comic way of moving; to all others he was the picture of a dignified gentleman walking sedately at the head of a band of retainers carrying silver-mounted sticks. But what made that fellow come to the Reredos of the Bhairavs and Bhairavis to spoil my game? *Life-in-Technikolor* had reproduced pictures of my hostel. He could have easily called on me there to quarrel with me.

'What makes you think he came for you?' Myna asked. Her exorcism came to an end with the departure of the dog boy and his gang! 'Now, you have been behaving like a spoilt child. Have I hurt you? Show me your hand.'

I received an unexpected reward when I told her that no one ever thought of spoiling me: everyone assumed that I never needed anybody's affection, while I was, in fact, living like an unwanted stray dog. She stopped my complaints with a kiss. My weals, too, received the touch of her lips.

'They are now cured.'

'But, tell me,' Myna asked. 'Philanderer, why do you call the Diwan the dog boy? And why do you think he has come here for you?'

VII

Perhaps Myna was right. Maybe the human seal came to the shrine of the Kala Bhairab simply to listen to her. Or, it was equally possible, to hear *kirtans* in the Pavilion, and it did not matter to him who sang so long as he had the satisfaction of hearing some singing.

Thanks to the articles in *Life-in-Technikolor* the ancient shrine of Kala Bhairab suddenly leapt into fame. Questions were asked in the Delhi Legislature about the decaying images and bas-reliefs of the sanctuary. The progress-at-any-price M.P.s had a quarrel with the Neo-Khadiwallahs about the intrinsic value of outdated icons and image-worship in general. The Delhi Government refused to be dragged into this dispute. The Prime Minister made a declaration to the effect that the Kala Bhairab shrine was not a national monument, hence all questions concerning it should be put to the Bengal Legislature. As the Diwan was a member of the Bengal Legislature it was not unlikely that he wanted to inspect the sanctuary that caused so much bad blood in distant Delhi and Chicago.

VIII

'Every man's first business is,' I declared with a grave face, 'and must be to take care of himself. I am looking after myself and let Emenroy look after himself. I find no reason why he should bother about my moral delinquencies.'

The emissaries of Emenroy talked a lot of nonsense about the obligations an intellectual of my type owed to society, and that was why it was my duty to dissociate myself from American super-capitalist concerns like *Life-in-Technikolor, Frank Confessions, The Living Era, et al.*

Before throwing those fellows out I reminded them that I had a strong dislike for all world-betterers, and as Emenroy and his camp-followers were avowed world-betterers they would do well not to waste their time and mine over tactics of world-saving by boycotting American popular papers. Though unacquainted with Chicago, I added that the cheques for my facile articles—written either under my own name or under various pseudonyms—emanated from Chicagoan concerns. Therefore I was feeling the urge to visit that wonderful city of perpetual progress. 'Chicago has progressed more in one hundred years,' a leader in *Life-in-Technikolor* informed its readers, 'than Paris in one thousand.'

'Money talks,' one of the Emenroyites jeered. 'You have been bribed to become pro-American.'

'Isn't that wonderful?' I replied, and swelled my chest.

It was plain common sense, as far as I was concerned, to make hay while the sun shone: in other words to make as much as I could of the temporary popularity of my lowbrow contributions. 'I shall have to save a lot. I can't afford the luxury of refusing good money for the sole reason that it comes from America.'

~

My freelance journalism distressed Gama for different reasons. 'Previously,' he sighed, 'you were a casual worker indulging in occasional midday naps. From now on it looks as though you were going to be the man about town, sleeping at day and roaming about at night. This will undermine your health. Moreover, a decent man ought to have a steady job, otherwise he runs the risk of getting married or going to pieces and finally emerging as a dilettante.'

'Well, I am a born dilettante. Like our Piram, I love leading a double life. Does not Piram spend his days here and his nights God knows where?'

'Don't be silly,' Gama grunted. 'I am worried because you may get into trouble with law suits. Can't you make your articles less scathing? Have you forgotten Foni Dhar? And then the Diwan? Who knows what he is up to?'

I saw the Diwan, the ex-dog-boy of my imaginings, from a distance, more than once, in the circle of Myna's listeners at the Kala Bhairab shrine. Professor Foni Dhar rarely crossed my path: there was, however, little likelihood of his prosecuting me.

In spite of his many misgivings Gama admitted, rather grudgingly, that journalism by itself was not bad: anyway, it brought me more money than his monthly pay-packets. What worried him was my absolute refusal to be polite to the rogues. Kolej Huzoor, in contrast to Gama, gave me his benediction. 'It is the era of the common man,' he said. 'A Regius Professor at

Oxford does not mind writing for *Picture Post,* Sinclair Lewis contributes to the *Ladies' Home Journal,* and why shouldn't you do the same? *Life-in-Technikolor* is not worse than these papers.'

~

Much to my regret the controversy with Professor Foni Dhar came to an abrupt end. The opening gambits were not at all bad, and at first it looked as though our game would be exciting and long drawn out. But unfortunately Professor Dhar refused to be baited when *The Modern Review* joined issue with *Life-in-Technikolor.*

Following my comments on the infamous *Anna Nosegay,* Professor Dhar did write a rejoinder: he did not justify his exclusion of good poetry in favour of poor verses; he simply attacked me on the basis of the *Institutions of Manu.*

'The degradation of the birth,' he quoted, 'is exactly proportioned to the degree of moral guilt of the transgressor. If a man, for example, has the temerity to censure his teacher, even though the censure is richly deserved, that man in his next birth will be an ass.'

'An ass!' I rubbed my hands with joy. 'Martin Tupper's ass has denounced Hinduism and Manu a thousand times. Now he has the temerity to quote Manu against one who has never been his pupil. Hurrah! I am going to give him tit for tat.'

Unfortunately just then a bigger scandal struck Professor Dhar and the University authorities.

A dissertation for the Doctorate degree which had received the professor's encomium turned out to be a parody! One of my school-mates, now a lecturer at the Islamia College, submitted a voluminous thesis for the Ph.D. on a non-existent German writer alleged to have been greatly influenced by Martin Tupper. The name of this Teutonic worthy was concocted by me: Herr Professor Doktor Pumper of Halle-on-the-Saale! Professor Dhar swallowed this undiluted parody, and proclaimed it to be good stuff; a work of high academic value. He recommended the candidate for the Ph.D. bonnet and parchment. Professor Foni Dhar's prestige was great, or it may be, his junior colleagues had to accept his decisions without questioning; anyway, they concurred with him. All went well. The candidate was informed that he was admitted to the Ph.D. degree.

And the candidate, Khuda Baksh, wrote to me that in future I should put after my name '½ Ph.D.' and he was going to do the same: 'Because our contribution to the concoction of the burlesque about Pumper has been in equal proportion.' In due course the official announcement of the names of the successful candidates to the Ph.D. degree was made.

Then came a bombshell in the shape of an editorial in *The Modern Review* expressing grave doubts about the existence of Herr Professor Doktor Pumper. It was followed by a letter to the same effect in *The Statesman:* the signatory was one Bhagwan Prasad, which, by the way, meant the same thing as Khuda Baksh—namely, *God's Gift*—one being the Hindu version and the other Mohammedan. By now, other papers commented on the slipshod method of Professor Foni Dhar's examination of the Ph.D. candidates. Why was not the German consul asked to give his opinion, especially as the dissertation dealt with an eminent figure of his Vaterland?

The German consul was a character and he looked a character: a living replica of Baron Munchausen. One of his forbears, Prince Heinrich XXVIII, donated, if we are to believe Horace Walpole, his own skeleton—before his death, of course—to Sir Hans Sloane's collection of embryos, cockle shells, and other curiosities. '*Schade!*' The German consul sadly declared, 'Sir Hans died before my forefather. Otherwise *jederman* would have seen his skeleton in the British Museum. Now it lies buried in a grave where *keiner* can examine it. I have also made a will about my own skeleton. It will go to the Senate House of Calcutta after my death.' 'What will they do with it?' I asked. 'Do with it? You surprise me, Herr Professor. You may know Sanskrit, but you are an ignorant man about science. I am Prinz Bosch XXXIII of Heuss, a descendant of Prinz Heinrich XXVIII of Reuss. My skeleton is of great value to men of science: men who are interested in creating beautiful citizens; I mean Calcutta's eugenists.'

The German consul, Prince Bosch XXXIII of Heuss, was a spiritual descendant of Baron Munchausen, but physically he resembled the well-known film star Erich von Stroheim, whom he declared to be the very quintessence of nordic masculine beauty. Things nordic interested him enormously, and he was trying to master the rudiments of Sanskrit from me, because Sanskrit was in his opinion a nordic language. His progress was extremely slow, and he often lamented that he would die before mastering enough Sanskrit to read the Kama Sutra in the original. His collection of erotica was remarkable and so was his cellar—probably the best-stocked in the whole East.

His eccentricities were many. Nevertheless, he was a fairly reliable man on questions concerning Germany. However, the dissertation on Herr Professor Doktor Pumper nearly undid him: his national pride gained the upper hand; he forgot to consult the German biographical dictionaries.

A doctoral thesis on the alleged German translator of Martin Tupper, the poet admired by Queen Victoria and the founder of *Reynolds Weekly*, filled his heart with joy and pride. He decided to give a sumptuous party in honour of Khuda Baksh—something to make his Russian opposite number gnaw his fingernails in despair. Fancy, therefore, his disappointment when he learnt that Khuda Baksh, being a strict adherent to the tenets of Mohammed, was unwilling to profit from his wine party. He became, metaphorically speaking, sick.

Khuda Baksh's refusal to pay even a courtesy visit to the Consulate for a cup of tea made the secretary of the Prince Bosch XXXIII suspicious. 'An Indian Herr refusing hock, Henckel, Heidsieck-Monopol, Moselle! That is *unmöglich*.' Something was wrong, he conjectured, with Herr Professor Khuda Baksh. 'He is not happy about his thesis,' I said. '*Nicht möglich*,' replied the secretary and decided to look up the German biographical dictionaries for the details about Pumper. Those voluminous tomes—some of which referred to Shakespeare as a German citizen—failed to enlighten him. His suspicion became greater, and cables were sent to the Kulturministerium in Germany. The cat was out of the bag: no archives, no library, no newspaper index furnished any clue whatsoever to the translator of Martin Tupper.

~

Professor Foni Dhar felt annoyed: not because he had made an ass of himself, but because he found out that I was the evil genius responsible for the major portion of that dissertation. I heard that he even became depressed to some degree and failed to attend for a fortnight the Vice-Chancellor's daily durbars; for a whole month he failed to offer his usual boxes of perfumed chocolates to his admiring women students.

Foni Dhar made about one hundred thousand rupees a year with his *Anna Nosegay*, and knew the art of currying favour both with the great and the small: to the Vice-Chancellor he made a daily offering of a basket of fruits, and to the girls candy-boxes. I wonder if the satirist Damodar Gupta had a man like Foni Dhar in mind when he penned the lines:

> His head's shining like a copper kettle
> Yet he makes pots of money with 'Baldness Cure.'
> Marry him? God! Who wants him as a pestle?
> But, dear friend, he has brass! And that's the lure.

Foni Dhar was a success with women undergraduates—especially with the teenagers, thanks to his candy-boxes.

The bald anthologist of *Anna Nosegay* deeply regretted the non-existence of the German critic Pumper whose views on most matters were the same as his. 'What a pity,' Foni Dhar sighed. Our imaginary Pumper claimed to have seen, according to the bogus dissertation, holographs of Ben Jonson's letters asserting that Shakespeare wrote his plays simply for reading aloud in an oval-shaped room of the Mermaid Tavern known as 'The O'.

However, Dhar regained his spirit when he heard that he was not the only departmental head to make a serious blunder. His opposite number in the University of Berlin was at about that time responsible for granting the Ph.D. parchment—not the bonnet, the German doctors were gownless and capless—to a candidate who had presented a thesis on 'Vanu Sing, the Indian Mystic Poet.' Mother India, though prolific in mystics, knew of no son of hers remotely connected with poetry and bearing the name of Vanu Sing. (Though Tagore's *nom-de-guerre* of his early years was Bhanu Singh.) So, our bald Dhar became bold.

To cover this bloomer of a lifetime Professor Foni Dhar proposed Khuda Baksh's rustication! But my friend was beyond the reach of the University of Calcutta authorities. He was teaching at the Islamia College of Peshawar, and the Governors of that institution did not care what the Calcutta Senate thought of him. Professor Dhar's futile threats came to the notice of the news-reporters—'Hickey's Boys'—always on the look out for scoops. And there was a big row in the press.

Some thought Foni Dhar would resign his professorship and retire to Benares and live there on his modest income of one hundred thousand rupees a year—a mere bagatelle of fifty thousand U.S.A. dollars: he could afford to do this without his professorial salary. They were, however, mistaken. Foni Dhar was thick-skinned, and he was determined to outdo the prudent vicar of Bray; he stuck to his post.

And my reply to his quotation from Manu remained for ever unanswered. This controversy, however, resulted in the introduction of a new word in the jargon of the journalists: funstar, a derivative of Foni the Fun-Star.

IX

As for the Diwan, he was an altogether different proposition. At first I had nothing very much for or against him. It was true that I did at one time seek employment as his personal secretary: that was the first occasion when I came across him in his back garden and mistook him for his dog boy. But after that I had nothing to do with him personally. It was not my fault if Piram attacked the *chobedars* who came to take him away from my hostel.

All the same, I must confess I did not relish his appearance in the sanctuary of Kala Bhairab. Night after night he came there and behaved as though it was Myna's duty to entertain him with songs and dances and stories. Whenever she was a few minutes late he fretted. If someone else replaced Myna he would get up and waddle away as if the sacred lore coming from other lips were not sufficiently sacred for him. Gradually I grew to dislike him: he seemed to present the spectacle of an elephant reposing on his stern.

Then, a casual remark of the cook made me positively unhappy.

The cook—the kind soul who did not know how to cook but who nevertheless did her best to appease the hunger of a score of voracious young men—started worrying over my nocturnal outings and frequent absences at evening meals. If her dishes were not to my taste, she feared, others, too, were likely to find fault with her culinary abilities. 'If you remove the keystone of an arch,' she reasoned, 'what remains? Nothing! Everything will fall.' And I was looked upon as her main support in the hostel. More than once the inmates, disgusted with her food, thought of giving her a month's notice and a ticket to Midnapore where she came from. But my intervention had prevented this. She was clean; she was honest; she was fairly reliable; quite attractive looking. These were the virtues that in my opinion counter-balanced her complete ignorance of the art of cooking.

'Now, Babu,' one day she whined, 'you are turning against me. Are my dishes worse than usual? Why have you stopped eating at home with the others? Where shall I go if they turn me out of here?'

I tried my bluff and told her that my journalistic activities prevented me from keeping regular hours.

'You are not telling me the whole truth. I have consulted the astrologer, and I know what is wrong with you.'

Which astrologer?—He was a smart turbaned man who sat in the Astrologers' Corner of a nearby temple.

'The astrologer told me the truth. "He sleeps, but not soundly.

He eats, but gets no satisfaction from his food." And that has made me think.'

The conclusion the cook derived from her cogitation was simply this: there must be a woman somewhere. Not only that, the charmer I admired was being courted by a number of rivals! Ages ago, as a child, I heard a story supposed to have come from Arabia, which propounded the thesis that it is not necessary to reveal a secret to a cook, she knows it intuitively; therefore a wise man would do well to consult his cook on all serious problems.

How much of my secrets did the cook know? Did she suspect that I was jealous of the Bahurupi and the Diwan? Was Myna at all interested in my rivals? And at the same time I wondered if it would be prudent to tell her anything about Myna. Therefore I struck the middle path and pretended indifference to her worries and asked as though out of mere curiosity if she knew anything about the Bahurupi—the street-musician.

'That man! The eel has gone back to his native mud. He is in gaol now and that is where he belongs.'

'Then why did Myna associate herself with him?'

'Babu, you know best. You have helped him, too.'

'When was that?'

'Quite some time ago when he tried to steal books from young students.' He was then caught red-handed, and the students gave him a thrashing: not one of them took any pity on him. As he was stark naked one of the young men gave him a woman's costume to wear: it was taken from the wardrobe of the students' theatrical society. 'And you were that student. And if you do not mind my telling you the truth, you did a wrong thing. You put ideas into his head. He became a Bahurupi.'

Perhaps the cook's information was correct. Yet it did not explain why Myna should be interested in him.

'He is a bit of a lady-killer.' The cook lowered her eyes. 'He courts women as boys catch flies. It is his second nature. Maybe the *kirtani* likes him. Maybe she wants to cure him. Who can tell? I, too, wanted to cure him. But he is not the type to care for a home and a wife. What can you do? There's something wrong in his blood.'

'I understand. We have some sayings of this kind about man's nature.'

> Hard it is to conquer nature: if a dog were made a king
> 'Mid the coronation trumpets he would gnaw his sandal string.

or

> Your nature is a thing you cannot beat;
> It serves as guide to everything you do;
> Give doggy all the meat he needs to eat,
> He cannot still help gnawing at a shoe.

'In the Penhari Parganas,' I added, 'our proverbs are mostly in verse.'

'You needn't bother much about that Bahurupi. It is the Diwan who has an eye on Myna. And that is bad.'

Myna, I heard from others at the Kala Bhairab shrine, had her philosophy of life, and it was extremely simple: if someone asked her for help she did not refuse it. The Bahurupi probably needed someone as his partner and therefore she gave her services to him—to put him on his feet. 'But,' I was also told, 'Myna never allows anyone to monopolize her.'

'The Diwan is a different story,' the cook began.

~

No, I did not want to listen to the cook. Most likely, I thought, she had a grudge against the Diwan, just as she had a grudge against the Bahurupi. Many aphorisms about gossips and scandal-mongers came to my mind. As an antidote to the cook's tittle-tattle I repeated to myself one of Myna's counsels:

> The deer, the fish, the goodman hunger
> For grass, for water, for content;
> Yet hunter, fisher, scandal-monger
> Pursue each harmless innocent.

I argued within myself: the Diwan was old and ugly; there was no reason for Myna to be charitable towards him. Yet in spite of arguments to eliminate the Diwan as a possible rival, counter-arguments came cropping up at odd moments.

~

What sort of a fellow was the Diwan? The *Indian Who's Who* gave his biographical sketch. Evidently it was his own thumbnail pen-portrait of himself. While semi-nonentities in that volume had taken every care to swell their entries with such ridiculous details as the names of the pamphlets dedicated to them or the number of times they went to prison for non-payment of taxes, 'in pursuance of Gandhian principles,' this man who was a Cabinet Minister and one of the biggest *zamindars*, owning estates as big in area as Calcutta itself, gave precisely three lines about himself! The only thing new about him that the *Indian Who's Who* gave me was that the standard text-book on Conic Sections was his: 'In other words,' I drew my own conclusion, 'he makes an additional one hundred thousand rupees a year like

Professor Foni Dhar with his brain-teasers.' (Of course, I ought to concede that the Diwan's text-book on Conic Sections was by far the best text-book on this subject available.)

Why was he so reticent about himself? What had he to hide?

'Lots,' said the cook. 'What about his son? He is no Gandhi. And even if he were one, is it not a shame that this son should become a Mohammedan?'

That reminded me of my inadvertent meeting with the Rajah of Luktam on the night of the full moon of Ashwin, and his bitter remarks about our legislators who were trying to 'modernize' India. 'Those who are fathers of rogues,' the Rajah held, 'should in decency abstain from foisting their new-fangled views about education on the country. Judge a tree by its fruits, and a man by his children. The father of a rogue is a rogue himself. The Diwan's brat changed his religion to get an easy divorce. Is that not a shame? Does that rascal believe in the tenets of Mohammed? Nothing of the sort. Religion for him is like a turban: you change it as often as you want to secure a new wife. I tell you the Diwan is a fool if he is not a rogue. He ought to stop the allowance of his good-for-nothing son.'

'Is the Diwan responsible for his son?' I asked the cook.

'As the mould is, so will the cake be,' she replied. 'Though the mould is not the same as the cake. In his case, the mould is hard, crusted. You can't bite at it.'

Did she guess what was worrying me? She went on talking and I listened.

'Call the Diwan old if you like, but he is like the crafty old squirrel that won't sleep on the ground if the females are up in the branches.'

Did she imply that the Diwan was like Naga Gangoo, interested in making conquests? That was hardly possible. At the

Kala Bhairab shrine there were heaps of women: casual pilgrims, regular worshippers, and stray visitors—once-a-yearers, once-a-weekers, and irregulars. If women had been his objective, he would not have been my headache. The trouble was that he found Myna alone interesting. The shrine without Myna was an empty place for him—in the same way as it was for me. What was I to do?

'If you are going out kicking,' the cook counselled, 'you had better wear boots.'

I shook my head. It would be most rash on my part to quarrel with him. That was bound to ruin my case with Myna: she had her theory about helping people. Whoever needed her service had only to ask for it. What service did the Diwan want of her?

'Babu!' the cook began, 'you don't understand me. I don't want you to get into trouble. Do I not know what it is to be dragged into a court? The law and the lawyers! May God save us from them.' She slapped her cheeks to emphasize her point. 'The law and the lawyers,' she repeated. 'Ashes if you lose, and cinders if you win, but it is they who gather up the charcoal. I know all this too well. And you need not put on your football boots to kick the Diwan. You can knock him down with a tiny frog, no bigger than your smallest toe. If you want to, you can do it any night and Myna will be yours.'

X

The cook's solicitude for my success was touching. But what was really behind her frequent visits to the astrologer? Why did she occasionally sigh, 'I don't think your Myna is as pious as all that'? Was she trying to be nice to me because I once helped—quite inadvertently—her former heart-throb the Bahurupi?

The answer I hit upon then seemed preposterous in my own reckoning. And because I thought it preposterous I am now putting it down in black and white. The cook must have assumed that Myna was the Bahurupi's 'moll' and it hurt her pride that she should have been ousted by a mere *kirtani* whose religious vow debarred her from getting married and running a home. What was Myna compared with her? Just nothing: a nomad, a homeless creature, a perpetual wanderer from one place of pilgrimage to another. Myna might have been half her age, but that, in her reasoning, was a handicap rather than an advantage. What did the Bahurupi need? A mother, one who would run a home for him, a good housekeeper. Certainly Myna could not play the role of a mother. Perhaps the Bahurupi thought a lot of Myna and maybe Myna, for her part, thought a lot of him, and that was why she addressed him as 'Uncle'. After all, the Bahurupi's sentence was not long: he was going to be released any day. What a triumph it would be for the cook to greet him on his discharge with the news: 'That *kirtani* Myna, for whom you left me, is a bitch: a mortar that needs always a pestle. Do you know as soon as you went to prison she decided to take herself a lover? She wanted to court the Diwan, but the Diwan won't have her. So she has taken to her cousin from the Penhari Parganas. I know all the details from her cousin. He lives in the place where I am cook. He is a bit of a rake.'

'These thoughts are wicked,' I said to myself when the cook presented me with her enchanted frog to knock the Diwan out of the ring.

'Here's the frog,' she said. 'And if Myna does not become yours before the week ends I will swallow a crocodile.'

I did not see any live frog. Two tiny white objects on the stretched palm of the cook's hand did not look like carved ivory frogs either. One was like a microscopic fishing-hook, or rather a minute wish-bone, and the other resembled a small spatula—the shovel, in the astrological jargon of the fortune-teller of Kalighat. 'What are these?' I asked. 'Where's your magic frog?'

The enchanted frog, I understood, was wrapped up in a piece of white linen and given astrological benedictions. It was then put on an ant-hill at sunset. The poor creature croaked on while it was being gnawed by the ants till it ceased to live.

'It is most cruel,' I interrupted her recital with my expression of thorough disapproval of what she had done.

'But love is cruel,' she replied in a voice that made me quake to the very marrow. 'Now that the frog is dead you may as well hear the rest of the story.'

She told the story in detail, but I barely paid any attention to what she said. I vaguely gathered that the dead frog, wrapped in a piece of red linen, was replaced on the ant-hill for three successive evenings: nothing remained of it save bits of bone, of these, two were selected—one shaped like a hook or a wish-bone and the other looking like a shovel or a trowel or a spatula, whatever you will.

All the while my thoughts were elsewhere, I knew I was out for trouble: it was imprudent to exchange confidences with the cook. I called myself an ass. 'Would to God,' I prayed in silence, 'someone would now come to my succour.' The hostel at that hour was empty but for the cook and me, and I did not like in the least the way she was edging towards me with her bits of frog's bones. Did I hear her say, 'The smoke of a burning home can be seen, but not that of a burning heart'? What did she want of me?

''Take this hook-shaped bone,' she went on with her eyes lowered as though excessive shyness prevented her from looking at me. 'Babu, just hook a woman's dress with this bone. And you will see what will happen. She will fall head and ears in love with you.'

'And,' I stammered, 'what's the other bone for?'

'That shovel!' She heaved a deep sigh. 'If you ever tire of her, you have only to touch her with the shovel, and her affection will vanish as quickly as it came.'

'I see,' I murmured. 'It is very kind of you to take all this trouble for me.'

She held out her hand and turned her face away from me. A cold feeling began creeping down my spine while beads of perspiration appeared on my forehead. Call me superstitious or whatever you will, I was saying my prayers with all the fervour I could command. The cook began sniffing. She was renowned for a special gift: she could weep at a moment's notice. 'Why don't you take them?' she asked finally in a voice choked with tears. 'Don't you believe what I have told you? And if you...if you don't believe me, you may try it on me.'

I was perspiring like a frightened horse. What was I to do?

The cook sobbed: 'Why don't you call me by my pet name?' It was Kusum, which meant 'Blossom'. I admitted it was most charming. This made her sob more noisily; she repeated she would not mind, for my benefit, having the hook-shaped frog bone stuck to her sari, and I was at liberty to throw the frog-shovel at her any time when I tired of her.

'You are in a fine mess,' my inner voice reproached me. 'Kolej Huzoor's formula will not help you.' I agreed with my inner voice. 'The best means of ridding yourself of a girl you don't fancy,' Kolej Huzoor counselled, 'is to be firm. Just repeat politely, "I am unworthy of you. You do deserve someone really worthwhile. It breaks my heart, because I do admire you. Yet for your sake it is my duty to withdraw." I think this formula will work for every country in the world except Paraguay. There, my boy, you will have to be very careful.' I wished I had asked Kolej Huzoor about the magic formula for Paraguay. What was I to do with Kusum?

Kusum was half my size and just twice my age. She wore ear-studs destined for maidens in her part of the country, though she was a widow with a number of married daughters, of whom one lived in Midnapore. Someone had told her that it was easy to find a husband in Calcutta: 'There are lots and lots of poets in Calcutta. They are starving and would be glad to get wives willing to feed them.' So she came to Calcutta and made the sad discovery that though there were about a hundred thousand poets and about ten thousand actors and would-be film stars, not one of them was prepared to accept the bonds of matrimony with her. The marriage bureaux and professional matchmakers pocketed their fees from Kusum and later told her that the competition with the younger hussies made her chances nil! Kusum then tried on her own in different hostels for bachelors, alas! With no better result. She dyed her hair prematurely grey and this, too, brought her no success. Finally, came her adventure with the Bahurupi, who fleeced her of her entire savings. Her case was hopeless. She did not dare return to Midnapore without a husband, ashamed lest her neighbours made fun of her.

'Why don't you call me by my pet name?' she demanded again as she wiped her eyes with a corner of her sari. 'You know the secret now. Only those who love me have the right to call me by my pet name.'

'But, Kusum,' I stuttered, guided by my inner voice, which insisted that I must not hurt her feelings. 'You know in the Penhari Parganas no child is allowed to call his mother by her name. I have always loved you and wanted to call you Kusum. But you see my difficulty. I looked upon you as a mother on the first day you fed me. And since then I have gone on doing so. That's why it is difficult to call you Kusum.'

I congratulated myself on my neat speech, though it was badly delivered. But it made no difference to Kusum. She was determined to verify what sort of an athlete I was—or rather, what sort of a lover I was likely to be. It was no use struggling against the inevitable, Kusum divested of her sari was already by my side. Myna's counsel came to my mind: 'Do not be unnecessarily cruel to anyone.' And to refuse Kusum would have been an act of cruelty. She was, in spite of her forty years, attractive, exceptionally well built, and had she not been the cook of my hostel I would most likely have courted her to win her favours. But she had a glib tongue, and that frightened me. There was no knowing how many cooks of Calcutta were going to hear soon about my adventure or misadventure with her.

A frightened man makes a poor lover, and I am afraid Kusum found me most unsatisfactory. Unwittingly I behaved like the boor described by a Sanskrit poet who specialized in naughty verses.

> Let me tell you, dear friend, of a singular thing
> A boorish lout of a lover did to me this morning:
> Hardly had I closed my eyes in the bliss of the moment
> When the frightened gallant hastily withdrew with a lament.
> Did he think I was dying, or perhaps dead?

To make up for my shortcomings I murmured my apologies, and willingly allowed her to make love to me in her own way, which was certainly novel and quite exciting. 'Not many women,'

I whispered, 'can boast of a shapely and firm bosom like yours.' This made Kusum sob softly. What was the use of a woman's breasts, she moaned, if they never nourished a son? She had the ill luck to bear only daughters. How she wished she had a boy to cling to her bosom.

This gave me a bright idea. Once the ordeal of the embrace was over I proposed a pact: henceforth she should look upon me as her adopted son and not as a lover; I was prepared to call her Kusum when no one was about; scandals must be avoided in the hostel. She agreed and added a clause of her own—the most onerous one of the agreement as far as I was concerned: she insisted that I must some time or other go to Midnapore to spend at least a few days in her cottage, and during my sojourn there behave as though I were a thoroughly spoilt child.

'You must act as you do on the stage,' Kusum explained. 'You must rave and shout and throw things about. And ask for this and that.'

'Why, Kusum? You don't want your adopted son to behave like an ill-mannered brute.'

'I want to have a good cry before my neighbours. I am sure they will all rush to console me and tell me that you are no good, and I was foolish to adopt a son of your age.'

'What good would that do to you?'

'I shall then have a nice quarrel with them.'

I did not know what to say. But then, I have never been any good at comprehending the complicated mechanism of a woman's mind.

'This evening,' Kusum declared, 'I shall go to the Kala Bhairab shrine to quarrel with the Diwan. I shall tell him what I think of him and his son. And you will hook the frog-bone to Myna's behind.'

'Come to the shrine, if you will. But, for heaven's sake, quarrel with no one. Myna hates noisy disputes. You don't want me to lose Myna, do you?'

XI

There was no Myna that evening at the Pavilion. And I derived a grim satisfaction in watching the Diwan sitting there on his stern and patiently waiting for her: he looked like a bulging rice bin. Did he know I was replacing her?

Of course, I missed Myna. Nevertheless I felt important: I was in the know, while the Diwan was not. It was also flattering to see Piram reposing beside Kusum: the bulldog refused to recognize the Diwan and his suite. Had Piram been somebody's else's dog I might have been tempted to tell one of the temple attendants to turn him out of the holy precincts. Though some women do make it a habit to drag their pets with them from one place of pilgrimage to another, this custom is strongly discountenanced in some shrines. In Jaunpur, if I remember correctly, the Mohammedan tradition of treating dogs as unclean animals has affected a large section of the Hindus, and the Hindu temples are out of bounds there to the members of the canine species. 'This is, of course, going too far,' in Kolej Huzoor's words. 'Dharma, our deity of moral and religious duty, appeared before King Yudhistir in the guise of a dog, and the Bhairavis ride on dogs. It would be against our tenets if we were to shut our temple gates on the lower creatures. Fancy a Hindu temple without cows and bulls, apes and monkeys, peacocks and parrots, doves and bats, dogs and cats! Why, we might as well turn cowbeef-eaters—Christians or Mohammedans—and start spring-cleaning or hoovering our sanctuaries for the benefit of the rogues who are ashamed of

Hinduism. Only noisy dogs ought to be debarred during prayers.' Though I agreed substantially with Kolej Huzoor's contention, yet I held the view that one should be guided by the local customs and tradition: 'There never was, nor ever should be a uniform general ruling for all Hindu temples.'

Anyway, Piram was the image of respectability itself. He was watching me in silent admiration. Kusum was doing the same with eyes brimming with tears. She was overjoyed to find me installed in the place of honour with a fat book in front of me. By signs and nods she was trying to convey me her instruction—not to read too fast.

Those who have never visited Kala Bhairab shrine should bear in mind that the Pavilion where I sat was something like the famous Painted Porch in ancient Athens where the Stoics used to congregate. Whoever cared to give any recital or readings from the sacred texts was welcome to do so. There were, of course, some singers who were universal favourites and they got precedence. As I was very often Myna's accompanist with my flute, in her absence I was asked to replace her. Myna herself left a message for me, advising me to give some readings.

Therefore I felt very proud, though, as I have said before, I missed her and wished she was there to listen to my elocution. 'Nothing but the very best is good enough for me,' I often told her. It was now up to me to show what I could do, especially as the Diwan was in the audience.

It was a mixed crowd; some of my listeners, I knew, were simple and devout, while others were sophisticated, and there were still others who came God alone knew why—perhaps out of curiosity; a few more came for the purpose of making fun of our sacred texts. At the end of each reading these last would invariably ask silly questions. For example, 'Do you really believe that Indra wields the thunderbolt? What makes you think that the god has a thousand eyes?'

It was, therefore, wisdom itself to choose a text which would not permit the mockers the opportunity of putting too many teasers. I felt nervous, not because I was afraid of being cornered, but because I was anxious to maintain some dignity in the sanctuary. Who feared squabbles or squawkers in College Square or University Union?—Certainly not I. But the holy precincts of the Kala Bhairab's temple demanded at least some semblance of decorum. How was I to maintain order if some of Chumchike Adhikari's gang or Emenroyites decided to kick up a row?

With Myna it was different. She was the universal favourite. Trouble-makers ran the risk of being manhandled if they dared interrupt her. So she could say, 'Those who want to scoff will scoff. Arguments won't change them. It is best to ignore them and talk only to those who will listen.' Her instructions to me demanded that I should choose a parable easily comprehensible to all.

Unfortunately, there was not much time for me to reflect. The Great Epic—the *Mahabharata*—is one of the fattest books in the world, and I took my plunge by opening it at hazard. Then I turned over a few pages when the name of Gautama attracted my attention: the story of the sage Gautama figures in the *Book of Consolation* of the Great Epic.

~

I began with a short prayer and read out the text, stanza by stanza, interpolating the Sanskrit text with my translation and commentary.

> Dwelt then in a forest hermitage
> Gautama the self-restrained sage...

One day Gautama came across a baby elephant that had lost its mother and was most disconsolate. The sage took pity on it and brought it with him to his hermitage. And there he nursed it and reared it till it grew to be large and mighty.

Now Indra, the Lord of the Firmament, decided to test the affection the sage bore to the elephant, and taking the form of a despot known as the Iron-handed, abducted the animal.

'Thankless King,' Gautama protested, 'do not take away this gentle and obedient creature from the hermitage. It looks after this place when I am away. It fetches my water and brings me my firewood of its own accord. It is indeed dear to me.'

'Would you not care to part with it for a hundred measures of gold, or a hundred handmaidens, or a hundred head of cattle?'

'You are certainly generous,' replied the sage. 'But what shall I do with what you offer? I reckon wisdom alone is wealth, and my needs are those of a temperate man. I cannot barter the friendship of this animal for gold, or for women, or for kine.'

'But elephants are royal animals. They are fit to serve kings only. It is natural that this animal, on account of its enormous size, should be stabled in my elephant-yard.'

'I would then follow it to your elephant-yard,' Gautama said.

'And what if I take it to the nether world which is under the sway of the red-robed Yama, Lord of the Dead?'

'Then,' Gautama answered,' I shall follow it there, and take it back from you. For Yama is known to be the Giver of Justice.'

'Gautama! Have you not heard that the nether world is destined for the unbelievers, the faithless, and the sinful? Is it a fit place for a sage to visit for the sake of an animal?'

'I, too, have heard,' Gautama argued, 'where justice prevails there the weak cannot be overcome by the strong. Is not the nether world—Yama's kingdom—the region for obtaining justice? How can it then be sinful for me to go there in quest of my object of affection?'

'If that be so, I shall withdraw to a higher region, taking the elephant with me.'

'Even if you retire to the exalted heights where dwell the *gandharvas* and *apsaras*—the choristers to the deities—there shall I follow you to take back the elephant.'

'Gautama! What if I seek a place still higher?'

'Scale if you will the very summit of Mount Meru where the air is filled with the chants of the centaurs and the centauresses, even there I shall not cease to pursue you.'

So it was said by each of every high-up place: the flowery groves of Narada, the scented highlands of Soma, the heavens of the enlightened, the heavens of Indra with its adoring angels. 'There,' declared the deity disguised as the despot known as the Iron-handed, 'in Indra's heaven you may not discover me.'

'Verily,' Gautama affirmed, 'even there I shall find you to take back the elephant. But now I know you despite your present form. You are no other than Indra himself, the Lord of the Firmament. You wander through the universe in diverse appearances. Pardon me, Lord, for my missaying you. For how could I recognize you in your guise of a mortal?'

The Lord of the Firmament tries man by devious means, and he was pleased that the hermit made his humble acknowledgment. 'Gautama!' he said, 'Since you have recognized me, I want to bestow a boon upon you. Ask for whatever you will, and it shall be accorded to you.'

The sage prayed that the elephant of the hermitage should be restored to him: 'For it is so young, barely ten years old. It needs love and affection, and is as yet too immature to undertake difficult tasks.'

'Is it then the only boon you desire of Indra who is the Lord of the Firmament?'

'Lord,' Gautama answered, 'I know you are the chief of the deities, the leader of the celestial host, the wielder of the thunderbolt, the bender of the terrible bow, the warrior of the glittering shaft, the immortal with a thousand eyes, the friend of the strangers, and the consoler of the wayfarers. And I know you have attributes many more than these. I know, too, that you bestow on man whatever he earnestly desires. Nevertheless, I repeat my prayer that the young elephant, which needs love and affection, be restored to this hermitage.'

'So be it,' Indra pronounced. 'Behold, the elephant that is so dear to you has returned: it is even now bowing down at your feet. Be it well with you both.'

Gautama made his obeisance to Indra, and took the elephant. And Indra blessed the sage, who, thereupon, was translated with his elephant to the Seventh Heaven, which even the righteous rarely attain.

Thus ends the account of Gautama who, with his elephant, went to the abode of the immortals.

And whoever reads, or recounts, or receives this apologue *with due understanding* shall reach the same goal.

~

'Will you allow me to ask a question?' It was the Diwan.

If thirty dozen rowdies had knocked me down and trampled upon me I could not have felt more flat.

An hour ago I had been bloated with my own importance, because I had assumed—quite erroneously—that I was in the know while the Diwan was not! There was Myna's message for me. But was there anything for him? 'Of course, nothing,' my ego whispered. 'How can there be anything for him? You are the only one in Calcutta for whom she has left a written message. Some of the temple attendants may have received her verbal instructions: she might have told them that she was going away from Calcutta for a short while.' As I have said before, I regretted Myna's sudden departure from Calcutta and at the same time rejoiced at the thought that the Diwan was not in the know. Now, however, I discovered that the case was the reverse, or almost so. The Diwan was there because he had been requested by no other than Myna herself to continue his visits to the Kala Bhairab shrine: to aid me with promptings and suitable questions if necessary.

The Diwan's presence was—in Myna's reasoning—an absolute guarantee that there would be no ugly scenes or unpleasant uproars over my possible indiscretions: she thought I was a hot-head, ready to come to blows with the Emenroyites, the *khadiwallahs*, the *topiwallahs*, and others of their sort—men anxious to modernize or abolish Hinduism. As the Diwan was a Cabinet Minister he was always accompanied by a sufficient number of plain-clothes policemen to quell any minor disorder. My humiliation was still greater when I learnt that Myna had sent one of her bangles to the Diwan along with her message: the offer of a bangle implied a humble supplication. No Hindu worth his salt must refuse a woman's prayer for succour if it is made along with the despatch of her bangle. 'She has done all this,' my deflated ego reproached me, 'because she thinks you are a fool, incapable of looking after yourself. And now the Diwan whom you detest has sent you a slip of paper with the answer to his question neatly written out. He has done this for Myna's sake. Perhaps he has won Myna's heart.'

My humiliation was complete. But I did not want to be pitied by the old Diwan, and refused to read out the answer from his slip of paper.

'Now,' the Diwan cleared his throat and went on, 'this is the question I should like to ask: what is the real import of the term *understanding*? "A parable," you say, "should be received with due understanding." I should like you to give an example of true understanding.'

'A very good question,' several people murmured. 'Very good.'

As I had meanwhile thrown away the Diwan's slip of paper I stared in all directions to encourage the curious to fire off their questions as well; so that I could gain time and think of a suitable reply.

An elderly man who had been snoring during the major part of my reading suddenly woke up. He asked his neighbour, in an irritated tone, what was happening? 'Understanding?' he declared, 'Why, it is the same as knowledge. And what is knowledge? It is identification.'

I encouraged the man to expound his thesis.

~

One of the greatest pleasures of coming to a place like the Kala Bhairab temple was, for me, the impromptu discourses of its frequenters. About a century ago General Sleeman, when travelling from one end of the country to the other, used to spend his nights listening to the discussions of his camp followers. In the dark he would sit behind a tree trunk and note carefully the comments of simple folk on such personalities as Plato (referred to as Al Platoun the Broadshouldered), Socrates, and Aristotle. (These three were the only Western philosophers he readily identified, but there were others whose names—owing to their transformation into oriental nomenclature—were unknown to him.) 'Those dark nights,' Sleeman records, 'were for me intellectual feasts: entertainments of a higher kind than any offered at Oxford or at any other university.' What was true of Sleeman was ten times more true of me. Like the Rajah of Luktam I was sick of listening to shibboleths on progress among the so-called educated, the town-dwellers who listened to the wireless, read newspapers and pretended universal knowledge. But in the temple-yards and on the steps of the *ghats* of the rivers, gathered men and women who barely knew the art of reading, but were infinitely better educated in the lore of the country's legends and history: they did not suffer from that feeling of inferiority which characterized Calcutta's 'cultivated people'—the feeling which made them admire with passionate fanaticism the regimes of distant countries like Russia or China or America. The better-off section of Calcutta's inhabitants thought it superstitious or undignified to take any interest in Indian myths and cults: for them civilization was equivalent to the general standard of material comfort and of mechanization of industries.

Like Kolej Huzoor, Gama, Balaban, and others, I detested their attitude. It is true I did not see eye to eye with Kolej Huzoor or Gama or Balaban or, for that matter, with anyone of my set; but there was one thing common to all of us, namely, our belief that those who were indifferent to India's past were incapable of appreciating India's civilization: 'Cosmopolitanism,' we held, 'is a poor substitute for patriotism. And patriotism is not mere braggadocio.'

To listen, let me repeat, to the discussions of those who regularly met in the temple-yards or on the stone staircases of the sacred pools and rivers was a sheer joy: they gave me courage, they deepened my faith, they sustained me in my days of trial.

My musing made me miss a good bit of the erstwhile snorer's exposition.

'To understand one's own limitations,' he was propounding, 'is the same as to acquire the knowledge of one's own failings. And what's the advantage of this knowledge or understanding, whatever you will? It's the surest starting-point for an eventual liberation: man becomes free as and when he becomes conscious of the strength and complications of his bonds.'

The Diwan, I noticed, was listening with bent head, but others were showing signs of impatience: as though they wanted me to bring the discussion on understanding to an end so that the gathering could listen to further readings from the sacred texts.

In a flash it occurred to me that there was something in the *Books of Esoteric Doctrines* that was admirably suited to my purpose:

'*To understand* the "nature" of a thing is *to enjoy union* with the thing. To understand Krishna, our ancient gloss says, one must seek union with Krishna.' The Diwan added, 'Radha understands Krishna because she joins herself with Krishna. Yes, I follow what you have in mind.'

**

I was congratulating myself on my narrow escape. To be truthful, I did not know how a parable should be received *with due understanding*. Anyway, my good luck spared me the dishonour of being a laughing-stock at the shrine of the Kala Bhairab.

I rose to leave the place.

'May I give you a lift in my car?' the Diwan asked, and my mood of elation vanished. 'I should like to have a talk with you. In fact I have been trying to meet you for a long time.'

I made some inarticulate sounds. I knew it was coming: this interview which I had been trying to avoid since the day I saw him in his back garden. I had no ready excuse to refuse his invitation. Moreover, it was quite possible that Myna was responsible for his stopping me.

'Is it true you owned an elephant at one time? No, no. Don't protest. I hear you fought for that elephant.'

'I can assure you it was not Indra who wanted to abduct my pygmy elephant.' I laughed, though inwardly I quaked, because I did not know what he was driving at. What did he want to discuss with me? 'He is a wolf in sheep's clothing.' I recalled Kusum's warning. 'I know all about him from his head cook; she is also from Midnapore. She tells me, "He may sit like a pussy, but he gobbles like a tiger." Never let yourself be lured into his home. You will not come out alive, and if you do you will not be the same again. He is simply a wolf.' Kusum, I knew, was liable to exaggerations. But what did he want of me? Did he want Piram to be brought back to his house?

XII

'He that has soft ears,' they say in my village, 'will get his ears tweaked.'

And I realized, rather late, that in the past I had been exceptionally soft-eared. The more I saw of the Diwan the more I felt guilty for having listened to Kusum and to the photographer who worked for *Life-in-Technikolor*. The Diwan was a different being from what the gossips recounted.

I greatly regretted my indiscretions: the stories heard from Kusum had been passed on to the photographer and through him to a wider circle. And one particular issue of *Life-*

in-Technikolor made me furious. It caused a big sensation on account of its pictures of 'the talking cow', and of Professor Foni Dhar arguing with the animal.

The incident of 'the talking cow' was of no great consequence. The animal was being taken to the slaughter-house when a ventriloquist decided to have his fun. He declared that the poor cow was crying for succour and made the appropriate semi-human sounds to convince the passers-by. Calcutta was then in a state of ferment over the issue of abolishing all slaughter-houses. 'The cause of cancer,' some papers declared, 'was meat.' A number of politicians keenly interested in the welfare of fishermen and in the promotion of fisheries took up the cue. They demanded that public sale of meat should be abolished forthwith. What about the traditional sacrifice of the goat to the goddess at Kalighat? That had, of course, nothing to do with public abattoirs: it was, they admitted, a religious rite, and they were not concerned with it. 'These politicians,' their opponents proclaimed, 'have cornered the fish market. Therefore they are interested in stopping the sale of meat in Calcutta. The cause of beri-beri is due to our deficient diet. Fish cannot replace meat.' The whole of Calcutta automatically divided into two camps—one for the immediate abolition of the abattoirs and the other for leaving things as they were. Petitions and counter-petitions were sent to Delhi. And the Hindu Maha Sabha launched at that time one of its periodic appeals for total prohibition of the slaughter of cattle. 'Hinduism means protection and preservation of cattle,' their manifesto announced. 'When Sivaji raised his standard of revolt against the Great Mogul he made a similar declaration. It is high time for us to finish what Sivaji began. A thousand-year-old injustice to the Hindus must be abolished.' 'Verily,' began a spokesman of the Marwaris of Calcutta, 'the cow is the embodiment of everything sacred in Hinduism.' (They all overlooked the fact that the Vedic deity Indra was a champion beefeater.)

In these circumstances it might be easily guessed that the news of the talking cow spread like wildfire all over Calcutta. The clever ventriloquist bought the cow to resell it at a high price to the Comradeship of Cow-worshippers of Calcutta. The beast was released in the *maidan* after being properly garlanded and duly worshipped. Professor Foni Dhar, being a Bramho—a puritan nonconformist—did not, naturally, believe a word about this cow's alleged gift of human speech. As he was a prominent figure in Calcutta, some fanatics of the CCCs decided to confront him with the animal in the hope of weaning him from his pristine puritanism. The professor himself was sufficiently alive to the fact that there was considerable publicity value in being taken to the *maidan* to lecture to a cow: already half a million people—consisting of 'believers' and 'unbelievers' in equal proportions—were gathered there. Accompanied by a battery of cameras, recording machines, televising devices, and a band of the CCCs, Professor Foni Dhar interviewed the cow. In the absence of the ventriloquist the beast remained dumb. Therefore, it was not much of an interview. But for some reason the animal manifested an intense dislike for the renowned anthologist of the *Anna Nosegay* and, like an enraged bull, tried to gore him. Professor Dhar saved himself by climbing a tree.

The issue of *Life-in-Technikolor* to which I have referred gave a series of shots to illustrate the incidents connected with Professor Foni Dhar's discomfiture. And these pictures did not disturb me in the least. I was not even annoyed at such captions as, 'Hindus worship cows,' 'The sacred cow suspects the learned professor of harbouring heretical thoughts,' 'The design of the temple to be built in honour of the talking cow,' etc. Even the most stupid newspaper reader in America or elsewhere must know, I thought, Hinduism is something more than venerating the cow. Did it then matter much if *Life-in-Technikolor* made a scoop with the animal's gift of human speech and the suggestion that it should receive the hon. D.Lit. degree?

However that may be, the same issue of *Life-in-Technikolor* reproduced a number of pictures showing the different entrances to the house of the Diwan in Hargila Lane, and the text embellishing them was in poor taste. And I felt like going to the Diwan immediately to offer my apologies. Not that I was responsible for those captions, but he knew I was associated with *Life-in-Technikolor,* and it was natural for him to conclude that I might have been the evil genius to inspire them.

I had a big row with the photographer over that issue of *Life-in-Technikolor.* The fellow who had introduced himself to me as the ex-punk on the full moon night of Ashwin was now one of my *chelas*—a disciple or admirer or whatever else you will. It was a nuisance to be called 'Guru'—the spiritual master—by him!

'Guru' is a term of high honour reserved for great personalities, people of outstanding abilities. The poet Tagore was called 'Gurudev' by his admirers, and this was as it should be; however dull the English paraphrases of his poems might be, he was a personality of the same calibre as, say, Tolstoy. And in my reckoning there was nothing wrong if anyone decided to elect Tagore his spiritual leader—his Guru: the matter was one which concerned no one except the self-appointed disciple. The poet was too big a man to have his reputation affected by a nonentity parading himself as 'Tagore's *chela*'. Did it matter much to Tolstoy that a briefless barrister with sticking-out ears called himself 'the only and the true disciple of Tolstoy the Sage of Yanaya Polyana'? But I was neither Tagore nor Tolstoy, and felt highly embarrassed when

I learnt that the photographer of *Life-in-Technikolor* went about all over Calcutta calling me his guru. At first Piram manifested considerable hostility to the fellow, but gradually he came to accept him as one of my acquaintances and stopped chasing him out of my room. This change of attitude on Piram's part affected me to some extent. And, maybe, my inner ego felt flattered to count a professional photographer among my admirers.

But why did that fellow need a guru?

Calcutta has been guru-ridden since the day of its foundation. Every inhabitant has his guru, one in whom he believes implicitly. There are a number of professional gurus who ride only in Rolls-Royces and charge heavy fees for giving spiritual guidance: very often the spiritual guidance degenerates into instructions about stock exchange speculations. There are gurus whose main function consists in selling to their disciples esoteric formulas—*mantras*—capable of solving every difficulty, spiritual and material: all that is necessary is to repeat the *mantra* with due reverence a certain number of times. There are gurus of all sorts: gurus whose blessings make their disciples expert wrestlers, unbeatable boxers, gifted actors, matchless dancers, remarkable footballers, and what not; gurus who cater for politicians and are themselves adepts in string-pulling; gurus of pickpockets and cut-throats; gurus of thieves and thugs; gurus specializing in women admirers; gurus interested in black magic and astrology. And very rare gurus who are genuinely remarkable people and most reluctant to increase the number of their disciples. As these last are not numerous, in Calcutta the term *guru* has come to mean *someone better than myself.*

Whatever my inner ego might have felt I thought it ridiculous to be labelled 'an Ex-Punk's Guru'. I did not deem it an honour to count a photographer working for *Life-in-Technikolor* as a disciple, and I told him so more than once. Yet somehow my very bluntness was interpreted by him to be a sure sign of my spiritual superiority. My familiarity with Myna, too, was regarded by him as a proof of my holiness. 'Only holy people are incorruptible,' the fellow told Kusum—of all the people in the world! And Kusum, instead of disabusing him of his silly notions, talked of me as though I were the Promethean god Balaram himself whom Myna would be only too happy to have as her companion and accompanist. My incapacity for compromising with men like Foni Dhar was considered to be a further corroboration of my spiritual strength, while my fairly extensive reading provided a confirmation of his belief that I must have been the occupant of the throne of the Dalai Lama in a previous existence. Evidently the young fellow wanted someone to be his hero, and he decided to worship me in his own way. Whatever fell from my lips he accepted as gospel truth. Being a man of East Bengal his sense of humour was naturally different from that of the rest of the world.

In these circumstances I had no reason to be surprised that he accepted my nasty aphorisms, spicy anecdotes, and improved versions of Kusum's tittle-tattle as statements of fact and profound verities and mysterious parables. I had only myself to blame. Nevertheless, as I have said before, I was furious when I read the captions under the illustrations of the Diwan's house.

'My ears have been tweaked,' I told the photographer. 'I must go to the Diwan at once to offer my apologies. I don't want to be thought a knave. It is galling enough to be considered a fool.'

The fellow stared at me with his mouth half open.

'I have no quarrel with the Diwan,' I continued. 'He has been kind to me. Don't you know that I have been working as his part-time secretary since the evening I read the scriptures in the Kala Bhairab shrine?'

'But why should he be offended with this number of *Life-in-Technikolor?*'

'What about these pictures and these captions, and your comments on the astrological bulletins?'

The fellow seemed not to understand me. Did I really believe in astrological forecasts? What was wrong in making fun of the statues at the entrance of the Diwan's house? Was it not comical to put up astrological bulletins at the different exits and entrances to the house?

~

My outburst was over the astrological bulletins. Perhaps at that moment I thought that the real cause of my anger was the frivolous fashion in which these were described. But there might have been a deeper cause. Perhaps I did not want the statues of Anadi and Ananta and of the other figures at the main entrance of the Diwan's house to be seen by profane eyes. Anyway, as I was now a part-time employee in the Diwan's household, my sense of loyalty might have been outraged. Since Myna's departure from Calcutta I had been working on the Diwan's behalf in the Imperial Library and also in his own library on a piece of research. Now I was his part-time assistant. My views about him were changing fast.

~

About those bulletins, it was—and it still is—believed among Calcutta's patricians that disasters and misfortunes foretold in one's horoscope might be warded off by posting notices in bold letters at the different entrances to one's house, giving the details furnished by the astrologers. 'Stellar combinations indicate,' such a notice may read, 'that the third son of the household is likely to be knocked down by a car on Thursday next between 2.50 p.m. and 6.54 p.m., and as a result of this accident he will probably lose the lower half of his left arm and the use of his eyes.'

The main thing, the astrologers hold, is to give the widest possible publicity to the impending accident: for that is the surest means of averting it. 'The evil spirits,' they say, 'are responsible for all mishaps. If they are propitiated they may not cause any disaster. But they are renowned for their contrariness, and it is not easy to satisfy their whims. However, one thing is clear: they can derive no fun from playing a trick that would cause no surprise to anyone. Herein lies the value of giving publicity to an impending accident.'

Like the photographer, I used to think at one time that these astrological bulletins were big jokes, and I did not keep back my views from Myna. Her reaction was unforeseen: 'Are they bigger jokes than the weather forecasts issued by the Alipore observatory? Can you always depend upon their bulletins?' 'Weather forecasts,' I argued, 'depend on many factors.' 'Astrological forecasts, too, depend on many factors. If natural phenomena cannot always be foretold accurately, what makes you think that spiritual phenomena are more easily foreseen? The value of an astrological bulletin depends on many things. But it is a fact that coming events do cast their shadows before.' 'This seems unbelievable,' was my final comment.

Myna argued that there was another way of looking at those bulletins: they were the means to bring to the fore our secret fears. 'And what good will that do?' I asked, and received the unexpected reply: 'Man is destroyed by secret fears and hidden sins and lapses, of which he is rarely conscious. Make them known, and they will vanish.'

This was certainly a new slant on those bulletins. And I well recall the evening when Myna expounded her views: it was shortly before she left for Gilani, in the hills. She was then in one of her mystic moods to which I have not yet referred: because Myna in her trances positively frightened me.

Her body was then burning hot. The slightest touch of her finger, I am sure, would have raised blisters on me. The expression on her face was unusually ecstatic: delightful to those who did not know her, but to me it was awe-inspiring because of its unearthly—or was it otherworldly? —comeliness. Her voice was endowed with uncommon melodiousness, like the note of the distant temple bells of the high mountainous regions heard in the stillness of the night. Her very gait had something exceptional. Her demeanour was commanding. The way she talked did not encourage any contradiction on my part.

The specific contents of the particular bulletin to which I had drawn her attention did not interest her. She was more concerned in making a general statement. 'It is the whispering fear,' she repeated, 'the fear unformulated, which is disastrous. It is the whispering sin—the feeling of guilt whose nature and form are not perceived, or at best very vaguely—that drives man to perdition. It is far better that the nature of the fear should be formulated and the character of the sin defined than that they should remain undiscovered to gnaw our hearts away.'

The hidden fear, I was told, unnerved and unmanned human beings more than open warfare. The unquiet mind, according to her, was like the slimy, slippery hagfish—the eel-like creature with rudimentary eyes and a round mouth surrounded with tentacles—that preys upon its unsuspecting victims by simply boring into their bodies and slowly devouring their entrails.

Myna in her mystic moods, as I have said before, frightened me. She then used words, phrases, and expressions as well as images and parables of rare significance. Where did she get them from? She illustrated her points with myths and legends and instances from natural history with uncommon acuteness. Did she create them from her own imagination on the spur of the moment? Why did she in such moments ask me to leave Calcutta and 'seek the world'? What did she mean by the statement that unless one understood one's affinity with the universe all knowledge was less than even a partial glimpse of the whole?

For the discoveries of physical science she had little curiosity and hardly any admiration. 'They are just tools,' she held. 'Tools by themselves are of little service if they do not help one to understand the nature of man and his oneness with the visible and the invisible world.'

A plain question about the worth of the astrological bulletins led her to propound doctrines beyond my grasp. I felt perplexed. And at the same time I was not in a position to question her views. Once a child had brought a ruffled bird to her. 'My pet has broken its leg,' the child cried. 'It can't fly any more. They want to kill it.' 'Let me have a look at it,' said Myna. 'Perhaps I can try to bring back its spirit to it.' 'Do, Kirtani, save it,' the child begged. 'Let me sing back its spirit to it. Meanwhile bring me a flower to tie to its broken leg. We shall then see what happens.' She began whistling, and caressing the bird. And when a tiny flower was tied to its broken limb it seemed to be cured as though by magic. Did she set the broken bones aright? Or was the cure miraculous? Myna's explanation was as enigmatic as her views regarding the oneness of the universe. The body, in her opinion, was sustained by thirty-two spirits, each one of them acting as the protecting angel of a particular limb, and the departure of any of them brought disaster to the member left unguarded. However, if the angel—or the spirit—could be cajoled back to its seat the broken limb would be whole again! Did I doubt that theory? How could I when I had seen with my own eyes the miracle she wrought with the bird? And at the same time it was difficult to swallow the view that each human being was being looked after by thirty-two angels.

Thirty-two, if I remember correctly, was her magic number. Was that why she wore at times thirty-two bangles and bracelets and armlets? Had those ornaments anything to do with the demands of the presiding angels? Why on certain days had she only floral ornaments—garlands and chaplets? Of course, it was out of the question to make inquiries on these matters without provoking a new mystical mood in her. So I preferred silence.

On one particular occasion I was so frightened that I could hardly speak, and the cause of my fright was the sudden discovery of the fact that Myna's steps hardly touched the earth. There was no sound of foot-falls. She moved as though sustained by invisible wings attached to her feet. Her whole frame glowed like an incandescent bronze figure. And I recalled that Myna's name before she became a *kirtani* was the Flame-of-the-Forest, or simply The Flame.

Had I any faith in Fakir Cheraguddin's stories about the supernatural, I should have said that Myna in her mystic moods was like a jinn, and that fire, instead of blood, flowed in her veins.

~

The question about the astrological bulletins was not, however, settled for good as far as I was concerned. It was the Diwan himself who furnished the most rational explanation. I raised the matter with him after I had come to know him better, and even then my query was put in a guarded fashion: I wished to know if the bulletins served any practical purpose.

'You will have to find your answer yourself,' he said. 'I shall, however, put some counter-questions to you. And it may be of help. Do you mind if I fire off my battery of questions?'

'Not in the least.'

'Suppose, purely for argument's sake, before our present rulers came into power, every householder in Bengal had put up a notice in bold characters at the entrance of his house, a notice as large as the cinema-posters, saying *They want to partition Bengal*. What would have happened then? How many votes would our present masters have collected if there had been such notices all over the land before the general election?'

The answer was, of course, obvious: 'Not one.'

'You may say astrological bulletins are not the same as political prognostications. But please try to put two and two together, and your reasoning will tell you "Forewarned is forearmed." These bulletins do serve some useful purpose. By the way, do you want to consult one of my astrologers? Just for fun.'

I was always afraid of peering into the future. Therefore I refused his offer with some polite excuses. They were lame, and I think the Diwan saw through them. To change the subject I raised a different issue: it must be, I wondered, difficult for a man like the Diwan to work with people responsible for the partition of Bengal and the division of India into a number of segments.

'There is a Gresham's Law in politics as in economics. Bad money drives out the good: this is universally true. And it is equally true that when you have universal franchise it is the irresponsible demagogue who will drive out the more sober-minded from the political arena. I am in the Cabinet simply because the *khadiwallahs* and the *topiwallahs* want a man not belonging to either of them. A stop-gap.'

'Do you not find your position rather irksome?'

'I do. But if I were to wait till I found colleagues sharing my views, I should have to wait till doomsday. I know both the *khadiwallahs* and the *topiwallahs* hate me. And I myself bear no great love for them. I hang on solely to remind them that there is such a thing as *matra*. It is fatal to overstep "the line of chalk" —one's limiting boundary.'

PART THREE

The Flame of the Forest

I

A desk and a chair were installed for me in the Diwan's so-called 'second sitting-room'. I was now, as has been stated earlier, his part-time private secretary. All the real work for him was done in the reading-rooms of different public libraries. Nevertheless, he wanted me to have a small corner all to myself in his house.

The Diwan's Estate Manager shook his head when he heard of the old man's decision. He had a long consultation with his second-in-command, Sircar. Sircar scratched his hairy chin and groaned, and called for a third man: this third man looked at me as though I were mad. These three then had a further confabulation, and finally I was asked exactly what sort of a room I wanted.

'Anything will do for me,' I said.

'Well!' Sircar murmured, 'since the architect will have to put up a new room for you it would be helpful if you said exactly what sort of apartment you would prefer.'

'Of course,' the Estate Manager added, 'an elaborate apartment cannot be put up overnight.'

'From outside,' the third man explained, 'the house looks big. But it isn't as big as all that. The grounds may cover six acres, but there are only some fifty rooms and all of them are full, crowded like a chicken-coop. Gomosta Babu, what do you say?'

Gomosta Babu was no other than the Estate Manager: he shook his head again and repeated his demand—some indication of the sort of room I should like to have built.

'If only,' Sircar remarked, 'the stables had not been pulled down, we might have found a corner for you. No, no. I didn't mean that you would have been given a room in the stables. No, nothing of the sort. Only one of the poorer relations might have been shifted over there, and you would have occupied the vacated apartment.'

'You see the situation,' the third man broke in. 'There are some two hundred people living in this house. Apart from the Diwan's drawing-room and the second sitting-room every nook and corner is filled to the brim. Of course, temporarily, you may occupy the guest-room.'

The Diwan cut the Gordian knot by installing me in his second sitting-room. It was quiet. From my corner I had a good view over the front garden: it was a blaze of colour with different flowering plants arranged in ornamental beds, in which Marechal Niel roses were conspicuous.

The room where I worked on alternate days—and mostly in the mornings only—served, I understood, the purpose of 'reception hall' when there were evening parties. At one time it might have been used as 'second sitting-room', but it bore no signs of being utilized as such when I first saw it.

It was about ninety feet long and sixty feet wide, with balconies on its east and south sides. The floor was of veined black-and-white marble, the slabs were arranged to give the appearance of a huge chess-board—a repetition, as it were, of the patterns of the open beams and rafters supporting the ceiling. The walls were plastered with highly-polished *chunam*—Indian cement of shell-lime and silver-white sand. At about ten feet from its north and south walls, all along the length of the room, there were two rows of ten pillars and two pilasters. The east end—with its musicians' gallery—opened not into an ordinary balcony, but into a broad-pillared verandah, while the west end terminated in a semi-circular apse containing a low platform, probably for stage-shows. Along the north wall there were twelve console tables with marble tops bearing bronze busts of Twelve Caesars, collected from a French man-of-war in the middle of the eighteenth century: these busts must have been executed in the time of Louis XIV, for they bore bronze periwigs and their profiles reminded one of the Roi Soleil. Behind each bust there was a Venetian mirror of dimensions not unworthy of the Hall of Mirrors at Versailles. And in the wall-space between the mirrors were oil paintings—portraits—of more than life-size figures: the pictures had evidently never been cleaned since the day they left the artist's studio, for though their heavy gilt frames shone brightly the personalities they represented could hardly be distinguished: annual layers of grimy varnish masked them almost completely.

The furniture of the room consisted mainly of light gilt chairs: they were massed in one corner. A number of massive chandeliers hung from the decorated ceiling: these were nearly covered in scarlet canvas bags. The raised platform, or the stage, was stacked with rolls of carpets destined, no doubt, for the floor when entertainments in 'the Indian style' were given: the floor was then covered over with the carpets and a milk-white sheet as large as the room spread over it and strewn with cushions.

A stranger, on entering the room, would in all probability have compared it with a concert-hall and commended it favourably: it was spacious, bright, and well appointed, capable of comfortably accommodating at least a couple of hundred people. But for me it was anything but comfortable. I felt lost in that immense hall. It looked depressingly empty: it made me comprehend the feelings of a tiny bird in an untenanted castle.

My preference was for dog-holes. I cajoled the Estate Manager and Sircar and wheedled out of them a folding screen. It helped me to build a little niche of my own in a corner by the side of the grand piano and a monstrously huge Chinese vase.

Only those who know what it means to work in a rich man's house in Calcutta will understand what a benefit I conferred upon myself by securing the screen and burying myself in my dog-hole.

A typical patrician residence is an open house—both metaphorically and literally. In other words, no door is ever closed and no one is debarred from strolling in and asking for odd things at all hours. Before putting up my barricade I was readily visible from a distance, and the curious made a bee-line for me. In the course of one single hour I was disturbed a dozen times with impossible requests. For example: Could I lend a helping hand to Toonoo? Did I ever fly paper kites? What was I doing there with a pack of white cards? When was the next express train to Nagpur? Did I know the fare? Could I go out immediately to buy a few yards of powder-blue organdie? Was there anything worth seeing at the Little Theatre on Friday next? Did I play whist? Would it be in order to leave the four-year-old Khoka in my charge? What was the precise nature of my work? What wages did I get? Was I sleeping in or not? What was I doing before coming to the Diwan's house? Was I married? Why did I scribble a few words on a white card and put it in a pigeon-hole?

These were only a few of the many questions asked by the intruders. (I must add that all the questioners were male.)

'I enjoyed as much privacy,' I told Gama, 'as a goldfish in a bowl, before securing the screen, and Piram's protection.'

However, the barrier of the screen and later the presence of Piram saved me from all encroachers. My desire for isolation enhanced my prestige in the zenana: the news soon spread in the women's quarters that I was queer: my card-indexing was nothing else than cartomancy—forecasting the future by means of cards. My watching out through the window was perhaps ornithomancy. And my walking round my desk, never venturing beyond the bounds of my own dog-hole, was a conclusive proof of my being gyromaniac—a person capable of divining the future by moving in a small circle and then falling into a trance.

Such a man merited scrutiny by the members of the zenana. They were, however, more discreet than the men, and instead of trying to question me they decided to watch me from the musicians' gallery. The screen was not high enough to shelter me from their gaze. Piram did not take any notice of them, nor did I, at least outwardly. One day there was an unusual hubbub in the gallery. The ladies who spoke only in whispers were on that occasion commenting quite audibly on my mental state: 'Poor man! He has gone off his head altogether. This is the result of his dabbling with magic. Fancy his putting up an umbrella over his head inside the house!' (I was trying to repair a bent rib.)

My alleged madness, I gathered later from Kusum, further enhanced my fame as a fortune-teller.

Next day I was honoured by a visit from the Diwan's second wife. (The first one, as I have said before, died long ago.) She asked me to stay for the midday meal. I tried to get out of this invitation.

'Your food will be brought here, if you like it that way. Of course it will be no bother. When there are two hundred meals to be served one more or one less does not make any difference. I want to talk to you.'

There was no escape.

II

I did not see her. She followed the orthodox custom of not appearing before a male stranger. Only those who called on her in the sanctuary of the zenana were admitted to her presence. I was not a caller; hence I was denied even a glimpse of her.

The screen stood between her and me.

She spoke in a low voice. Evidently she was anxious that no one should overhear our conversation. And that was why the musicians' gallery was cleared and the room itself put out of bounds to all.

'Do you think,' she asked, 'the Diwan has really gone to Benares? Are you sure?'

It was for her, I thought, to answer that question. After all, I was only a part-time secretary, especially engaged for a piece of research work, and therefore in no way concerned with his movements. Nevertheless, I said that I had every reason to believe that the Diwan was attending a political convention in Benares.

'I hear,' she murmured, 'Ek Nambur will be speaking there.'

'So you know as much as I.'

'Maybe,' she went on from behind the screen, 'I know more about Ek Nambur than most people. That's why I am so worried.'

'Why should you worry?' I spoke with my tongue in my cheek, for I had a profound dislike for Ek Nambur the arch-demagogue. 'There are many who admire him.'

'They may. But do you? Let me have your frank answer. What do you think of him?'

No diplomatic answer came to my lips on the spur of the moment. The thought uppermost in my mind was, 'Once a rogue always a rogue.' Ek Nambur, in my reckoning, was an old rogue.

~

I had the opportunity of knowing Ek Nambur when he was just nobody, or to be more correct, a *fils-à-papa,* not interested in anything except hanging round Santi Niketan. Ages ago I had the doubtful privilege of spending a few nights under the same roof with him at the Chinese Institute of Santi Niketan. My sojourn was in connection with the visit of a cultural mission from China, and I was one of the so-called interpreters.

My participation in this mission would have been forgotten but for an ugly incident: a child of ten had his jaw dislocated and Ek Nambur was held responsible for this mishap.

It was alleged that the boy in question had stealthily crept into the room where Ek Nambur was giving a demonstration of his hypnotic powers to a Chinese model—one of the many who had turned up from Calcutta to have a good look at the Chinese artists and to explore the possibility of being hired by them, and the youngster had taken a number of snapshots of the pair, and left the room as silently as he had come in. In fact, his coming in and going out would have remained unknown had not the Chinese model innocently asked Ek Nambur for prints of the snapshots. 'What snapshots?' asked Ek Nambur. 'Those the little boy took,' was the reply, 'when you were...er...tickling me. Don't you remember? I was lying on my back, and you were leaning over me. You kissed my toes, then my knees and thighs.' 'Show me the boy,' Ek Nambur interrupted.

Ek Nambur was furious, not because he had been photographed *in flagrante delicto*—yea, in the very act—but because the Chinese model was not ashamed of his lecherous caresses. She was no virgin, far from it; apart from posing as a model she practised the art of a light-o'-love, and she had no reason to feel squeamish about anything: she did not suffer from the inhibitions of her Hindu sisters. Ek Nambur's chief joy in life was to make the innocent blush. As a matter of fact some suspected that it was the very reason why he hung round the colleges of Santi Niketan: to exercise the art of seducing the immature. It was therefore a terrible let-down for him when he found out that the Chinese model, who looked so young, was not a teenager, but a mature tart. Like all Chinese women she had no superfluous hair on her body, hence Ek Nambur's mistake. He raved like a madman, and gave full vent to his wrath by smacking a tiny boy.

It was the wrong boy that got his face bashed and jaw dislocated. Ek Nambur then went to the local photographer and there made a scene. Thus the story of the snapshots in question got wide publicity. The pictures were all underexposed, but they revealed enough to bring about the *fils-à-papa's* immediate expulsion.

It was hard for him to leave Santi Niketan, because apart from the hobby of tampering with the innocent and the immature, he loved to bask in the reflected glory of the Gurudev, the poet Tagore. But there was no choice. He had to go. And his humiliation was all the greater when he found the Chinese tart installed in the same coach as himself.

For this ravening rascal was excessively prudish in public, though behind barred gates and closed doors he was the most prurient rake in existence. He was brutal and foul-mouthed: he hated work, hated his parental home, hated everything except giving demonstrations of hypnotism to young girls and immature boys. However, he loved to talk about Mother India's sorrows.

After leaving Santi Niketan he found his vocation: professional patriotism—liberation of Mother India. 'India,' he proclaimed, 'must be freed from all exploiters. We must get rid of the wicked capitalists and imperialists. They—the brown and the yellow, the pink and the green bloodsuckers—must go.'

The turn of events produced strange results.

> When the sea is churned
> Up comes froth malignant.

The newly introduced universal adult franchise wrought havoc among the sedate moderates. They lost their seats at the general election, and Ek Nambur scored a magnificent victory. The bazaar demagogues came into power with this *fils-à-papa* as their leader.

Ek Nambur's eyes were like a serpent's. He could hypnotize not only innocent girls and flighty maidens, but sedate matrons and aged widows as well. He had sticking-out ears, and this defect was found to be an additional attraction for them. They thought he was full of charm, and some of them freely declared that his sex-appeal was irresistible. Their mood has been described by a satirist:

> Do I not lower my eyes to avert his gaze
> And with my hands shut my ears to his voice?
> Do I not cover my blush with my thickest veil?
> Tell me, dear friend, what black magic is it
> That the seams of my bodice should burst
> When his image unasked haunts my thoughts?

It must be admitted that Ek Nambur could talk beautifully about the sorrows of the exploited and bring tears to the eyes of his listeners—both female and male. And they all voted for him and his followers.

'He that has a goose will get a goose.' With the unexpected success at the polls Ek Nambur's hypnotic powers increased; his gift of the gab doubled; and his arrogance knew no bounds. It was rumoured that he made mesmeric passes over his opponents and turned them into imbeciles; foolishly they left their home and hearth to seek safety in exile, and thus brought about their own destruction. For the foreign governments were not interested in ageing Hindu refugees: they were handed back to Ek Nambur. Ek Nambur was a nominal Christian.

~

The Diwan's wife was in a paroxysm of fear. She had tried every argument to prevent her husband's journey to Benares.

'Do you think,' she asked me, 'Ek Nambur will try to hypnotize him? I know he hates my husband.'

I told her that the Diwan knew all about Ek Nambur. 'He has taken his journey with his eyes open. To be forewarned is to be forearmed. You have warned him in advance. Now he is not going to fall a prey to Ek Nambur's wizardry.'

'But,' she whispered, 'I have received a message from Ek Nambur himself. And that frightens me. He hopes I shall join my husband and both of us stay with him for a few days.' She then recounted that at one time she had been under the spell of Ek Nambur, and her admiration for the serpent-eyed *fils-à-papa* used to distress the Diwan. 'That was some time ago. And I was wicked enough to spread the story that my husband behaved like a jealous mongoose. I did this to please Ek Nambur. Now I am thoroughly ashamed of myself.'

What was I to say? What could I say? I knew the trickeries Ek Nambur played to ruin his opponents. He was not ruthless like a Renaissance prince. He had nothing of the Teutonic brutality. But he was far more thorough. He 'liquidated' those he did not like by robbing them of their means of livelihood: he made them destitute and forced them to commit suicide.

'Do you understand what I should like you to do? You should go to Benares to fetch my husband. Ek Nambur will surely kill him. He will hypnotize him first and then humiliate him and finally make him take his own life. He is more dangerous than a serpent. He has hypnotic eyes.'

~

I thought of the mythical Nahush who possessed the gift of enchanting common mortals with his honeyed words and putting them in a trance with his unblinking gaze.

'Have you ever ridden a red horse with a green tail?' he asked Khyati, the king's daughter. And Khyati was delighted when Nahush promised her a ride on this uncommon steed after sunset. For she was a mere girl, not old enough to divine Nahush's thoughts. 'But keep my story secret,' he advised her. 'I shall take you out when no one is about.'

The innocent princess succumbed to Nahush's wizardry, and soon came to be corrupted by him. When the seducer knew that she was entirely within his power he threatened to divulge her secret unless she obeyed him implicitly. Though ashamed of herself she readily gave her promise and begged him to do everything possible to spare her public humiliation.

'Then go and tell your father,' Nahush demanded, 'that you are expecting a child, and that he must have me as his son-in-law. Ask him, too, that I should be made the successor to the throne.'

Hardly was the wedding over when Nahush destroyed the king and mounted the throne, and Khyati was driven out of the kingdom in disgrace.

No one, however, rose in revolt against him, for he had bewitched the people with prodigious promises. Khyati's father, he declared, knew nothing of the sorrows of the common people; but he, Nahush, was well acquainted with their trials for he was one of them, and he was determined to transform the kingdom into an earthly paradise. Provided, he made it clear, the people whole-heartedly cooperated with him for the attainment of this highly desirable objective.

'Nahush!' The people cried, 'Give us your command. We will do whatever you bid.'

'Bring me, then,' he ordered, 'those men commonly known as sages. Bring me every one of them. These men are arrogant and selfish. They have not congratulated me on my accession to the throne. Nor have they sympathized with you on your victory in securing me as your ruler. They have never drawn water nor have they hewn wood, but have led the life of parasites, subsisting on the fruits of others' toil. They are sycophants, and their chief pleasure has been to interpret the laws of yore, which as we all know were formulated for the sole purpose of grinding down the poor. Such men are dangerous. The prison-house is the only fit place for them.'

Thus all the wise people of the land came to be gaoled.

Nahush denied the imprisoned sages food and drink till they were all nearly dying. He then bewitched them with his gaze, and made the proposal that thenceforth they should be allowed some sustenance provided they replaced the horses that drew his chariot.

Strange to say, this humiliating condition was accepted by the famished sages, and from then onwards Nahush rode out every day in a chariot drawn by them. He used to chastize them whenever it pleased him with the goad or with his kicks. To inflict greater indignity upon them Nahush took to corrupting their children before their own eyes.

Yet the people did not rise in revolt against him, because he used flattering words and spell-casting glances; and also because they found it agreeable to see the humiliation of those who were once counted among the more fortunate.

And it so happened that one day Bhrigu, a disciple of Agastya, came to Nahush's city from a distant land to pay respects to his master; he asked of the people the whereabouts of the great Agastya, the Master of the Law. 'He is about to be yoked to Nahush's chariot,' they said. 'You will find him where the king's vehicles are kept.' And there Bhrigu found him and heard from him the treatment Nahush was meting out to all the sages of the land. 'But,' Bhrigu asked, 'why do you allow yourself to be treated thus?'

'He gazes upon me,' Agastya replied, 'and my will to resist dissolves. I do then whatever he bids me to do.'

'In that case, don't look at him.'

Agastya promised to bear Bhrigu's counsel in mind, and when Nahush, as was his wont, mounted his chariot and ordered the sages to pull, Agastya refused to move. At this the enraged usurper cast his glance upon the Master of the Law, but the latter refused to look back. This made Nahush still more infuriated and he spurned the Master of the Law with kicks. Even then Agastya did not move. Nahush fumed and cursed, but Agastya paid no heed to his imprecations. He stood as still as before. And his example was followed by the others.

Thus the spell cast by Nahush was broken. A single man's refusal to obey an unjust command brought the reign of tyranny to an end.

And because he forgot his *matra* Nahush found himself transformed into a reptile, a crawling creature at the mercy of whoever cared to cast a stone at him.

~

Whenever Ek Nambur's name was mentioned the story of Nahush automatically came to my mind. However, I did not mention anything about the legendary Nahush to the Diwan's wife. Nor was there any use frightening her still more with my own misgivings about the political convention. So I tried to divert our conversation to something else: the Diwan's views on education.

Did she realize what constrained the Diwan to attend the political convention at Benares? They were going to discuss the drafting of a new education bill, and the Diwan was anxious to present his point of view.

~

In his younger days it was customary among men of his class to admire Plato's *Republic* and Mill's essay on liberty. The spread of literacy, it was thought, would automatically transform India into an America, and India's age-old traditions would vanish to give place to a new and heroic conception of life. What this new and heroic conception precisely meant neither the Diwan nor any of his contemporaries had tried to visualize when they were young.

It was nebulous at best: of course it implied certain benefits, such as abolition of the poverty of the masses, a higher standard of material well-being, a form of government then prevailing in Great Britain, full employment for the intelligentsia as well as for the manual workers, an improved—that is to say, mechanized—system of agriculture, and general industrialization.

Now he no longer believed in the dreams of his youth. 'America is certainly literate,' he often told me, 'but what is America reading? Germany is certainly the richest country in Europe: her resources are greater than those of all her neighbours put together; but what has she done with her wealth? What profit has she derived from her system of education?'

The views of the Diwan were by no means novel to me. But what I wondered at was his stand against the rising tide. It was fashionable for everyone to shout, 'Give education to the masses,' and yet no one bothered to define the precise implication of the word 'education'. Was it as the French understood it? Or was it as the Russians interpreted it? Was education equivalent to character-building? 'If so,' the Diwan held, 'home is the best place for receiving education, and the school for obtaining instruction, technical knowledge.' (However that may be, the Diwan had my full sympathy.)

And when I heard what was the reason that led him to carry on, in spite of his age, an active political life I felt really sorry for the poor man.

'It is worth while,' he held, 'to remind them of *matra*. For Ek Nambur and his followers are in reality "After-us-the-Deluge" doctrinaires. They have no thought of tomorrow. Some of the *khadiwallahs* believe that the New India can afford the luxury of quarrelling with every nation in the world. They would be only too happy to see a world conflagration. It would give them the excuse to rob both Peter and Paul. If they had any love for India they would not have burnt the nation's money in their present reckless fashion. We are heading towards bankruptcy and anarchy.'

'Do they listen to you?'

'Perhaps they don't. Yet I can't afford to resign. I have no means of livelihood, except the income from my textbook on Conic Sections.' His landed property, I understood, did not bring him a cent: almost everything went in the salary of his retainers and the rest in taxation. He was the sole breadwinner for two hundred mouths. 'And the only source of income worth mentioning is that text-book. If I resigned they would remove that book from the school and college syllabus. Do you see my dilemma?'

Could he not have cut his costs by turning out the hangers-on, the poor relations, the indigent friends, and others who crowded his fifty-roomed house? 'That is hardly possible,' he said. 'Where are these people to go? I have a moral obligation to them. You know as well as I do there are no jobs for intellectuals. And the jobs for manual workers are not many. Can I send these helpless people away?'

The Diwan's dilemma, I knew, was the dilemma in most households, whether patrician or not. No one knew the solution. No one dared raise it or discuss it dispassionately. The *khadiwallahs,* the *topiwallahs,* the Emenroyites, the Trotskyists, the Neo-Trotskyists, the Communists, the Ram-Rajyaists, and others had one cry: 'Give us absolute power, you shall then see how the country would be changed by us in no time.'

Nahush, too, wanted the same privilege.

III

The Diwan was taking the line diametrically opposed to the line of least resistance. It was suicidal from the point of view of practical politics.

'He is not over-fond,' I told Gama, 'of Ek Nambur and his hangers-on. Neither does he care for the Communists, Trotskyists, Socialists, Neo-socialists, and other of the Opposition.'

'What does he really want?'

'He would like to see the country as it has always been during the centuries. Not transformed into a China or a Russia, nor made into an imitation America like Liberia.'

Gama whistled. 'Poor man, I am sorry for him. He will certainly lose his seat at the next election.'

That was what I thought. I wished I had never met him nor sought the privilege of working under him. 'Would to God,' I said, 'I had parted company with him for good the day I saw him exercising his pigeons.'

'Then you would have laboured under the impression that it was not the Diwan, but the dog boy you met.'

'That's true. But that would have done me no harm, whereas now I am upset.'

'Upset? Upset over what? At having stolen Piram's affection! Don't be silly.'

'Not so much over the dog as over something else: something much more serious.'

'For example?' Gama raised his eyebrows to make fun of my grave expression.

'For having known him.'

It was not easy for me to explain my feelings. The more I saw of the Diwan the more I realized my incapacity for judging men at first sight.

The Diwan might have looked odd when he wobbled on his feet: the lower part of his body was ill-proportioned; it seemed not to fit at all to his trunk. He was corpulent. His head was strangely moulded. One could not have called him an incarnation of majesty when one saw him in his back garden dressed in a short dhoti. But the same person who looked ridiculous when poking at his pigeons was the picture of dignity itself when he held his durbar, seated cross-legged on a throne, clad in ceremonial garments, with clusters of pearl necklaces round his neck and his head crowned with a massive turban bearing an agrafe.

The durbar had nothing particularly official about it. It was a monthly semi-informal gathering of his estate officers, pensioners, and leaseholders. They came to pay him their respects and to submit their petitions of complaint, if they had any. Not all his tenants and officers came to the second sitting-room every month: only those who had any special favours to seek; some, however, came for the simple pleasure of seeing him and talking to him for a few minutes. The sittings generally lasted for an hour. The callers were entertained with music and sweetmeats. They dispersed when the Diwan had heard what each one of those present had to say. The actual termination of the durbar took place when *pan*—betel nut and spices—and attar were distributed among the party.

The Diwan then reminded me of the late Rana of Udaipur, a scion of the Rajputs, who, too, had deformed legs, a defect which did not in the least diminish his princely majesty and natural stateliness when he gave his audiences. Like the Rana of Udaipur, the Diwan belonged, I felt, to an India that was passing swiftly away.

How I wished there were some Basholi or Paharpuri painters to portray the ceremonies connected with the Diwan's durbars.

(I would have hated the idea of a modern oil-colour painter—an expert in three dimensions—daubing a canvas to represent a function associated with a tradition that was more than millenarian.) A canopied seat of solid silver, resembling the *howdah* on an elephant's back, was placed on the platform at the apsidal end of the hall: it was for the Diwan. Garbed in a brocaded long coat of rich material he sat cross-legged in the customary Hindu fashion, while surrounding him on three sides stood a number of attendants in scarlet liveries with orange sashes, bearing silver sticks or ceremonial peacock-feather fans designed to look like immense *ficus religiosa* leaves. (These fans were his insignia of office: the Diwan was a hereditary title-holder and his rank was that of a minister of state. He was not entitled to the ceremonial umbrella, reserved for the Rajahs.) On his right, facing east like him, sat the Estate Manager on a crimson velvet cushion: he was dressed in yellow silk with gold and silver embroidery, and his function was to introduce each caller and collect and read out such petitions as were presented to the Diwan. Near the Estate Manager there lay a white silk cushion: no one ever sat on it, for it was reserved for the Diwan's son. As has been mentioned earlier, he was a modernist and did not see eye to eye with his father; in fact he was not on speaking terms with him. His higher education in America, it was said, led to his joining the Communist Party, and though he lived on the allowance from his father, he never attended any of these gatherings. Nevertheless, the white cushion was there for him to occupy in case he condescended to visit his parental home during a durbar.

Bright silk curtains, gorgeous awnings over the doors, arches and windows, and the festooned garlands of flowers round the pillars and pilasters transformed the general appearance of the hall into an audience chamber of an ancient Hindu palace.

The periwigged Caesars and the canvases of Hudson (Joshua Reynolds' master), of Reynolds himself, and other Western artists were thus purposely hidden from view. The floor was strewn with rich carpets and priceless rugs, and on these sat cross-legged the callers in their varied costumes and colourful headgear to complete the picture. The only ones in white, conspicuous by the simplicity of their dress in that colourful throng, were the widows, and they were not many. (For only those women who looked after their own affairs attended the durbar, and they were all widows. Married women met the Diwan's wife in the zenana, and I did not know if the gatherings there were as dignified and as impressive as the ones I was privileged to witness.)

Here was a tableau of the India of yore, whose magnificence surpassed the best that the modern world could offer.

'Don't you dare say such things in public, old boy,' Gama advised. 'If any one of the bright young people you are coaching comes to hear of your love for ceremonies you will have one student the less on your list. They all admire either Ek Nambur or Emenroy, and both of these worthies have made their pronouncements condemning traditional Indian ceremonies.'

I said:

> 'The ill-bred and the base-born
> Hate the ceremonial horn.'

'All the bright things are ill-bred and maybe they are ill-born as well. But what about it? They are all for progress. They will tell you that a technicolor show is worth all the durbars of the world. Don't forget the formula about vox populi.'

'Are you suggesting that I should obey what the crowds bid and swim with the tide?'

'What else? The Devil must have goaded you to seek your birth in a family with a devilish motto: *Frangas non flectes.* You are bad enough, but that ring of yours with the device *You may break, but you cannot bend me* has changed you into a real devil. Throw it away and start brushing up your Chinese.'

~

The Chinese, Gama thought, were being courted by Ek Nambur, and the day Nehru died they would be invited to occupy Bengal. And the first thing they would do as soon as they reached Calcutta would be to liquidate all ancient families, whether they were wealthy or poor did not matter. I was probably on their black-list because I had once acted as interpreter to a Chinese cultural delegation that came from Canton, led by the artist Hsu-Pi-Hung.

'You can't stem the rising tide,' he concluded. 'Be philosophical and take what comes. It's no good sighing over the past. The Lord Almighty cannot now change the trend of events. Ek Nambur has seen to it.'

The political convention at Benares passed off without any hitch, thanks to Ek Nambur's clever manipulations. He got the almost unanimous support of all the leaders of the splinter parties: the only persons to vote against him were the Diwan, representing the zemindars of Bengal, and the delegate from Rajputana.

I told the Diwan what Gama thought about Ek Nambur and also my own views.

'Maybe,' he said, 'Ek Nambur has seen to everything, and your friend is right. But there is something worse than tyranny, and that is anarchy.' Men will submit, he believed, to any rule by which they may be exempted from the domination of caprice and of chance. 'Bengal was in a state of anarchy when the men of John Company came here in the eighteenth century. And the people of Bengal begged the Company's men to save them from perpetual insecurity—from the raids of the Vargis, from the ravages of armed brigands, from the arbitrary imposition of taxes. It did not matter to the Bengalis that the men of John Company were foreigners. "Better security under strangers," they said, "than anarchy under marauders." When Ek Nambur goes the Bengalis of tomorrow may raise the same cry. Our nationalism is only skin deep.'

I interrupted: 'You might as well give up the game, then, and withdraw from politics altogether.'

'That I must not. "Not by abstention from his duties," Krishna said, "does a man obtain freedom from evil. Not by mere renunciation does he attain salvation." Nothing in the world should make a Hindu cringe: I mean, a true believer in our traditional Hindu faith ought not to accept anything as inevitable. His first obligation is to perform his duties to the best of his ability.'

Of course, he admitted, that there were stages in a man's life when he should retire from active work and practise contemplation. 'For,' he quoted again Krishna's saying, 'both renunciation and unselfish performance of duties can lead to salvation.' However, he was not for running away from his post when everything looked dark: 'That would be cowardice.' Circumstances demanded at times retreats in the battlefield, but these manoeuvres did not imply abandoning the struggle. So far as he was concerned, he found no reason to feel frightened at the trend of events: the situation was certainly discouraging, but when was it anything but that in the several thousand years of India's history?

'For brief periods we have had respites, and these were mostly periods associated with non-Hindu emperors. So, why should I feel downhearted? Before leaving for Benares I was somewhat in your mood. But now I am different. Can you guess why?'

Had he made a pact with those who came to Benares? That seemed hardly possible. After all, there was the likelihood of his being hypnotized by Ek Nambur. Perhaps his wife's fears were justified. Anyway, I told him that I did not know my answer. He asked me to make three guesses.

'Perhaps,' I said finally, 'you have overheard some conversations on the *ghats* of Benares—those long flights of steps where people sit down and converse.'

'Almost correct. I overheard Myna's remarks on the steps of the temple of Hanumanji—the Great Monkey God. I was very upset that day because of a newspaper report. It said, "There is no truth in the report that the Diwan from Calcutta was attacked by some hooligans in the Dal-ki-Mundi district of the City." Do you understand the implication? Of course, it was inspired by Ek Nambur. "You gay bird!" was his greeting. "You went there for a good time." Now, tell me is it possible for me to walk through streets of steps of Dal-ki-Mundi? Can I climb a dozen steps without being helped? Do you now see the implication?'

I saw clearly what Ek Nambur had in mind when he had that news item inserted in the local papers. It gave him a splendid weapon to use against the Diwan when it suited his convenience. I could visualize a press conference at which Ek Nambur would announce, 'Gentlemen, I want men of integrity in the Provincial Governments: men of moral integrity. Much against my wish I have been constrained to ask the Diwan to resign. I do gravely deplore the circumstances that have forced me to take this step. You will recall some time ago there was an incident in the Dal-ki-Mundi district of Benares, and at my request the newspapers were good enough to hush-up the matter. There were, however, certain hints in some of the papers. This I could not prevent. I believe as much as you do in the freedom of the press. Now, the Diwan, who ought to set an example...etc., etc., is known to be a person given to sexual orgies, and his visit to the Dal-ki-Mundi district was to contact traffickers in girls and minors...etc., etc. Therefore he must go. Long live Mother India.' I told the Diwan what was uppermost in my mind.

'Well,' he said, 'I was depressed. But when I saw Myna gay as a linnet, and heard her story, I became a changed man. What do you say to this story of hers?'

~

When Bhim Sen entered Indra's heaven at the end of the many trials imposed upon him by Saturn, he bowed to this deity of misfortune before saluting any other immortal.

All the divinities were amazed. 'Why,' they asked, 'Bhim Sen, do you give precedence to Saturn, the cause of your sorrows and sufferings on earth?'

'Yea, even unto him,' he replied. 'But for Saturn I should not have had the good fortune to prove my worth while I was on earth.'

IV

Myna—always as gay as a linnet—was like that.

She flitted in and out of one's orbit without rhyme or reason. Once I received a message from her uncle, the Rajah of Luktam, asking me if I would care to come to his place for a *kirtan* ceremony.

The Rajah was the same person who had asked me to find him a few brick-bats for smashing the window of the Diwan's son on the night of the full moon of Ashwin. Among other things he had promised me a fakir's rod similar to his. There was, therefore, every temptation for me to go. But the idea of taking part in the procession that generally preceded the singing of *kirtans* did not appeal to me. And there was another hindrance: the problem of tips. What sort of gratuities did one offer in a Rajah's residence?

A brief week-end at Chatrapara in the palace of my classmate Tarak Nath had once cost me a small fortune. 'How am I to tip the servants?' I asked the Manager of Tarak Nath's residence. 'I shall prepare a list for you,' he said, and I felt thankful.

Later on he presented me with a long list: the names and the status and the services of domestics who merited gratuities from me. There were some fifty names on that list, and I was expected to distribute largesse to the tune of two hundred and fifty rupees! I told the kindly Manager that I had not that sum with me. 'Oh, that doesn't really matter,' was his condescending reply. 'I have already given them the tips on your behalf. You may send me a cheque at your convenience.'

'Surprise,' an expert humorist said, 'is essential to wit.' Was that fellow joking? As for me, I was stunned: two hundred and fifty rupees for a week-end in a Rajah's residence! Why did the Devil tempt me to accept Tarak Nath's invitation? I cursed myself.

'Some of the people,' the Manager went on, 'so rarely get the chance of being tipped.'

I nodded. What else could I do?

'Two rupees for the bath attendant, Gobar.'

I bit my tongue. My guilty conscience reprimanded me.

Officially, the only service Gobar had rendered me was to lead me to Tarak Nath's private bathroom. There at the doorstep I had dismissed him in spite of his loud protests. I had no need, I told him, of a general massage; no rubbing of the limbs with scented oils for me, nor any delicate application of depilatory unguents. An athlete like me was capable of looking after himself unaided. 'No,' I told Gobar firmly, 'I don't need a maid, either, to soap or to scratch my back in the Japanese fashion. I do my own soaping and scratching.' The fellow went away with a long face, which did not please me at all. He must have pulled a longer face, I reckoned, when he returned to clean the bath: for inadvertently I had foisted upon him several hours of unofficial toil: something which did not figure in his regular schedule.

My friend Tarak Nath's personal bathroom deserved to be placed in the category of national monuments. It was a fairly spacious hall with a marble floor, slippery like a sheet of ice. Its walls were adorned with incrustations and mosaics of multi-coloured mirrors. It must have been built a couple of centuries ago for the delectation of the later Moguls who rejoiced in water sports and in wallowing in their baths for hours. It had a large, partially-sunk-in, tiled bath along the whole of one wall, with crazy china steps leading up to its brim and then going down right to the bottom: the affair was huge enough to permit an august personality like the Emperor Farrukh Siyar, who weighed a ton, along with his entire harem as well as a couple of Manipuri elephants a good swim.

But this tiled bath itself was, I knew, a delusion—a pure snare: in fact, it was no bath at all, neither a swimming pool. It was simply a reservoir of drinking water—or a tank, in the builder's jargon—from which the bather, while standing, or squatting on the marble floor, was expected to pour water over himself with the dipper provided for this purpose.

All this was perfectly clear to me, as clear as the limpid,

translucent water of the tank. I was not foolish enough to assume that because two hundred years ago the Emperor Farrukh Siyar bathed in it, therefore I was entitled to do the same. However, the dipper of the princely family of Chatrapara undid me. It was an extraordinary one: an elaborately chiselled solid silver pitcher of mammoth proportions, with a highly polished neck. I had difficulty in raising the empty thing with both hands. (I was almost sure that this extra-heavy affair had been taken out of the family strong-room in my honour.) I cursed the country tradition which insisted, 'The heavier the silver dipper the greater the dignity of the user.' A second later I was cursing myself: for the moment I dipped the pitcher into the water I slipped and slithered along the floor while the wretched thing escaped from my grip to sink to the bottom of the tank. So all that I could do in the circumstances was to plunge after it, and make the best of a bad bargain by having a decent swim. When I had had enough of splashing about in the reservoir, I discovered to my horror that there was no plug nor any other visible means for letting out the water. Princely houses, it dawned on me, rather late, prefer animate, mortal water-carriers to inanimate pipes and mechanical gadgets for emptying out or filling in their private tanks. In parenthesis, I ought to add here, for the benefit of such people as might like to profit from my experience, that it is most unwise to get into a reservoir of this kind whether in the palace of a prince or in the house of a plebeian. For apart from the grave risk of slipping and drowning, it is the surest means of making oneself thoroughly unpopular in Bengal—and in such countries as have succumbed to Bengali influence in matters connected with the daily bath, thanks to the Bengali Ramayana, e.g. Java, Bali, Laos, *et al.* The water of the so-called bath tank is used in orthodox households—even when tap-water is readily available—for drinking and cooking purposes. Before foolishly dismissing an attendant, a prudent man should also verify the size, the shape, the weight and other details of the all-important dipper.

Gobar must have laboured hard to get the tank emptied, scrubbed, and refilled. Certainly he merited his tips. But what about the others?

'You will see,' the Manager said, 'I have included the railway level-crossing man. A couple of rupees will gladden his heart.'

'What has he done for me?'

'He closed the level-crossing barrier for one full hour—in your honour.'

What was the use of arguing with such a man? I gave him a cheque there and then, though it meant overdrawing my banking account. Since then I have not been on speaking terms with anyone remotely connected with the Chatrapara Raj family.

~

'A portable gnomon may be a pleasant toy,' I confessed to Kusum. 'But I am not going to Luktam. I have just posted my letter to the Rajah.'

'Oh! How wicked of you,' Kusum exclaimed. 'You could have stayed in my daughter's cottage, or in the pilgrims' resthouse. My daughter will be so disappointed. My youngest child, you know, lives at Luktam. And then what about that frog's bone?'

To my bitter disappointment I heard that Myna, too, was expecting me. In fact, everyone that Kusum could think of was looking forward to my visit. Thanks to *Life-in-Technikolor,* I was not an unknown figure in that tiny place on the Rupnarayan river; my reputation was, I understood, further enhanced by Kusum's letters to her daughter extolling my virtues as an expounder of sacred texts and as a magician of uncommon ability, an expert in hypnotizing dogs, men, and women.

'In the Barga-Bhima temple,' Kusum added, 'they read out from the Great Epic just as they do in the Kala Bhairab shrine. Oh! You are really wicked. One must not disappoint so many people out of sheer pride.'

'It's now too late to do anything about it. The next time I shall certainly consult you.'

The Kalinjar temple, too, deserved a visit on its own merits, I gathered. I was really a fool to refuse the Rajah's invitation: for I heard later that he did not live in a palace of a thousand rooms, but in a small corner of the ancient pilgrims' rest. (Some sort of a decree under the Defence of the Realm Act constrained him to vacate his palace for the experts invited from abroad by Ek Nambur. The modern Nahush was determined to humiliate the ancient families of Bengal. The papers announced that a scheme bigger than the Tennessee Valley Project for damming the Rupnarayan river was being hatched in Delhi. I did not realize that the first person to be victimized for this purpose was the Rajah of Luktam.)

~

In spite of myself I had to turn down a second invitation from Myna. It came from Badrinath. Her address was simple: the shrine of Badrinath. Her advice was: 'Come as you are.'

'The temple of Badrinath is at an elevation of over ten thousand feet,' I reminded Kusum. 'And at this time of the year all the paths leading from Hardwar to even Rishi Kesh are likely to be snow-bound.'

'How far is Rishi Kesh from Hardwar?'

'About fourteen miles.' It was not the distance but the altitude that mattered in that Himalayan region. As Kusum knew nothing of the high mountains it was not easy for her to grasp that an autumn mountain-climb was no joke. She was so solicitous about my responding to Myna's invitation that I became somewhat intrigued: however, she was too clever to give away her secrets.

'But,' she expostulated, 'you may go as far as Hardwar by bus and train. And send her word.'

'Who will take my message?'

'Why, the Kamli-Wallahs. Aren't they looking after Myna?'

Yes, that was a fact. The Kamli-Wallahs were a religious body, somewhat like the Quakers: they garbed themselves in black blankets. The founder of this order wore a goat's-hair blanket in the form of a loose cloak with a cord of black rope round the waist. And the disciples followed the master's example. How did Kusum know about them? My question elicited no answer.

I tackled Gama about this body of people who took infinite pains to help the Hindu pilgrims doing their round of various mountain shrines: they maintained hospitals, dispensaries, rest houses, pilgrim shelters, and supplied the poor with food and drink. Did he know anything about them? When were they first mentioned in our travel literature? Myna's invitation gave me the opportunity of indulging in our periodical fencing over historical data. (He scored a point over me when he made a rough guess about the time of the Kala Bhairab statue in the Indian Museum.)

Gama's account was substantially the same as mine. When the intrepid Chinese traveller Hiuen Tsang visited India in the seventh century A.D. he noticed these black-blanket wearers. 'Even in those days,' Gama said, 'they were pretty active.

Mayapur, Hardwar's suburb, was their headquarters. Of course, being Chinese, Hiuen Tsang had to change the name Mayapur into Mo-Yu-Lo. Afterwards, when Tamerlane honoured Hardwar with a visit to sack the place, the Kamli-Wallahs dispersed. However, they came back a year later and in 1400 A.D. rebuilt the stone encased stairs on the banks of the Ganges known as the "Steps of Krishna". That's all that I can tell you.'

'I have not anything new to add,' I replied.

'Anyway,' finally Gama said, 'the Kamli-Wallahs will look after you. Why don't you accept Myna's invitation? Only some time ago you were dying to meet her. And now that she sends you an urgent message you are complaining about snow! You are really funny.'

So, I thought, Gama was in league with Kusum. What was the reason for their trying to get rid of me for at least three months? That was the time I calculated would be necessary to go to Badrinath and come back. The fact that they encouraged me to go was probably the main reason for my staying on in Calcutta.

~

Sol Mischkon of *Life-in-Technikolor* was positively distressed when he heard of my final decision. Through his photographer he had assured me that his paper would bear the cost of my mountaineering kit. Aware of my fanatic fervour for 'up-country' things he had made, I understood, discreet enquiries among alpine clubs and also among mountain climbers. I was touched by his consideration for my 'up-country' taste.

Never in his life had he seen a *sambur*—the giant Indian elk—which has a maned neck. Nevertheless, for my sake he secured shoes made of sambur leather for walking safely on the slippery hillsides. His informant was right: the local people—and not the pilgrims—preferred the sambur-leather footgear to any other. From the same source he must have gathered that the loose-fitting Afghan *poshteen* was the most suitable coat for the Himalayan heights. A *poshteen* is a skin coat, or a fur coat, turned inside out, that is to say, the furry side is the inner surface of this convenient garment. It is, however, made in three sizes, waistcoats, sleeved jackets reaching almost to the knees, and the great robe that hangs in heavy folds right down to the ankles and is worn slung over the shoulders like a cloak, or the blanket of the Kamli-Wallahs, its long sleeves not being used. The poor man, not knowing my preference, had one of each kind made. Then, he had also secured a Kabul tent weighing, I believe, a ton, and the necessary camp furniture, such as a folding bed, a collapsible table and chairs, a portable stove, tinned provisions, hurricane lanterns, electric torches, a collection of hats, caps, and turbans, and various other articles: all of these would, no doubt, have rendered great service to a member of a mountain-climbing expedition.

But they were of no use to a pilgrim.

'If I did go at all,' I told the man from *Life-in-Technikolor,*' I would have gone like any other pilgrim—bare-foot.'

The man gasped. He murmured something about frostbite and physical discomfort.

'If millions of people can manage it every year, why can't I do the same? Do you think Myna uses sambur-leather boots to go to Badrinath?'

He mumbled something about the poverty of the average pilgrim and also about superstition: in America a mountain resort attracting such huge crowds would have had a funicular or a hanging-wire railway built for the general convenience of the worshippers as well as the priests!

By now I was seeing red, and the pity I had originally felt for the Chicagoan vanished. I felt like giving him a lecture on what we people of the Penharis thought about pilgrimages. But then it would have been only words wasted; in certain respects Americans of the type I met in Calcutta and the Marxists were the same—they were worshippers of the Golden Dynamo and of material comfort. I might, as well have discoursed on the art of mixing colours to someone totally colour-blind. So I brought the interview to an end with the remark: 'You may tell your Chicagoans that I am superstitious. Padre Johan has American degrees yet he visited the shrines of Jerusalem barefoot like any Hindu pilgrim on his way to Badrinath.'

It took him some time to grasp that no amount of money would induce me to go to Badrinath just then, and I went on harping, 'I am superstitious. I don't think creature-comfort is of greater consequence than spiritual consolation.'

V

'I am superstitious,' I told Gama. 'Just as Padre Johan is superstitious. So, what about it?'

'It is not a question of superstition,' Gama argued, when he had heard what I had to say. 'It is the devil in you. At times you must be listening to this hidden demon and following his advice. That's the trouble. You want to go, and then you don't want to go, all because you would love to go. What sort of reasoning is this?'

I was reproached for refusing to do what would have given me the greatest pleasure. My argument was: 'It's so easy to do what is pleasant. I am trying to resist the temptation.'

'Why not succumb to the temptation, and be happy about it?'

'What's bred in the bone won't go out of the flesh.'

'You are the limit.' Gama shook his head and stared at me in a way as though I was mad. 'You are a gentleman at large. A rare creature in these days. A fellow who can write cheap captions and popular nonsense and make more money in a week than a barrister in a year! And yet you won't profit from your freedom from care. If I were you I should go to the ends of the earth.'

'Whatever for?'

'Just to see things. Only a week ago you said you were saving money for an air jaunt to Chicago and Boston, and now you can go to a place which is only a day's journey by train. What has happened to you? Something to do with women, or what?'

'No,' I answered. 'There is nothing to detain me in Calcutta. Yet I can't accept this new invitation from Myna. I am simply afraid of the place where I am to meet her.'

'What's wrong with the place?'

'This time it is not Badrinath, but Gilani.'

~

Gilani is a most attractive village in the foothills of the Himalayas: it affords a wonderful view of the great mountain Nanda Devi.

I knew this village well: because once in every twelve years people from the Penhari Parganas undertook their pilgrimage to the traditional source of the Ganges, or rather, the spot where the first streams of the Ganges touched the soil of India, and I was in their company. The great gatherings of many millions of pilgrims took place on the slopes of Nanda Devi, and a curious custom, whose origin no one knew, led the visitors from the Penharis to choose Gilani as their centre during these Ganga Jatra festivals.

Gilani was a small place. It consisted of some fifty houses clustered together with one main street in their midst. The houses were two storeyed, the lower one of stone and the upper one of wood; the roofs were gabled like all mountain chalets with this peculiarity, that they had long projecting eaves and their fronts bore elaborate carvings in geometrical patterns. The main street was fairly wide and paved with huge flagstones covered with inscriptions in Deva Nagari characters.

It was impossible to decipher these writings. They were rubbed off almost beyond recognition. The local tradition maintained that these stones covered the tombs of a number of Brahmins who once came to the village to bless a wedding that never took place. These Brahmins had expressed the desire that their bodies should be placed in tombs beneath the road leading to the slopes of Nanda Devi.

Why did the wedding never take place?

And what led the Brahmins to choose the main road for their burial place? Were they expiating some sin?

The explanation they gave was this: in times long past a Rajah of Kanauj, the greatest potentate of his day, became so inflated with pride that he desired for his harem the choicest handmaidens of the presiding deity of the mountain Nanda Devi—the Bestower of Benison. Apparently his proposal, transmitted to the deity by a set of misguided Brahmins, brought no satisfactory reply. This so infuriated the Rajah that he came to Gilani with a powerful army to storm the citadel of the deity and to abduct her handmaidens. He brought with him his Brahmins as well to consecrate his wedding.

The Rajah's camp was pitched at Gilani because the village was judged to be the most convenient spot for commencing the assault on the mountain.

The villagers were upset. They tried to dissuade the Rajah from his mad project, but he refused to listen. They then approached his Brahmins and begged them to lay an interdiction on the Rajah because his undertaking was unholy. 'You must not forget your duty,' they pleaded. 'The Rajah may have lost his sense of *matra*. But what about yourselves?' However, they too refused to pay any heed to the villagers. And not only that, they went to the length of uttering benedictory prayers when the Rajah with his army began climbing the mountain slope.

'They were,' I understood, 'led by an ibex. It had the largest recurved horns ever known, with the broadest transversal ridges. The bouquetin knew where to go, for the Brahmins had dedicated the animal to Nanda Devi, and naturally it took the path that led to the Devi's throne.'

The description of the enormous size of the ibex and its powerful horns led me to assume that the beast must have been as big as the extinct ovis ammon of the Gobi desert. However, to come back to our story, the army followed the steps of the ibex, and it went up and up towards the eternal snow-line.

The Brahmins stayed behind at Gilani to conduct ceremonies that would, they thought, bring victory to the Rajah. When darkness fell, signals of flares from the mountainside informed these Brahmins that all was well with the invading legions. The next night, too, they saw the flares, but the pinpoints of light were feeble. The army was now approaching the snow-line. But after the third night neither the Brahmins nor any of the villagers saw signals. They all, however, heard the sound of drums that the wind raises when the Devi is angry and in her wrath dislodges mountains to bury the habitations of men, to reduce hills into valleys, and change the courses of rivers.

'What's the meaning of these drum-beats?' the Brahmins, it is said, asked.

'The Devi is angry,' the villagers whispered. 'The Rajah and his soldiers have been exterminated.'

'Nonsense,' the Kanauji Brahmins jeered. 'We worship the god Siva. What fear have we of Devi? Should she destroy any of us, bury our corpses in your main street.'

The next morning they found the decapitated head of the ibex with enormous horns: it had rolled down the slope right to the middle of the village square. 'The Devi,' the villagers concluded, 'has accepted the offering. Let us take it to the Brahmins of Kanauj.' But there remained not one Kanauji Brahmin to witness this miracle, for all of them were found with their heads severed. Evidently the Devi's invisible servitors had beheaded them at the same time as the ibex.

The Kanauji Brahmins were buried by the villagers in the main street of Gilani and their tombs were covered with huge flagstones bearing inscriptions in Deva Nagari characters recounting their story. An abiding warning to all foolish people who dare accord any earthly ruler the same status as the divinities and the semi-divinities.

Did any of the villagers know what really happened to the Rajah and his army?

'Not one of them escaped. They were destroyed to the last man by the Devi's servants. If you care to go up to the snow-line in summer time with an ibex as your guide you will find a huge heap of petrified human bones—complete skeletons, some of them still holding their weapons in their fleshless hands. They are there to remind us of *matra*.'

Whatever may be the truth of this story, about one thing I was certain: if the Rajah did come to Gilani he must have been impressed by the beauty of the spot and the industrious perseverance of its inhabitants. The soil was rocky everywhere, yet the villagers had succeeded in transforming every yard of cultivable land into profitable little gardens.

The skill with which they ploughed tiny plots of agricultural ground on the slopes of the mountain was astonishing. These doll's-house fields were surrounded either by hedges of iris or by raised borders of boulders, and were irrigated with the water of distant mountain springs, conducted with infinite care through meandering channels and the hollow of the bamboos—serving as pipes—and many ingenious devices to regulate the distribution and the flow.

In early summer these tiny fields, rising in tiers one above the other, were yellow with barley. The villagers knew how to brew, and when enjoying their drinking bouts they took from time to time spoonfuls of chillis to augment their thirst.

When summer ended the yellow of the terraces gave place to the brilliant emerald-green of sprouting mountain-rice. Still later in the year, different varieties of amaranth were grown in the same fields. These bear flowers of bright red and flaming orange, and they set the hillsides ablaze with their vivid tints, rendered all the more gorgeous by the contrasting coniferous green covering the landscape. In winter, a heavy pall of snow and mist covered the whole area, but high, very high above the village glittered the crests of the Himalayas, like fringes of cloud-banks burning in the rays of the hidden sun.

Nearby were the forests: these were different from the jungles of the plain. Whereas those of the Penhari Parganas teemed with life, here in Gilani and its neighbourhood they seemed to be devoid of living creatures. This was the first impression one got, but gradually one learnt that the silence was ominous: it was the absence of monkeys that made a world of difference, for they spot the lurking tiger or the clumsy bear and sound their warning, which is immediately taken up by all the other animals and birds. The red-faced langurs, however, visited Gilani's forests for a couple of months in summer and then only in rather small troops.

I did not know the altitude at which Gilani stood. Its flora was what the botanists would call Alpine. Though it was high enough to deter the common langurs from infesting its forests, it did not discourage tigers and bears. These latter frequently visited the village at night-time to cause depredations. It was said they preferred to hide in the woodlands covered by the deodars—the Indian cedars renowned for their fragrance, the beauty of their shape, and the stateliness of their trunks. The tigers, on the other hand, sought shelter in the forests of giant bamboos which rose to a height of fifty feet and whose culms are as thick as the human thigh.

It would, however, be absurd to dwell on the trees or the birds and the beasts of Gilani, or even on its Chinese stele—or headstone—bearing the inscription: General Wu at the command of the Son of Heaven traversed the land of singing sands and the country of the lamas to penetrate into Intu (India)... For the most significant thing about the village was the atmosphere of eeriness. something difficult to define and still more to describe.

Let me repeat that its surroundings were weird and beautiful. The giant white mountains towered above it, and gauzy white clouds hovered round their crests as though to enhance their mysteries. There was solemn silence all around: the stillness was awe-inspiring, and so, too, the sound of the wind, which, in a curious way, reminded one of the distant beating of drums and the playing of reed instruments. These sounds, in some mysterious fashion, seemed to augment rather than diminish the all-pervading peace and quietude; and the silence became all the more frightening when the wind dropped and the aeolian choir became mute. To gaze upon Nanda Devi and the other heights on a moonlit night was an experience never to be forgotten: one felt that the ground one stood upon was holy and the sight before one's eyes an unveiling—a foretaste—of the mysteries that led the sages to say: 'I will look up to the mountains.'

The vision inspired a sense of the utter insignificance of man. In the light of the moon, the slopes of Nanda Devi seem exceedingly simple to climb; they then beckoned all beholders with a magic call...

~

It was difficult to tell Gama all these things. Gilani was a bewitching place and it was best for me to keep away from it. It was like Nahush, who could hypnotize anyone with his unblinking gaze.

'What would happen,' I asked myself, 'if at the end of a *kirtan* singing on a moonlit night Myna said, "Come with me." What would I do if she proposed, "You will play on the flute and I shall sing, and we shall move on and on till we reach the throne of the Bestower of Bliss"? What would prevent me from accepting her invitation?'

Self-preservation, I repeated to myself, is a man's first duty. Ulysses tied himself to the mast of his ship lest the siren songs should tempt him to plunge into the sea. But where was my mast? What was there to hold me back?—Nothing.

It was this fear that prevented me from revisiting Gilani when Myna was there.

~

Gilani, I have said before, was a beautiful but eerie place. And it was here Myna received her first mystic call that led her to become a *kirtani*.

VI

'Let Kumbhakonam boast of its Brahmany bulls,' was the usual saying among my villagers in the Penhari Parganas. 'But we have our Padre Johan: he is worth all the holy zebus of the south.' And no pilgrimage was ever undertaken by any of us without listening to his special sermon: the oration he delivered for our benefit before our annual peregrination to the holy sites started.

Padre Johan was, as I have said elsewhere, a vastly-learned man and a *prêtre défroqué*. Once he belonged to the Church of India, but that was long ago; he left the official Church to preach the Gospels in his own way among his own people—the backwoodsmen of the Penharis, where I come from. It is doubtful if he ever succeeded in making any converts, but that was of secondary importance, I believe, both to him and to the villagers. What mattered most to him, I do not pretend to know; but his benediction was of major importance to all of us. We admired not so much his erudition as his integrity, his oratory, his fearlessness, his gift of inspiring others, and his permanent concern for the spiritual welfare of our people. He was for the pilgrims and the would-be pilgrims and their friends and relations, a true *sadhu*—a man of God. Did it matter much that he was a Christian and not a Hindu? Could anyone be fearless without the assurance of divine succour? Did he not worship the Virgin with the Child?

'Let others say what they will, but we shall always ask for his blessings before we start on our pilgrimage to Nanda Devi': this was the usual burden of the villagers. And Padre Johan never denied his blessing to the least of us. He never turned anyone out of his corrugated-iron chapel at Jamtara when the pilgrims crowded it to suffocation to hear him preach and to receive his benediction at the end of the service.

That year—the year to which I have referred in the preceding chapter—the Rajah of Luktam was in the congregation; for he, too, was going on pilgrimage with his suite. His presence, however, did not attract any special attention because the pilgrims were particularly worried on account of Gokul's death.

Gokul was the fellow who usually served as the Penhari villagers' guide to the places of pilgrimage. 'Not that a guide is essential,' the villagers whispered among themselves. 'Yet it is good to have in one's company a man who knows his way about. And Gokul, after all, was a decent chap though he loved a drop too much when he quaffed rice beer.'

The year in question was of particular importance. Every twelfth year, the planet Jupiter being in Aquarius, the feast of Kumbha Mela occurs; it is of peculiar sanctity and brings at least a million men, women, and children to the holy sites. 'Without Gokul,' one pilgrim whispered to his neighbour, 'we shall perhaps get lost among other Kumbha Mela people.' 'Cannot Padre Johan suggest someone to be our guide now that Gokul is no more?' 'He has not yet heard of Gokul's death.'

Gokul the Drunkard was commonly known by his nickname: Brother-to-the-Ox. For that was his profession, looking after the oxen and bullocks. But he met a hero's death. Therefore no one referred to him any more as Brother-to-the-Ox. He died struggling with a black bear—a most dangerous beast especially after its long winter hibernation—that had attacked a woman. 'Death is better than disgrace,' was Gokul's last uttering. The black Himalayan bear is considered to be a disgrace in the animal world—a reincarnation of Nahush: it is reputed to ravish a woman before destroying her. Hence dying Gokul was happy to know that his intervention had spared the woman from being defiled by Nahush's beastly manifestation. 'It would have been a terrible disgrace,' Gokul murmured, 'if the rascal had his way when a Penhari man was about. The shameless brute. Death is certainly better than disgrace.'

Some thought it was not Nahush, but Ek Nambur in the form of the black bear who wanted to assault the woman. The people of the Penhari Parganas hated Ek Nambur, and when it was rumoured that this popular idol suffered from occasional attacks of lycanthropy, they concluded that he was capable of transforming himself, through the aid of black magic, into a wolf or a bear at will to satisfy his lust for beastly propensities. 'If only Gokul had shouted for help,' they sighed, 'we could have saved him. And taught that bear the lesson of its life. We would have brought it in chains to Padre Johan and had it branded and exorcised.'

It was, however, too late to tell Padre Johan about Gokul's death and their worries. He was already mounted on the pulpit to deliver his sermon: generally he read out two texts, one from the Bible and the other from the Hindu or Mohammedan sacred books, and commented on them, linking them up as though his excerpts were from one and the same scripture. They did not grasp the implication of the passage from the Bible, but the other quotation was perfectly clear to everyone: it was the story of the great famine in Sravasti long, long ago.

~

'In heaven,' Padre Johan continued his exposition, 'when there are errands to be undertaken, I feel, the Lord does not seek such messengers as have never erred, never defaulted, never deviated from the straight path during their sojourn on this earth. He would not send, my reasoning persuades me, the innocent-most of the angels, nor the most immaculate of them to come down to this world in human form to dwell in our midst and set a good example to all of us by his way of living and by his mode of dying. For such an angel would lead during his tenure on earth an existence certainly most exemplary, but far beyond the capacity of creatures of common clay to emulate.

'That there are distinct orders of heavenly messengers I do assuredly believe; and I am equally convinced that they at times converse with men, even when they are not sojourning among us as men; and I hold it also to be true that some of them are commanded by the Lord to live with us as plain human beings, no whit different from you or me or any of our neighbours.'

There was a stir in the congregation. Gokul the Drunkard was an orphan. He lived in a cottage apart from the rest. Some thought that the reason of his dwelling in complete isolation was probably due to his being sent from heaven to test the faith of the villagers.

Perhaps there was no truth in the story that he ogled the girls. Or, who knows, that, too, was a part of the task imposed upon him by the Lord. Anyway, no woman had ever lodged any complaint with the headman against Gokul. Whatever might have been his apparent faults, or failings, he was the perfect guide to the holy shrines. He was not like Ek Nambur the Lady-killer who believed neither in God nor in the Devil, and whose main preoccupation was to humiliate the God-fearing.

'Therefore,' Padre Johan continued, without suspecting for a moment that his listeners were attributing to him a superhuman gift of perception of Gokul's death, about which he really had no knowledge. 'I repeat, it is my firm belief that when the Lord needs heavenly messengers for his mission on earth he does not convoke the absolutely innocent, the absolutely pure, those without any experience whatsoever of human temptations and follies, of human errors and shortcomings, of human trials and agonies...

'I imagine he would rather call for those who have mounted to heaven after having learnt how to triumph over sin: those who by their mode of living and toiling have made the earth a better place for Adam's children to dwell in: who lived to serve and served to live, who brought joy to others though they themselves lived in conditions which seemed joyless...'

By now they were all convinced that the Padre was talking about Gokul, about the services he rendered ungrudgingly to the villagers on their long peregrinations. And when the Padre's discourse dwelt on Supriya, a frail woman, who undertook at the request of Buddha the Enlightened One the difficult task of feeding Sravasti's entire population during a great famine, they believed he was giving them the plain hint that Gokul's successor was destined to be a woman.

'He means,' they began discussing among themselves, 'a woman who is frail. But our women are all frail.' 'That's the trouble,' some sighed. 'Padre Johan is a man of God, but he has never married. That's why he does not know anything about women.' 'Perhaps, he means the frailest of the frail.' 'But have they not all ogled Gokul? They are all among the frailest of the frail.'

Just as the sermon came to an end Padre Johan's spectacle case fell off the pulpit, and a girl of the Rajah of Luktam's party got up to pick it up for him.

'Thank you, my daughter,' said Padre Johan. 'Thank you. I don't think I have met you before. What's your name?'

'They call me the Flame of the Forest,' she replied shyly. 'But that's not my real name. I am Myna.'

'You have pretty names. Now I know you, my daughter. I remember even the very day you were born. You live at Luktam nowadays, but you are one of us.'

~

'Of course,' they all said at the end of the day when they gathered under the peepul tree to discuss the final arrangements. 'Of course, she is one of us. Was she not born at Latikagram? Is not Latikagram in the Penhari Parganas?'

They all knew the exact date of her birth. It was associated with a near-miracle for the people of the Penharis: it was a day of general rejoicing.

~

For several years in succession the flowering trees on the banks of our Latika river had refused to blossom. 'What's wrong with them?' people wondered. 'They are not ordinary trees.' 'To salute a grove of trees is an act of merit, but to have even a look at those sacred flower-bearing trees is an act of exceptional merit.' These were the very flames-of-the-forest which had inspired the seventeenth-century poet Senapati to compose some of his best verses. The villagers fretted. 'The trees are dying,' some said. 'Maybe they foresee the end of a *kalpa*—the last stage of an era—and they have gone into mourning.' 'Maybe,' others whispered, 'the gods are angry with us. Something ought to be done.' Prayers were offered to propitiate the deities yet the sacred groves remained as barren as before. Then the scribes of all the villages of the Penhari Parganas got together, to talk things over and to prepare a suitable petition to the district authorities to save the trees. The district officer finally sent a shellac-chemist from Ranchi to report on the matter, and this expert declared that nothing could be done: 'The trees are dying because they are very old.' There the matter ended as far as the authorities were concerned. But as the months passed the villagers became more and more worried. The trees on the banks of the Latika river were the pride of the Penharis. They were the flames-of-the-forest, perhaps the most beautiful flower-bearing trees to be found anywhere: because of their beauty they were deemed sacred; many legends of their heavenly origin enhanced their sanctity. Then, when all hopes had been given up, suddenly one morning they burst into blossom.

The banks of the Latika river became once more a blaze of colour; a gorgeous sight, more ravishing than ever. In mass, the inflorescence resembled sheets of flame. The branches were still bare of leaves, but the bright orange-red petals contrasting brilliantly against the jet-black velvety calyx were in great profusion. The groves looked as though they were on fire: their splendour dazzled the beholders.

All the villagers of the neighbourhood rushed to the river banks to admire the sight. Soon the whole district came to know that a child was born at Latikagram in the early morning at the same time as the trees had blossomed. Naturally the child came to be named the Flame of the Forest, though to her parents and friends she was just Myna.

~

'We are sinners,' they said to each other. 'We do not deserve any merit from our pilgrimage. Fancy not understanding what Padre Johan meant when he hinted that a frail person should lead us! We are deaf as well as blind. That's why we did not immediately grasp the true import of his message: *A little child shall lead them all.*'

To them Myna was this child. True she was not quite a child, yet she was not a woman: just a grown-up girl.

'Does a sinner merit the sight of Nanda Devi?' one of them asked. He was particularly troubled over Salomon Benisraeli's voyage to Jerusalem. Salomon's son Daud and I were fellow students at one time, and I heard from him that Daddy Salomon had come back bitterly disappointed with his pilgrimage, while the Padre Johan had thoroughly enjoyed his! In fact the Padre declared that he would, if he could, revisit Jerusalem any day... The villagers drew their own conclusion: unless one is really worthy one will not profit from a pilgrimage.

'What shall we do,' they whispered to each other, 'if Nanda Devi refuses to appear before us?'

~

Nanda Devi did not withhold herself from any of the pilgrims led by Myna, the Flame of the Forest. She proved no whit less gifted than the best-trained guide. Being a lay sister of the Kamli-Wallahs her party received greater consideration than any other group in the village of Gilani. Gilani was exclusively inhabited by the Kamli-Wallahs, and they were most generous in their hospitality.

'The eye is wellnigh blinded by the vision of Nanda Devi's glory,' this was what every one of the pilgrims whispered to his neighbour. And they were telling the truth.

For I know from my own experience that no picture can evoke, no pen describe, no tongue delineate the awe-inspiring grandeur of nature's marvels to be seen from Gilani: Nanda Devi stands towering over the very sea of hills and ranges, broken up into a thousand billows flowing in different directions, stretching over a distance of sixteen hundred miles.

'Verily,' the headman of Gilani said, 'Nanda Devi is the throne of the Great God.'

"And what's the Great God like?' asked a student of Hathkhura Training College, who was with the pilgrims. He was there not to acquire merit from his peregrination, but simply because he wanted to see the Himalayas: it was more convenient and inexpensive to join a party than to undertake a journey all on one's own. He wanted to make fun of the headman, and repeated his question. 'Has the Great God four arms or ten arms?'

'A silly question,' Myna replied on behalf of the headman, 'deserves a silly answer. But I shall tell you, no one knows the Great God and everyone knows about him from his *avatars*—the incarnations of the Great God.' She then told a story, known only to those well versed in Sanskrit scriptures.

Everyone was amazed. 'Our Flame of the Forest,' the villagers murmured, 'has been inspired by Nanda Devi. Now we know why she wants to stay behind. She wants to converse with the deities of the mountains when all the pilgrims have departed.'

They understood her, but not the student from the Training College. He continued his silly questions right to the moment of his departure.

~

The story Myna told was this:

Once upon a time, because the Spirit Supreme willed it, the deities wrought a victory over the demons. And they gloried in that victory. 'Ours,' they thought in their pride, 'ours, indeed, is this triumph. Ours alone is the palm.'

And He read their thought and made himself manifest to them in the form of a phantom.

They, however, failed to recognize him. 'Who is this?' they marvelled: 'He fills us with wonder.' They then spoke to Agni, the deity of fire and light: 'O thou all-seeing and all-knowing Agni, without whose blessing nothing is engendered in the universe! Wilt thou go and see who is this being that fills us with wonder?'

'Indeed, I will,' said the deity of fire as he ran towards the phantom.

And the phantom asked, 'Who art thou? What puissance is in thee?'

'I am Agni, the divinity of fire and light. I am omniscient: the deity who knows all things, sees all things: one who can kindle and consume everything in this wide world.'

'If so,' the form said, presenting a blade of grass to Agni, 'then burn this up.'

And the deity of fire strove with all his might and yet he could not kindle it. Thereupon he returned to the other gods and declared, 'I cannot find out who or what is this that fills us with wonder.'

They then addressed Vayu, the deity of the wind and the air and the ether: 'O thou Vayu, who are omnipresent! Wilt thou find out who or what is this phantom that fills us with wonder?'

'Certainly, I will,' said Vayu as he rushed towards the form.

And the form asked as before, 'Who art thou? What power is in thee?'

'I am Vayu, the lord of the wind and the air and the ether. I am omnipresent. I am in the heart of everything. I ride the whirlwind and direct the storm. Indeed, thanks to me the stars move in their courses.'

'If so,' the form said, presenting a bit of straw to Vayu, 'blow then this away.'

And Vayu strove with all his power and yet he was unable to move it. He then returned to the others and confessed, 'I cannot find out who or what is this that fills us with wonder.'

At this they all turned to Indra, the wielder of the thunderbolt, and said, 'O Indra, thou who are omnipotent, wilt thou find out who or what is this phantom that fills us with wonder?'

And as Indra hastened towards the form it hid itself; it vanished. In its place there appeared a damsel of radiant beauty who was no other than Nanda Devi, the incarnation of divine wisdom. And Indra asked her, 'Do you know who it is that fills us with wonder?'

'The Spirit Supreme,' she answered. 'Rejoice in Him. Since through Him you have triumphed and attained the glory of victory.'

Thus only did the deities themselves learn from Nanda Devi all that they know of the Great God.

~

After the pilgrims had left, Myna wandered all by herself in the direction of the forest of the flowering bamboos.

She had not gone far when a red-faced monkey coughed from a low branch of a mulberry tree to attract her attention. It sounded so much like a man clearing his throat that Myna took no notice of it.

Moreover, she was in a distracted mood. Was it right on her part to enter into a debate with the student from the Training College? Did not Padre Johan recount that the Redeemer never wasted words on scoffers? Who was she to talk about the Great God? All that she knew was the precepts of the Kamli-Wallahs. They counselled her to help only those who sought her help. 'It is God's world,' they told her. 'Both good and bad go to make the world. You will be wasting your time if you try to drive every unbeliever to see his folly. Do good in your field and that is the highest service expected of you.' But what really was her field?

By now she was far from Gilani. She did not, however, realize the distance she had covered. Nor did she hear the coughings of the monkeys from the branches of the trees: for it was not one but several of those red-faced apes that were now sounding their warning. In the stillness of the sunset hour the monkeys were giving their cautionary message to all the beasts of the forest: 'Beware! Beware! There is a law-breaker. Keep away from the drinking-pool. Keep away.'

Myna was going in the very direction of this drinking-pool. The sun had set, but the crests of the mountains still glowed: they were giving back the light of that sunken sun. The shadows had already gathered in the valleys below. It was time for the animals to come to the pool. But the warning given by the monkeys kept them away: 'There is a law-breaker.'

In the *Book of the Forest* of our Great Epic, the Catechizer asks, 'What upholds the universe?' And the neophyte responds, 'The law.' 'Who have no faith in law?' 'The demons.' 'What happens when the demons break the law?' 'It means the end of a *kalpa*.' And what is a *kalpa*?—A *kalpa* may mean an age, an epoch, an established order, an acknowledged tradition, a way of living. The end of a *kalpa* ushers in a period of storm and stress, a time of troubles till a new order with a new code of law takes shape. Woe to them, both individually and collectively, who experience the breakdown of the law—the end of a *kalpa*—for they will go through great tribulations. Must they inevitably suffer? No, not necessarily: for if they have faith they will die in this life to be reborn into a new one.

Myna mused, absentmindedly.

The monkeys kept on their strange calls: 'There is a law-breaker.' But Myna did not hear. And even if she had heeded she would not have understood the language of the monkeys.

A little fawn came out from nowhere and began trotting in front of her. It was not afraid of Myna, nor of the coughing sounds made by the monkeys. Probably it was so thirsty that it did not care whether there was a law-breaker near the pool or not.

'Kaza! Kaza!' came the wheezing sound from above the branches. The monkeys were no longer coughing, only one of them—perhaps their leader—made the ominous uttering, 'Kaza! Kaza!' Still neither the fawn nor Myna took any notice of this warning.

Everyone knows the meaning of 'Kaza'—it is *kalpa* of a sort: some call it *the hour of fate*, the critical moment when you become a willing prey to the demon who breaks the law. The law sustains the universe, and the law prevails in the jungle, too. The law of the jungle has nothing in common with the oft-told tale of permanent lawlessness: jungle life does not consist of the hunter and the hunted; it has little of the popular 'talon and tush and claw' whether in the jungles of the Penhari Parganas or in the forests of the Himalayan slopes. Had that been the case our sages would not have recommended the neophytes and the acolytes to dwell in the forests at least for some time. From time immemorial the *munis*, the *rishis*, and the *sadhus*—

the sage as well as the seeker—would not have sought lessons of peace and serenity in the deepest and wildest woods of Hindustan. To forget for a while the strains and stresses of the outer world, nothing is so helpful as a sojourn in the jungle. However, let it be repeated, the jungle has its laws and these cannot be violated with impunity; any breach would lead to swift retribution, irrevocable punishment. A false step may lead to total annihilation. There is no mercy for the absent-minded, and no charity for those who do not know the meaning of the word 'Kaza'.

A growl from the undergrowth brought Myna back to her senses and she saw in front of her two glowing balls of greenish fire—the eyes of a tiger: the demon law-breaker squatting near the water pool to destroy any unsuspecting animal that came to quench its thirst. In a fraction of a second she realized the hopelessness of her situation, and made no attempt whatever to escape. Vaguely she remembered the little fawn that had kept her company up till then. Where was it? She stretched out her arms to snatch it away if possible from the jaws of imminent death.

Then the earth suddenly reeled like a storm-tossed boat, and she reeled, too, and hit the back of her head on the stony ground; the next moment she found the pair of greenish balls of fire gazing into her eyes, while her hands held a warm, palpitating bundle of flesh, no bigger than a baby—the mangled fawn. What happened after then she did not remember clearly. She heard the curious barking of a doe that had rushed at her almost at the same time as the tiger. The earth reeled again, and a sharp pain on the back of her head made her close her eyes.

~

When she opened them again she found she was bathed in blood, lying on the ground, and her hands still clutching at a mass of shredded flesh: it was no longer warm; it was the remnants of the dead fawn. Instead of taking her the tiger had taken the doe that came to the rescue of its young.

It was all quiet now. Lying on her back she saw Nanda Devi draped not in the usual mantle of spotless white, but in silvery resplendence—like a warrior in shining armour; a wisp of a cloud was moving about the summit—it was like the banner of victory. The moon was high in the sky and it made a silvery day of the landscape; it spread a veil of weird phosphorescence over the mountains, the ridges, the hills, the trees, and the tarns.

The wind rose to chant the choir of the elements. The tall conifers waved their arms, while the flowering bamboos whistled. High up in the sky, skirting the crests of the mountains, curiously-shaped clouds ran about hither and thither as though they were wild horsemen searching for an unsaddled rider. Then there was the sound of drums accompanied by the clash of cymbals coming from the higher reaches of the hills.

Myna listened while her eyes began to dilate oddly: for everything she now saw was enveloped in a silvery haze, and her hearing caught whisperings of voices and sounds hitherto unknown to her. What were they trying to tell her? She strained her ears as best she could. The hills were trying to convey some message to her. The trees, too, had something to say. Even the grass beneath her was whispering a tale whose import eluded her.

Only the small fawn, or rather the torn and broken remnants of what once was a fawn—did not say anything. Its silence was to Myna far more galling than a vociferous rebuke. 'If only,' she said to herself, 'I had been more alert I could have saved it. Why doesn't it say something? Why does it not reproach me?'

Then everything, every incident preceding her encounter with the tiger came back to her mind: The warnings given by the monkeys, the awesome stillness of the forest trees, the mutterings of the drongo bird—*kaza, kaza, kalpa*—and the rustling in the undergrowth... Fear and trembling seized her and she covered her face with her hands.

~

What was this fear? Was it the dread of dying? No, it was something else. Was it, then, solicitude for life? Myna did not know. But why was she spared the tragedy of being torn limb from limb? Why was the doe accepted in her place by the tiger? Was everything written down in the Book of Fate? No, that could not possibly be the case.

A scurrying herd of mountain deer passed by her, soon to scatter in all directions, and the growl of a beast of prey reached her ears. No doubt, she thought, the tiger was coming back. She closed her eyes to compose her thoughts. But even with her eyes firmly shut she went on seeing that Nanda Devi was now draped in a dazzling mantle of flame and myriads of snow pigeons with flaming wings were circling above her. And music filled the air: at first faint, like the sound of distant temple bells, but gradually it grew louder and louder and their swelling peals made the earth tremble and the mountains quake.

Myna was no longer afraid. She was now on her knees with her hands outstretched towards Nanda Devi: the altar of the gods seemed almost to be within reach; Nanda Devi was an effulgence of light, brighter than any fire lit by man's hand... She understood now the language of the trees, the bamboos, the flowers, the blades of grass: they were singing in unison to the voices in the air, to the music of the unseen bells, and to the rhythm of the *damaru* drum of Siva: 'Glory! Glory! Glory!' The mountains, the hills, and the crags and chasms, and the valleys below responded, 'Rejoice! Rejoice! Rejoice!'

And who was she in that rejoicing throng? As voiceless and as insignificant as the smallest ant.

'In vain,' she heard the singing voices reproach her, 'the mighty elephant is asked to collect the drops of nectar hidden in the heart of the lotus. In vain will the proud lion try to collect the grains of corn scattered in the sand. In vain will the leviathan be called to collect the droplets of dew from the petals of the rose.'

'But I am as insignificant as an ant,' Myna whispered.

'He asks the ant to drink the nectar of the lotus, to gather the grains in the sand, to bathe in the dew of the rose.'

'I am like mere dust,' Myna sighed. And that very moment she heard that unless a man was reduced to dust he could not be moulded anew. So she cried, 'Reduce me to dust, Lord, and fashion me anew. Teach me to understand you.'

'Who dares understand the Great God?' a drongo bird chirped. And it dawned upon Myna that these were her very words to the student of the Training College. 'Who dares?' the bird asked again.

'Forgive me,' Myna sobbed. 'I am foolish. I am frightened. I don't know what I am good for.'

'Sing with me. Sing and rejoice. Listen to my song.'

What did the bird sing? Myna understood that the Bridegroom was looking for the Bride, and the bride Radha was playing at hide-and-seek with the divine spouse Krishna; Purush was rejoicing with Prakriti; and she, Myna, was Radha's handmaiden.

'Yes,' the drongo assured her. 'It is you who have been called. You are the Flame of the Forest, Radha's favourite. You were born at Latikagram, and the trees flowered at the hour of your birth. Sing a song to please Radha.'

'But,' Myna answered hesitatingly, 'I can't sing. I mean I can't sing well enough for this company of heavenly hosts.'

'The least gift offered with rejoicing is most welcome. You can sing. That's why you have been named Myna. Sing to my tune.' The drongo bird began whistling.

And Myna sang like an oriole pouring out a stream of golden song: Krishna's ditty in praise of Radha.

If I were a reed, a singing reed, my Radha!
I would list where'er you tryst
to keen love's secret sorrow.

If I were a bell, a ringing bell, my Radha!
I would sway night and day
to tell the lover's credo.

If I were a star, a moving star, my Charmer!
I would bend where'er you wend
to shine in Radha's halo.

Myna regained the village shortly before dawn. The sky was then a canopy of green jade and the air scented with the perfume of musk roses. Nanda Devi wore a mantle of the deepest blue—Radha's favourite colour. And far, far in the distance, a peak rarely visible from Gilani, appeared clad in the glittering saffron of the newly-wedded bride: it was Hari-ki-Piari the Beloved. Seven stars formed a chaplet round its crest. And Myna recalled that Hari-ki-Piari was one of Radha's many appellations.

~

So, she reasoned, the visions seen during her hours of agony were not mere fancy. She was from now on not an aspirant or a neophyte, but an initiate.

Lying on her bed she scrutinized the ornamental frieze that formed a band round the four walls of her room. She had seen it many times, but never examined it as carefully as now. The frieze consisted of decorative figures in low relief, and though it made a continuous band, it constituted duplications of one and the same motif—elephants and lions, satyrs and men, horses and geese, following in the wake of each other, each trying to trample down its forerunner.

These figures, she concluded, were symbols of each *kalpa*—an age in the history of man. This thought led her to deduce that during her trance near the drinking-pool of the forest she was given an insight into the past. 'To be ignorant of what occurred before you were born,' the voices told her, 'is to remain as ignorant as a child.' So she was shown the ascent of the Himalayas from the depths of the primal sea, the descent of the Ganges, the battle between the angels and the demons, the advent of the different avatars of the Great God, the visitations of conquerors, and destroyers like Genghis Khan and Tamerlane. Other epoch-making events right from the dawn of history to the churning up of the present-day world came to be unfolded before her eyes as though on a screen. She was also accorded a glimpse into the future: each *kalpa* was followed by an ugly diminutive demon representing the era of turmoil, the period of storm and stress, the years of transition between the death of an age and the birth of another. The ends and the beginnings of the *kalpas* looked very much the same: this helped her to grasp the meaning of the Sanskrit saying, 'The end is my beginning, and the beginning is my end.'

She never explained to me precisely what led her to assume that the coming *kalpa*—the era ahead of India—was symbolized by an ugly, misshapen, evil-looking dwarf. This devilish figure had tusks for canine teeth, claws for fingers, and curling worms formed a wig on its bald head: an altogether horrid creature—this symbol of the coming age. The more she scrutinized it the more she felt disgusted.

Was she expected to love it?

The visions counselled her to love all things, to bear all things, to cherish all things—to be compassionate even to the demons, for they, too, belonged to the universe of the Great God. The tiger was the symbol of his fierce embrace.

How could she love the horrible demons that rejoiced in destruction?

'O Visions!' she prayed, 'teach me how to love, or else let the mountains grind me into dust. O Unseen Voices! You told me that the Lover is nigh, but I know I am unworthy of his company. I cannot have any charity for the demons. Therefore I am not fit to be the companion of Radha the Beloved.'

Sudden gusts of fire surrounded her and a tongue of burning flame pierced her heart, penetrating to her very entrails.

'What would you have of me?' Myna sobbed.

She found her answer as she prayed:

The love for Krishna and Radha is like the cloud of fire. It sweeps the mortal from the earth to the haven of all souls, by burning up every atom of dross and the least particle of impurity. It lifts up the body to the soaring throne of the deities.

She now understood that love meant many things: the union of the lover and the beloved; the blending of the male and female principles—the necessary cause of production and reproduction as well as the source of strength, vigour and enterprise; comprehension; admiration; compassion; affection; charity; tenderness; pity; and passion, and other feelings as well.

And there were different degrees of love. Each was to be accorded what was due to each, and no one was to be totally denied: she was to refuse her love to none—not even to a plant or to a rock. For love was the key to the understanding of the universe.

'Heaven,' she heard the voices say, 'is not far off. It is round about you on this earth as it is also under the earth and above it. You hold the key to the Golden City, and it is now yours to enter it. All that you are asked is to believe, and to pray. Prayer will augment your faith.'

'But,' Myna whispered, 'I do believe. I have seen with my own eyes the Hari-ki-Piari peak in flames. Yet my flesh is weak. Tell me, how can I love the demons?'

'There are different degrees of love.'

That was true. But how was she to use her discretion? Her capacity of discernment was so restricted.

'Meditation will give you the gift to discern.'

'But I am so feeble.'

'Concentration will give you strength. Be like the sand, the yielding sand of the Jumna's strand that gladly accepts the imprint of a little child's hand. And be also like the sand, the unyielding sand on the sea's strand that stubbornly resists the storming waves' aggression.'

'I am trying to understand,' Myna murmured. 'I ought to understand.'

'You will be judged by your measure of love and the measure of your love. Love brings the supreme blessing—*Maha Sukha*.'

'What is *Maha Sukha*?'

'As a lover in the arms of the beloved, even so the soul in the embrace of the Spirit Eternal, ravished in bliss...'

But how was she to manifest her love? She knew Krishna was the avatar of the Great God. She knew, as everyone in the Penhari Parganas did, the songs in praise of Krishna the Divine Shepherd and of Radha the beloved Shepherdess. But she knew, too, that her knowledge was so limited, her accomplishments were so few.

—Did even the learned know all that was to be known of Krishna the Divine Bridegroom? Of Krishna the Divine Warrior? Of Krishna the Divine Consoler? Of Krishna manifesting himself in a thousand forms? Not even the immortals ever dared describe all the manifestations of Krishna. Jaya-Deva, the master poet of the Penharis, dealt with only one aspect of Krishna in his Song of Songs. Why could not Myna do the same and sing only songs in Love's praise and bring joy to all her listeners?

~

Myna dreamt that she was lying in an olive grove and by her side sat the *gopis*—the companions of Radha. One of them whispered to her, 'Tell all that you have seen and heard.'

'But words fail me,' Myna murmured.

'Tell, all the same, what you know. That is one way of serving Krishna and Radha.'

'Won't you first tell me your story?' Myna asked.

'Certainly, I will,' the *gopi* replied. 'Listen to my song and you will understand.'

Lord, when you came to me where I had lain
Long summer evenings, indolent and still,
Unstirred as olive branches where my hill
Melts in the vapours of the windless plain—

The night was shattered! Stars lashed from the mane
Of your great stallion, crackling hooves of fire
Beat on me so with terror and desire
That I was blind and fainted in that rain.

Give me the power to look upon your face!
Release my limbs from fear until I run
Out free to meet you! Seize me! Sweep me high
Into your mighty saddle! Up let us race
The dark steeps of the world to catch the sun
On the white summit of the morning sky!

Myna fell into a deep sleep that lasted without any break for several days and nights.

Meanwhile, the weather changed. It began with a thunderstorm that came up with dramatic suddenness. Its violence and duration surprised the inhabitants of Gilani. Then came heavy downpours: a terrifying deluge of thrashing rain, whose roar was so deafening as to drown even the terrific crashes of thunder: a frightening maelstrom of sound. The trees, the hills, the mountains and the valleys were blotted out, and the incessant lightning illuminated nothing but a silver-grey curtain of falling water. The day was changed into night, while biting squalls lashed the hillside and the earth groaned. The villagers were too preoccupied to miss Myna. The unpredictability of the weather was the only theme of their conversations. Was it an event like this that inspired Panini to write his rare verses?

At midnight in the season of showers
When the dark clouds thunder
Earth longing for the moon's lost visage,
As a widowed mother moaneth.

Myna's host, the headman of Gilani, started worrying about her after the fourth day. 'I don't mind her sleeping,' he told the villagers. 'She must be tired. But what I do mind is her refusing drinks. About eating I have never been very particular, but fancy a hefty girl denying herself my own home-made brew.' He wondered if he should not convey her in a litter to the hospital at Ghatwal.

Ghatwal was, however, in the valley, and the men of Gilani hated anything that had to do with the depressing lowlands. 'Haste is waste,' they told the headman. 'Let us take it easy. The poor girl had a hard time looking after the pilgrims from the Penhari Parganas. She evidently needs rest. Sleep won't do her any harm.'

'To take her out in this downpour would be a cruelty.' This was the view of the headman's wife. 'We ought to wait till it becomes better.'

~

Finally, Myna woke up on her own. The weather, too, changed. It became fine as usual. As usual?—No, not quite. Certainly it was fine, but there appeared in the sky some strange haloes round the sun: with mock suns on the horizontal diameter of the outermost halo and tangent arcs at its highest point, extended in the shape of cattle horns covering the sky. It was a magnificent sight: a sign foretelling, so the villagers said, a miracle.

Myna was no whit worse for her long slumber. They, however, noticed that the tone of her voice was altered; it reminded them of the music of mountain rills in summer. And when she sang her songs in praise of Radha and Krishna, they thought the angels were lauding through her lips.

'Krishna,' the headman's wife whispered, 'the Lord of the Universe is certainly glad to hear her songs.' Myna was then chanting to herself:

> Shouldst thou, O Zephyr, come to where tarries my lover,
> Tell him of me, O thou wanderer,
> Tell him from Radha that spring never lingers for ever;
> Fearful am I of dread summer –
> Summer that scorches and sears with its cloudbursts and thunder;
> Tell him to loiter not now that short spring stays in flower.

When she sang, her whole frame radiated brightness: she became like a luminous angel herself.

'What have you done, my Flame of the Forest, to become so pretty?' asked the headman's wife one day when she and Myna were together in a little bamboo shelter on their way to the market of Ghatwal. They were caught in a sudden mountain storm and had sought refuge in one of the tiny coverts, built of bamboos and roofed with *bogla* leaves, called 'resting cottages.'

Here and there where the mountain paths meet one will find these shelters, built not to provide rest but to procure protection when sudden downpours or storms strike the hillside. At such times the resting cottages are a great boon, and one may find all sorts and conditions of people there, chattering away the half hours of forced respite due to the malice, as some think, of the mountain spirits and the restless souls of the Brahmins buried under the heavy flagstones of Gilani's main thoroughfare.

'Are you in love, Myna?' asked the headman's wife. 'If so, with whom?'

Myna tried to explain as best as she could her adventure in the forest.

The headman's wife shook her head. She knew of the five paths, or rather the five phases which Kamli-Wallahs declared to be the means of serving Krishna and Radha: *santi*—calm contemplation of the godhead; *dasya*—active servitude or willing service; *sakhya*—friendliness; *vatsalya*—filial attachment, like that of a child for its parent; and *madhurya*—the tender affection of a girl for her lover. 'Of these,' she said, '*madhurya* is the most difficult. Few are worthy of it. Are you quite sure, my Myna, that you were not imagining strange things?'

'Imagining,' said the doctor of the Ghatwal hospital: he, too, was there, cooped up in the shelter for the duration of the storm. 'Imagining,' he repeated. 'That's the word. If it gets out of hand it can cause havoc. In fact, most mental catastrophes can be traced just to this: to phantasy blocking up the ways of our senses.'

'What happens then?' asked a charcoal-burner.

The doctor said something about the actual solution of a problem and its substitution by an illusory satisfaction: a mirage mistaken for a miracle. 'In high mountains such occurrences are not infrequent,' he said. 'Specially with those coming from the plains.'

'My mother-in-law suffers from phantasies,' the charcoal-burner complained. 'But she wants the real thing. No substitute will do for her. She wants a large nose-ring in gold. She imagines she is young, and insists on my giving her a gold nose-ring for her birthday. Now, what do you say to that?'

'That's nothing,' remarked a peon of the forestry service. 'The good lady wants a piece of jewellery. That's all. But my elder sister thinks that she is so very young in her sixtieth year that she can find a husband if only she reached Calcutta. I think her reasoning has gone totally wrong. How can one cure her? She has lost her senses.'

The doctor got fidgety. He looked at his wrist-watch. The storm outside did not show any signs of abatement. He wished that Myna would give some further details of her visions, but she did not open her lips any more. Had she not been told, 'Never make a laughing-stock of yourself. Never waste words on those who refuse to believe—'?

'Say what you will,' began a woman who sold cheesecakes at Ghatwal, 'people do see things at Gilani. Our Pugla Pir once went there to beg for a donkey. Since then he has not been the same as before.' For Pugla Pir did not get the donkey which he badly needed for his pilgrimage to Mecca, but he received instead two disembodied spirits on each shoulder.

'What makes you think he is possessed by two ghosts at the same time?'

'You have only to listen to him when they quarrel, and this happens pretty frequently. "You two have no business to perch on my shoulders," Pugla Pir shouts. "I don't want your advice," shrieks one of the ghosts. It uses Pugla Pir's lips to make itself heard, but, believe me, its voice is all its own: an old woman's voice. And then the other ghost says, "Mother! You won't take anyone's advice. That's the trouble with you." It, too, makes use of the poor Pugla Pir's tongue to vent its feelings, and its voice is different: it is of a young giddy girl. And they go on quarrelling in this way.'

'And what does Pugla Pir do?'

'What can he do, the poor man? "I have enough of this quarrel between a mother and a daughter," he says. "Both of you have hanged yourselves. What's the use of carrying on the squabble now that you are dead?" Pugla Pir is really sick of these two ghosts.'

'What do they quarrel over?'

'Each calls the other a slut, a mean creature, for depriving the other of a young man's attentions. And all this trouble with Pugla Pir started because he went to Gilani on a Friday.'

Murmurs of sympathy for Pugla Pir soon changed into hostile mutterings: for the company heard with surprise that he could, if he wanted, exorcise himself any moment, but he stubbornly refused to do so.

'All that is necessary is to take the name of the Sultan Solomon three times. But he doesn't want to. For he hopes to come across the young beau whom the spirits admire.'

'What good would that do to him?'

'He would love to throw him down a precipice for tempting the mother and the daughter at the same time.'

'If God can bear with the young man what business has Pugla Pir to think of murdering him? Maybe the poor man is good-looking, and it is not his fault if the women hanged themselves for his sake.'

During all this time Myna did not open her lips once. She reminded herself of the injunction of the invisible voices: she was to advise only those who sought her advice; she was a pilgrim and she was to think of the fellow pilgrims before all others. The benediction of the angels rang in her ears:

> Be thy journey auspicious: may the breeze,
> Gentle and soothing, fan thy cheek; may the lakes,
> All bright with lily-cups, delight thine eyes,
> The sunbeam's ardour cooled by shady trees,

The dust beneath thy feet the pollen be
Of lotuses, and thy path pleasantness and peace.

VII

What led Myna to assume that I was a fellow pilgrim?

It was a Friday morning when I received a further message from her: 'Balaram! Come as you are. Don't hesitate.'

The expression 'Come as you are' evoked sinister memories, and I trembled. Just then I was having the devil of a time. And I nearly got the hangman's rope round my neck. All for taking this delightful formula to be a mere metaphor while my newly-arrived guest accepted it as a literal truth. My trouble began in this way:

'Padre Johan says,' so started a rambling telegram, 'you might be able to put me up for a night or two.' And it ended with the request, 'May I come as I am?' It bore the name of the sender: Charlie.

'Charlie?' I asked myself, 'Who is he?' I knew of no one familiar enough to send me a wire for a night's lodging. Anyway, Padre Johan's recommendation decided the issue, and I wired back—most foolishly—'Come as you are.' And the next morning Dr Charles Andrews Anstruther, D.D., LL.D., did turn up in a scarecrow's rags; he had in his hands a bundle of books and a suitcase slightly bigger than a snuff-box and on his face a beatific smile. He embraced me cordially as though I were his long-lost son. 'How good of you,' he murmured, 'to accept me as your guest. How kind of you.'

I had not yet recovered from the shock of meeting one of my heroes devoid of his university gown—the useful robe which hides many things—when Charlie murmured again, 'Do you think I may have a bath?' He spoke like a child asking for a great favour. 'I feel rather dirty.' This I could easily see for myself: had he not asked for a bath I would have suggested one. Anyway, I felt a momentary relief when he got into the bathroom. This respite, however, was of short duration. Charlie called for me: he wanted something.

And from that time till my near-hanging I was kept on my feet, running to and fro, doing this or that for Charlie.

'Have you by any chance a spare shirt?' Charlie asked like an innocent child. 'The one I have is rather dirty. It needs mending.'

Dirty was not the word for it. It was filthy. And it was worn to shreds. So was his coat; the same with his shoes; the same with everything he had with him. No rag-and-bone merchant would have cared to collect Charlie's outfit. I offered Charlie the best of everything I had, and felt somewhat elated by my sacrifice: I considered myself a better man for the privilege of entertaining Charlie. He was, let me add, the hero of all the younger graduates of the Teachers' Training College: he was a friend of Tagore, and we were all Tagore fans.

To some of us Dr Charles Anstruther was the incarnation of one of the Twelve Apostles. Before the privilege of knowing him personally I used to say, 'He is like St Francis of Assisi while Padre Johan is St John of Patmos reborn.' However that may be, Charlie proved to be more than a handful to me.

Charlie, if I remember correctly, came to India to teach at a Scottish Missionary college in Delhi. As a teacher he was not very successful, but as a man he was greatly admired. He would perhaps have stayed on at this college, leading the life of an average lecturer, till his retiring age, had there not been a reshuffle among the lecturers and professors. One day Charlie found himself elevated to the principalship of his college. Others would have rejoiced at this promotion, but Charlie felt downcast. 'There are others better than I,' he told the Board of Governors. 'Choose one from them.' 'You have the gift of getting along with your difficult colleagues. You are the man for us.' But Charlie was adamant: 'The better people ought to come before me.' The Governors felt annoyed. They wanted Charlie to explain what made him think that he was not good enough to be the principal. 'You see,' Charlie confessed, 'I am no longer a good Christian. I mean a Christian as you understand the term. As it is a Christian college I think a true Christian ought to be its principal. And I shall, if you do not mind, continue to serve as a lecturer.' This was too much for the Board of Governors. There were on the staff of the college a number of Hindus, some Mohammedans, one Jew, a few agnostics, and only three Christians—Christians of the type that regarded the rest of the mankind as steeped in stygian darkness. 'When did you cease to be a Christian?' they asked Charlie, and he meekly replied that it was his eternal endeavour to lead a truly Christian life. 'But,' he added, 'I cannot possibly make any converts. I have requested Crockfords to remove my name from their directory. For I think of Christ as most Hindus do: He was an avatar of God.'

'An Avatar!' They were profoundly shocked. Charlie was accused of being drunk and ordered to withdraw. But he refused to move and, to make matters worse, repeated his remarks. 'Has Charlie taken to whisky?' someone said.

From the theological point of view Charlie's concept of Christianity was all wrong. He was asked to resign. This he did, but he did not know where to go. He had not saved a cent. His concept of Christianity taught him not to keep any money in store: a practice he had learnt from the Hindu sadhus. A sadhu, however, could count upon his followers, whereas Charlie could not: in those days he had hardly any acquaintances outside his college. He knew of no Kamli-Wallahs, and even had he known them it would not have been of great help, for the Kamli-Wallahs helped only the worshippers of Krishna and the pilgrims to the Himalayan shrines.

Charlie was virtually starving when he received a letter with a cheque from Tagore, requesting him to come to Santi Niketan to teach Greek. Thence onwards Santi Niketan became his home: he was lodged and fed there, but I do not know if he ever collected any salary. That did not, however, prevent his long peregrinations: his newly-won Brahmo admirers bought his railway tickets, just as Myna's journeys were at the expense of the Kamli-Wallahs.

~

There was, however, one great difference between Myna and Charlie. Myna could earn her keep wherever she went: if she whistled, money would come pouring in from all sides. Who would not pay a week's pay—and sometimes more—to see her dance? And when she sang it was not necessary to pass round the platter. Her listeners, even the skinflints and the close-fisted Jains, felt it an honour to put their tokens of homage at her feet. She did not collect the gifts, it was for her accompanist to pocket them, and he usually made a good job of it. (Had she stuck to the Kala Bhairab shrine for a few months, I, as her flautist, would have made enough brass to take me round the world twice.) Moreover, her comings and goings were like a bird's: she asked for nothing, sang her songs, danced her dances, gave everything that even the most covetous could ask for, and then flitted away as she had come, unobtrusively but not unregretted.

But with Charlie I ran the risk of being charged with murder: I did not know how to get rid of him.

'I have a few letters to dictate,' Charlie said shortly after his arrival. 'Where do you think one may borrow a typewriter?'

I could not possibly deny him the use of my latest American acquisition. But when I saw him hammering away with a single finger and manhandling my machine, I became alarmed. I took pity on my typewriter and suggested that it would be worthwhile to hire a stenographer.

'That's very nice of you. Do you think it would be possible to phone for one?'

I did phone for one.

And when I came back home after an absence of eight hours I found Charlie busy with not one stenographer, but three! He was dictating to one, a second person was busy copying out what had already been dictated, and a third one engaged in making clippings from newspapers!

His one night's sojourn was prolonged to seventy long days and long nights. Scores of people came from all over Calcutta to see Charlie. He was going to Geneva for an international conference as a delegate of the Indian Trades Union Congress. So, it was necessary for him to get certain things settled. Telegrams, cables, wireless messages, long-distance telephone calls were absolutely necessary for his mission to Geneva.

His capacity for work was prodigious.

He tired out during the day his stenographers with continuous dictations and during the night he kept up his activities with interviews, readings, prayer-meetings. All these took place in my room and I was expected to settle his bills: this apostle sent whatever he earned from his writings to Santi Niketan in recognition of the service Tagore rendered him when he was in a dire plight in Delhi.

My nerves were not of steel and when I received the bill for his long-distance telephone calls I felt they were frayed beyond recovery. I did my best to keep up appearances and dropped polite hints that the Trades Union Congress ought to look after him.

'Yes,' he admitted. 'They have invited me to stay at the Great Eastern Hotel at their expense. But as your room is so comfortable I find no reason why I should leave it. By the way, I should like to have some paper. Do you think it would be possible for you to spare a few sheets. There are none in your cupboard. I say, who is that pretty girl? The one whose photo I found inside your blotting-pad?'

'She is called Roma.'

'A Roman Catholic? Hum. Hum. You associate with a Roman Catholic girl!'

'I used to. But I don't now.'

'Have you discovered the folly of the Roman Church? In that case Roma has rendered you a great service.'

I remained quiet. I had not the heart to tell him that Roma was not interested in theology, but in security. She thought I was not the right type of person to associate with. And that picture of hers inside my blotter ought not to have been there: it should have been returned to her long ago.

'The Roman Church,' Charlie continued, 'exercises a most pernicious influence on the country. It is a superstitious body. I have been examining your books. It seems you are indifferent to Scottish theologians. You should make a beginning with John Calvin.'

'To know a thing,' Myna once expounded to me, 'is to become a thing, by being one with the thing.' Any doubts that I might have entertained at the time this thesis was presented to me completely vanished when I heard Charlie mention Calvin in the same breath as the Scottish theologians. My nerves, as I have said earlier, were in a bad state, and I fear I said something rude about the Frenchman Jean Cauvin, commonly known as John Calvin, an honorary Scot.

This let loose a flood of arguments from Charlie. He spoke at length on the different theological views of various puritan bodies in Scotland. And I realized why an English historian died of brain trouble: after studying various religious movements in Europe the poor man had the temerity to think that he would be able to master the niceties of Scottish theology. Naturally, his brain gave way.

'None but a Scot,' I said to myself, 'can appreciate Scottish theology.'

Meanwhile, Charlie continued his discourse. He did not believe in making converts and was charitable enough to bear fools gladly. He enjoyed the dullest of the dull hymns sung in Gandhi's circles but he hated Mozart's masses. He loved the music of the bagpipes and the beauty of bare walls and barren heaths. He found Sibelius entertaining and Haydn unbearable. He equated discomfort with virtue. He was, I discovered, a dour Scot at heart, and the Roman Catholic Church for him was the Devil's own organization: and—the most interesting of all—his love for India was based on his contempt for England.

The long debate with my ex-St Francis of Assisi gave me a terrible headache, and I went out to consult a druggist. I badly needed some sleeping tablets.

'Here you have a month's supply,' the druggist said, 'these tablets will steady your nerves as well. But you must not take more than two before going to bed.'

I do not remember the name of the stuff he gave me: it was a 'Bengal-Chemical' product—pheno-something.

~

Charlie believed in self-abnegation. He made a fine art of it. In this respect he was like his hero, Gandhi. Whether the Jain prophet of Hindu India enjoyed saccharine tablets or not I do not know, but Charlie certainly did. He insisted on these tablets and refused sugar cubes. He preferred 'Milk Maid' brand of tinned milk to fresh 'Cantilever' milk.

Was he diabetic and therefore avoiding sugar? Had he some Gandhian principle which constrained him to take tinned milk only? No, nothing of the sort.

'Poor people,' he explained, 'cannot afford sugar.' It was the same with milk. I was asked to read, or re-read as the case might be, Somerset Maugham's *Liza of Lambeth*, issued in 1898 or thereabouts.

'You will see Liza opened a tin of condensed milk for her tea.'

I understood his point of view: as the spokesman of the poor and the unprivileged of the world, he considered it his duty to practise self-abnegation. Again I had not the heart to tell him that in 1898 condensed milk of the 'Milk Maid' brand might have been cheaper than fresh milk, but it was no longer the case. As for sugar, the highly-taxed imported saccharine tablets were far, far more expensive than the best-quality sugar in Calcutta. From his talks, I gathered that since 1898 he had not bought a single article of food or clothing: he was leading the life of the Christian apostles in the days of Augustus Caesar and—like the sadhus of Mother India—was allowing his admirers the privilege of acquiring merit by looking after him. The sadhus, however, accepted whatever was placed before them: things good, bad, or indifferent. But Charlie, the Christian sadhu from St Andrews, made it clear that he would rather go without any food than take a mouthful of what contained a drop of fresh milk or a grain of natural sugar. 'The poor cannot afford articles of luxury'—was his constant burden.

'*Vous l'avez voulu, George Dandin*,' my inner self reproached me. 'You wanted it. And now you have it! Did you not tell him, *Come as you are*? What right have you to complain?'

'Only for a night's lodging,' I argued. But I knew in my heart of hearts that I was at first elated to have the privilege of entertaining a man of God, a friend of Tagore, an Interpreter of India's soul, etcetera—Charlie Anstruther, the theologian who was the pride of St Andrews and of Oxford.

Finally I told him that I could not afford to entertain him and his innumerable callers any more. The bills of his stenographers, photographers—because Charlie believed in supplying the press with his own pictures—grocers (Charlie preferred Brazil nuts, they were probably inexpensive in St Andrews in the year of grace 1898, but they were expensive rarities in Calcutta) and other caterers reached staggering figures. Charlie laughed; the innocent laughter of a boy who does not believe in a cock-and-bull story.

'I shall stay on here till we leave for Geneva. You will travel with me. I am so helpless without someone. By the way, your new saccharine tablets have a rather strange taste. I think you ought to take them back to your chemist.'

The next morning I found Charlie fast asleep when I brought him his morning tea at 5 a.m. Like Gandhi, Charlie loved to begin the day early, only to snooze for hours after breakfast. Out of consideration for my irregular hours of work he made the concession that his early-morning tea should be served at 5 a.m. and not at 4 a.m. (Women were Satan's snares! And Charlie would not let Kusum serve him.) I tried to wake him: he was a light sleeper; once he complained that lizards were noisy creatures and disturbed him considerably! I shook him. Yet Charlie refused to open his eyes. He went on sleeping as before. I knew he had the habit of placating his transcendental God once in a while with heavy doses of Scotch. But, I thought, whisky could not be the cause of his profound sleep. What was wrong with him?

I found my bottle of sleeping-tablets—a month's supply of phenobarbutol—nearly empty, while the new saccharine tablets were untouched. Both bore similar white labels, and there was no mistake about the real cause of Charlie's comatose stupor.

'Bless the Lord!' Gama said. 'Charlie is still breathing. You run to the police station to surrender yourself. I will take him to the Presidency General Hospital. Maybe the stomach-pump will save him.'

At the police station they treated me as though I were a professional poisoner. I was asked if I had tried out sleeping-tablets on other people as well. 'Not yet,' I replied without realizing the implication of my stupid answer. This, however, cleared the atmosphere: the officer sized me up as a mental degenerate, and declared curtly that he could not be bothered with silly people troubling him at impossible hours.

'You want to get your picture in the papers,' he declared as he led me out of his office. 'Well, I am not going to give you the chance. Try some other method. But for God's sake, don't come back here. Go to some other police station.'

Fortunately for me, Charlie recovered. He left the Presidency General Hospital for his plane to Europe. He was, as has been said, a member of the Delegation of the Indian Trades Union Congress to an international gathering in Geneva. Charlie's parting instructions to me were characteristic: I was to open all cables and telegrams addressed to him and forward them to Geneva by wire, of course; as for his letters and packets, these were to be readdressed to Santi Niketan.

The first cable I opened was from Geneva: it exhorted Charlie to come as he was to stay with the Tombs, and for as long as he wanted! I gave a sigh of relief, and murmured, 'Charlie! I hope you will remember your *matra* and not overtax the patience of the Tombs.'

'I have had enough of this man of God,' I told Gama shamefacedly. 'His simple needs nearly ruined me. I have used up the money I saved for my trip to Chicago.'

'When you give,' Gama replied, 'try to give with both hands. What's this new streak of meanness in you? Isn't Charlie a great man? Is it not a privilege to entertain him?'

I shook my head. 'The money on Charlie has simply been wasted. He does not realize the sacrifices I have made.'

'Don't be so materialistic,' he said. 'You may yet need a man of God to save you. Have you seen the papers? The Diwan has been dismissed from the Cabinet. He is under house-arrest.'

VIII

'This is nothing surprising,' the Diwan remarked, 'in fact, I have been expecting it for some time.'

I was amazed at the Diwan's coolness. 'Ek Nambur wants you to leave politics. Can nothing be done to bring him to his senses?'

'You see,' the Diwan spoke quietly, 'Ek Nambur is the mouthpiece of the country. He will come to his senses when the people who have voted for him come to theirs.'

In principle, it was all right. But one could not let a tyrant do what pleased him. My indignation gradually rose to white heat. The Diwan, however, remained as he was: unperturbed.

'No country gets what it does not deserve,' he repeated.

'This is poor consolation. You mean to say we of the Penhari Parganas, we deserve Ek Nambur. We did not vote for him. Of course, we were in the minority. But does not the minority matter?'

The Diwan smiled. The minority, he held, did matter. He himself belonged to that generation which claimed that the aristocratic families were the authentic voice of India, and though they were a minority they were entitled to rule India. 'Good government is no substitute for self-government! That was our slogan. We thought that the Rationalists of the West were great thinkers. We talked a lot of rubbish about the value of literacy, because we thought John Stuart Mill was a prophet. We must pay for it. Parliamentary democracy can work only where the Protestant Christian faith prevails. We had overlooked that fact.'

Did he, then, support a policy of no action against Ek Nambur?—No. Certainly not.

About collective action he had nothing to say, 'Because,' he added, 'I don't know how the masses should be approached. I cannot promise them paradise on earth as Ek Nambur is doing. But individual action is a necessity.'

In which way did he suggest that a man like me should act in the present juncture?

'Well, you are a friend of Myna, and you ought to know the answer. Has she never made you read the *Gita*?'

His long quotation from the *Gita* I found most irritating. Instead of giving a direct answer to my question he discoursed on the necessity of each individual human being fulfilling his obligations to the best of his capacity. (I had no objection to this thesis, on the contrary I was for it.) This was followed by an equally interminable and tiresome account of his mistakes in his early manhood, a list of his sins and shortcomings. The sum total of all this was that he should have followed the traditional method of retiring from active life: a *kalpa* was over and a new *kalpa* was beginning; he belonged to the one already past, and Ek Nambur's drastic measure was all the more welcome because it forced him to retire.

I found it was useless to argue with him. His mind was made up: he was prepared to take Ek Nambur's kicks lying down, apparently on the authority of the *Gita* and Krishna's injunctions!

~

However that may be, I was not prepared to leave the matter as it was. I knew Ek Nambur was terribly sensitive to comments in the foreign press. 'In this respect,' Kolej Huzoor thought, 'he is on a par with Abdul Hamid, the last Sultan of the Ottoman Empire.' So, I hit upon the bright idea of sending a long cable to Charlie in Geneva, asking him to refer to the Diwan's house-arrest in one of his inevitable press interviews.

I ought to add here that Charlie, though a man of God and an ascetic in every respect, was great in giving interviews. When press reporters manifested any indifference to his movements or to his views on such burning issues as the salt tax, or the erection of a new abattoir, or the naming of a new street, or the renaming of an old one, or on other questions of similar world-shaking importance, he made it a point to badger the news-editors in his own inimitable way, and they, if only for the sake of peace, acceded to his demands. Charlie, therefore, was the ideal person for my purpose. 'Let the Diwan's house-arrest be known to the world,' I told Kolej Huzoor. He shrugged his shoulders and said, 'Don't be a fool. Ek Nambur may be like Abdul Hamid. But the world is not the same as it used to be. Today's democratic West cares mighty little for India's internal affairs.' 'But it is simply awful that a man should be driven out of politics on the false charge of collecting obscene objects.' 'My boy,' Kolej Huzoor replied, 'when the ape is king, dance before him. What business have you to quarrel with Ek Nambur over the Diwan's house-arrest? I should advise you not to get involved in this affair.' I refused to listen to him: anyway, my cable was sent. And it was acknowledged the next day.

I was highly elated with Charlie's reply: he was willing to help me. But he demanded further details by cable and also suggested that I should try to speak to him over the telephone at midnight G.M.T. 'Mont Blanc 6735 on Friday next,' was his instruction. His message ended with the encouraging words: 'Meanwhile I shall contact Delhi.'

~

Charlie's ready response made me feel that I was a mean worm. He was so friendly to me, while I was, of late, one of his embittered critics.

One of the last conversations I had with Charlie before he was taken to the Presidency General Hospital was about his stubborn refusal to learn Sanskrit or any other Indian language—ancient or modern. 'It is a marvel,' I told him mockingly, 'how you have managed to live in India for more than fifty years without mastering a single word of Hindi or Bengali or any other Indian tongue.' Had Charlie been slow in picking up a language I would have pardoned his shortcoming on this score. But this was not the case: he was a gifted linguist. Most of the European tongues, both ancient and modern, as well as Hebrew and a number of African dialects were as familiar to him as English. Yet why did he never make any attempt to master at least the Sanskrit?

The answer he gave was characteristic: he was afraid of getting confused! Shortly after his arrival in India he had tried to read a translation of the *Mahabbharata*—the Great Epic. And that settled it.

'The boundaries between the natural and the supernatural,' he stated, 'between the divine, human, and even animal creatures on the one hand and the vegetable and the inanimate world on the other, are singularly vague and undefined in the Hindu scriptures.' But was that any reason for the man who enjoyed his Homer to ignore completely the *Ramayana?* Poor Charlie felt uncomfortable. When pressed hard he elaborated his thesis:

Troops of divine and semi-divine personages appear on the Indian scene on every possible occasion. Gods, angels, men and animals, plants and rocks are forever changing places in a bewildering fashion. A constant communication is kept up between the visible world and the invisible, and such is their mutual interdependence that each seems to need the other's help. If distressed mortals are assisted out of their difficulties by divine interposition, the tables are often turned, and the perturbed deities themselves reduced to pitiful straits, are forced to implore the aid of mortal warriors and worshippers in their conflict with the demons and the titans.

'All this,' Charlie concluded, 'is extremely confusing. I have, of course, tried hard to wade through the Hindu scriptures in translation. And you won't be offended if I tell you that these are just abracadabras. Fancy gods looking to mortals for their daily sustenance! I believe your Great Epic says that the immortals are sustained by human prayers and sacrifices. Not only that, they are actually living on them. Now, that's going too far.'

'But,' I said, 'Charlie, that is India: this intermingling of the divine and the mundane. Now let me quote a sacred formula and you will judge for yourself its implications:

> *Were ye to drink deep the waters of life, even unknowingly,*
> *Then shall ye have tasted, says Krishna, of my pool of eternity.*

Charlie shook his head. He did not want me to proceed any further: the sound of the Sanskrit words grated on his ear.

'All right,' I replied. 'I won't quote anything in Sanskrit any more, but just give you the substance of a *mandala* in English.'

He would not have that either!

'Now, son,' he protested, 'I don't want to be confused. I feel very much at sea when I am dragged to admire images of the gods and goddesses. I must confess that some of them are really revolting, and when I am told that the male and the female figures embracing each other represent Krishna and Radha, well, I don't know what to say! Such statues are pornographic.'

I made a further attempt to explain the meaning of the *mithuna* images, but he refused to listen.

'It's no use quoting the Sanskrit authors to me,' he interrupted. 'About Sanskrit I feel somewhat like Macaulay. What can one make of a language that sounds like: *Na nonanunno nunnono nana nananana nanu?* No, son, it's wicked to justify pornography on the authority of Sanskrit poets.'

How could one understand Hinduism without some knowledge of the Sanskrit epics and other works?

Again Charlie shook his head, 'Hinduism is all confusion.' He contended that a confusing theology would produce men with muddled minds: 'You can never predict a believing Hindu's reaction to any unforeseen situation. That's why the Hindus take recourse to astrology. They do not want to be caught unawares. Take, for example, the Diwan. He is an excellent man, I don't doubt it for a moment. But in a time of crisis, I am almost sure he will lose his head. But Mahatma Gandhi, being a Jain, will stick to his principles. Tagore, being a Bramho, will do the same.'

I remembered all this, and called myself a cad. Charlie was as excellent as John Ruskin; like Ruskin, he thought Hindu art was beyond him and Hinduism an impenetrable and foetid jungle.

~

But Charlie was perfectly right about the unpredictability of the Diwan's future action. However, he was taking up the matter of his house-arrest, and that was enough to make me think that the thousand rupees spent on entertaining him were well spent.

Then came the thunderbolt: a further cable from Charlie suggesting that I should ring him up at about four in the morning, Calcutta time; 4 a.m. in Calcutta was about 10 p.m. in Geneva. The address he gave was 2 Tacconnerie, Geneva Quaker Centre.

Our telephone conversation was brief: Charlie declared that he could do nothing because he had heard from Ek Nambur that the Diwan had obscene images at the entrance of his house, and not only that, he worshipped those images in public. I told him that his information was wrong: the images were of Anadi and Ananta—the symbols of eternity overcome by God. 'In that case,' he assured me, 'I shall see what can be done.'

Two days later, at a still more impossible hour, a further telephone conversation took place.

'Son,' Charlie's voice announced, 'I did ring up Delhi and had a long talk with Ek Nambur about the Diwan.'

Ek Nambur, by the way, belonged at one time to the same college at Oxford as Charlie. Therefore, in spite of his sternness, Charlie had a soft corner in his heart for this modern Nahush; though it was incomprehensible to me why a Doctor of Divinity of St Andrews—a most upright Presbyterian—should have any sympathy whatsoever for an unscrupulous demagogue and a dirty-minded rogue like Ek Nambur. But Charlie's reasoning was not mine. He found Foni Dhar's *Nosegay* a fascinating anthology simply on the score that it contained some verses by the poetaster Montgomery. 'Some of Montgomery's hymns are wonderful,' Charlie proclaimed, and that, according to him, was reason enough to rejoice in that abominable collection of mediocre poems by nonentities. Professor Dhar was also a graduate of Oxford, and maybe it was on this score that Charlie went to the length of justifying this crazy man's predilection for such modern 'English' (!) authors as Edith Wharton, Ellen Glasgow, Ella Wheeler Wilcox...and E. M. Forster. Dhar simply adored the successful and particularly those old women whose Christian names began with 'E'! What was E. M. Forster doing in his list of Hypatias? 'Because,' Foni Dhar asserted, 'E. M. Forster's knowledge of India is as profound as Ethel M. Dell's, and he is as successful as Ella Wheeler Wilcox.' I believe it was his sense of loyalty to all Oxonians that constrained Charlie to reprimand me for my evil habit of teaching my students to hum in the hearing of Foni Dhar a doggerel to the melody of *Frère Jacques*.

> William Shakespeare, William Shakespeare,
> Forster as well, Forster as well,
> Ella Wheeler Wilcox, Ella Wheeler Wilcox,
> Ethel M. Dell, Ethel M, Dell.

To come back to my long-distance talks with Charlie, I heard over the telephone how the nominal Christian Ek Nambur was trying his best to rid India of her many superstitious habits: the *holi* festivity—the Hindu Saturnalia—was going to be suppressed in the towns as soon as circumstances would permit Ek Nambur to frame a new law; later on, it was going to be prohibited in the villages as well; Ek Nambur was going to modernize the Hindu calendar to suit the requirements of an American Association for Uniform Dating; Buddha's relics were to be distributed among the neighbouring—and backward, in Ek Nambur's estimate—countries: these and various other schemes of Ek Nambur were lauded by Charlie. Finally, he announced that I should not try to mislead him about the obscene images in the Diwan's house: I had only referred to Krishna's triumphing over the Nagas and the Naginis at the back entrance, but I had no business to overlook the far more shocking statues at the main entrance: these were life-size copulation figures!

'If you can get them removed,' Charlie said, 'son, you would be doing a service not only to the Diwan but to the whole country. I hear they are simply revolting. Ek Nambur tells me that they are filthier than any at the Black Pagoda. Now it is up to you to do a good job. Get those obscene statues destroyed, and the Diwan's house-arrest will come to an end.'

Here our conversation ended. I did not tell him, though for a moment I felt like doing so, that to have those statues destroyed would have meant the same thing as asking the Diwan to give up Hinduism and hang himself. Those images, which Charlie and Ek Nambur found revolting, were worshipped; they were family deities as precious as the household gods to the ancient Romans.

It was perfectly true that those green chlorite statues at the main entrance of the Diwan's house depicted *mithuna* scenes—

the male and the female representations of the Divine—Purusha and Prakriti, or Krishna and Radha—in close embrace. But they were no more obscene than Leda enfolded in the wings of the Swan or Europa ravished by the Bull. Whereas Leda and Europa belonged to the long-dead pagan Hellas, the *mithuna* images belonged to living India, the Hindu India of today. They were the visual embodiment of the theme of the tenth *mandala*—the hymn-cycle—of the most ancient Hindu scripture, the Rig Veda: something similar to the contents of the thirty-eighth chapter of the Book of Job in which the Lord asks, 'Where wast thou when I laid the foundations of the Earth?' The tenth *mandala* raises that very issue, 'Where wast thou at the dawn of creation? Knowest thou the story of the very beginning?'

> And in Him desire, the primal germ of mind
> Arose, which the prophets and the searchers say,
> Is the first subtle bond, connecting Entity
> With Nullity. This ray that kindlest dormant life ...
> Where wast thou then? ...

'John Silver is a good man,' I mumbled to myself as I left the telephone box. 'But he is no Scot. The Diwan is a good man, but he has never been to Oxford or to St Andrews. Charlie's reasoning baffles me. "A nicht dacent sort o' chiel." That's all he can say.'

Someone drew up his car by the kerb-side. I recalled vaguely that I had seen that car and the motorist somewhere.

'May I give you a lift?' the motorist asked as he threw open the door for me.

I shook my head: I preferred walking.

Only a drunkard ever proposes a free lift in Calcutta. No one in his senses, I thought, would dream of offering a man any help at five o'clock in the morning in this strange city where friendliness is uncommon. I was, as might be surmised, returning from the Central Post Office at Dalhousie Square to my lodging. I had to go there for my telephone call to Geneva. My conversation with Charlie was made from a special box fitted with earphones for the convenience of the Censors: censorship had recently been introduced by Ek Nambur over all international communications. On the whole, the new arrangements were satisfactory: the boxes looked like huge glass bowls and you felt like a fish watched from all sides, and I could see for myself the faces the censors made when I had my international phone call. I was told that there were mechanical devices for recording every word one uttered. Nevertheless there were censors with earphones and shorthand pads to intimidate you in case you said anything against Ek Nambur or the *khadiwallahs* and their associates the *topiwallahs*.

'Won't you come in?' the motorist asked again. 'You won't find a taxi at this hour.'

I thanked him and told him that I was opposed to such lifts on principle. The last occasion when I had enjoyed this sort of hospitality left a mark on my mind and a gap in my heart. I was then walking along the Strand with Roma when a chauffeur-driven duck-yellow car stopped by our side and a big bald head peered out of the window of the back seat. 'Hello!' the owner of the bald head shouted: it was my friend Daud Benisraeli. 'Come on in,' he cried. I did not care for Daud's invitation for a lift, but Roma did. We had a brief altercation, and finally Roma alone got into the luminous duck-yellow limousine, while Daud whistled provokingly:

> If wealth is thine, the maid is thine
> For maids are won by gold:

But wealth is now no longer thine
And her you may not hold.

I retorted with some blunt remarks about the advantages of owning a speckled bald head: Daud's head was as hairless as a green coconut-shell, and spotted like a tree-climbing toad's back. This made Roma furious. Perhaps the word 'speckled' reminded her of the Sanskrit stance we two had translated into Latin that very morning—a variant of the lampoon on Professor Foni Dhar.

His speckled pate shines like a copper kettle:
Yet his business roars with his 'Baldness Cure.'
Marry him? Good God! No!
I am just a friend, and his wellwisher, too.

'Don't be rude,' Roma cried. 'I have had enough of you,' she hurled at me as the car drove off. And that was the last I saw of Roma. Since then I never felt like responding to any motorist's invitation for a free ride.

But the motorist was insistent. 'I know you very well,' he said. 'You ought to remember me. Did you not captain the Calcutta University F.C. when we all went to Nagpur?'

I was still hesitant. 'Maybe,' I said to myself, 'you were with me when I was in Nagpur. But that is no reason why you should go out of your way to give me a lift.'

'I want to talk to you,' he continued. 'I was waiting for you at the corner of the General Post Office when you were telephoning Geneva, Mont-Blanc 6735?'

How did he know that I was talking to Dr Charles Anstruther, and my communication was with Geneva?

'You see,' he whispered, 'I belong to the C.I.D. Headquarters at Elysium Row. The moment an international telephone call is fixed we are informed. In fact, no long-distance communication can be arranged without consulting us.'

'Now I understand. But what do you really want?'

IX

He broke the news gently: in brief, I would do well not to return to my hostel just then. My room was being searched under the Defence of the Realm Regulations and the newly-enacted Anti-Communist Emergency Measures. It was likely that all my books, pamphlets, manuscripts, and other belongings would be sealed and taken away to the C.I.D. Headquarters and kept there until the police received further instructions from Delhi.

'Have you a summons for arresting me?' I asked.

'No,' he assured me. 'There are no orders for arresting you as yet. Only your papers will be carefully examined—not here, but in Delhi. And then you will hear what they have to say.'

'Hear what?'

'You know what I mean. They may discover things that are seditious. I don't mean to say that you are a communist. But in these days someone in Delhi may plant anything.'

'Of course,' I said, 'they may also find some obscene pictures. I have reproductions of the statues of the Black Pagoda.'

'Well,' he interrupted, 'you understand. That's why I have made it a point to see you. Now let me be brief. Would you care to be my guest till the storm blows over?'

What could I say? The news was a bolt from the blue. However, I still wanted to know why he should go out of his way to be helpful to me? Did he by any chance come from the Penhari Parganas?

'I want you to take a boat trip,' he went on, 'as my guest. There is a Portuguese steamer leaving the Prinsep Ghat soon. We have just fifteen minutes. I think we can make it.'

Did he suggest that I should go to Portugal as a stowaway? No. He did not propose my getting into a ship destined for Europe: she was only a coasting steamer—one of those 1,000-tonners that plied between Calcutta and Karachi, touching at the French settlement of Pondicherry and at the Portuguese foundation of Goa, and occasionally went to Timor and Macao as well. He repeated that he was most anxious that I should make myself scarce for a few months. He had bought a ticket for me to Goa, but I could, if I wanted to, get off at Luktam and stay there as the Rajah's guest.

'How do you know that the Rajah of Luktam would care to have me?'

'I shall tell you in a minute. There's hardly any time to waste. You know Myna? The Flame of the Forest? She wants you to come as you are.'

~

'Did I hear you say,' I asked, 'I should come as I am?'

'Yes,' he answered, somewhat puzzled at my question.

By now I recognized him; he was Sunjoy Dutt, one-time cheer-leader of the University Football Club. I was apologetic for my absent-mindedness and slowness in recalling faces. (A cheer-leader is an important man in a football club—in fact, in all organizations in Calcutta. A political demonstration without a cheer-leader would end in a fiasco. The Liberals and the Moderates suffered defeat in the general election because they foolishly refused to hire cheer-leaders at their meetings. An able cheer-leader is an asset and he commands a higher fee and greater esteem than the most gifted lecturers in Calcutta.) How stupid of me not to have recognized at first sight Sunjoy Dutt as the man responsible for the University Football Club's victory in Nagpur and in many other places? I renewed my apologies, but a moment later, as I scanned his face, I burst out laughing.

He thought I had an attack of hysteria due to the sad news he had broken to me. He murmured that he was very sorry on my account, and repeated that I would be doing no one any good by staying on in Calcutta.

'Now, Sunjoy,' I said, 'don't look so miserable. I can't help laughing, because I have overdrawn my bank account thanks to Charlie. You know Charlie Anstruther of St Andrews? We nearly blew the roof off the Senate House with our cheers when he received the D.Lit. *honoris causa.* This man of God came to spend a night with me and stayed on and on till I became broke. Would you believe it? I asked him to come as he was. And now Myna wants me to call on her as I am!'

He did not get my point: he just reminded me that my berth in the steamer had been paid for, and he was prepared to lend me all he had on him.

~

As we drove towards the Prinsep Ghat I told him that my chief worry was not myself, but the Diwan. 'He ought to have put up a fight,' I repeated more than once.

It was better, I propounded, to have fought for the right, to have done one's best and to have failed, than to accept the order of things that the modern Nahush proposed. Ek Nambur wanted to destroy all *mithuna* images because they irritated the susceptibilities of his American admirers. 'Naturally, the Diwan cannot give him the backing he needs for his new iconoclastic frenzy, but the old boy ought not to have taken things lying down. Before his house-arrest he should have made an attempt to expose Ek Nambur.'

Sunjoy did not appreciate my point of view. He held that at times it was prudence itself to lie low. Perhaps the Diwan was more concerned with his dependants than with his own reputation. He was the only breadwinner for two hundred mouths. How could he afford to quarrel too openly with Ek Nambur?

'As for you,' he added, 'say what you will, prudence has never been one of your distinguishing qualities. Take, for example, your conversations with Charlie. Are you innocent enough to think that your talks with Charlie in Geneva have not been listened to by Ek Nambur?'

'That shows Ek Nambur's bad breeding. You know our Penhari saying, "It is well to hear, but it is bad to listen." Anyway, it must have warmed his heart to know that an Oxonian always backs an Oxonian. Do you know that Charlie belongs both to St Andrews and to Oxford?'

We were now beyond the Holkar Monument on the Hooghly river.

'Forgive me,' Sunjoy said as he stopped his car. 'I think it would be prudent if I were to leave you here. I don't want to be seen by my colleagues at the jetty. There is your steamer. She is called the *Maria*.'

He gave me my ticket and produced, curiously enough, a string of *tulasi* beads—prayer beads—similar to those that Myna offered me when I met her for the first time in Calcutta. Without my knowing it I made the same gesture as the Diwan on the day when I saw him with his dog in the back garden of his house: I joined the palms of my hands and bowed my head. Sunjoy seemed to be moved by my spirit of reverence. I ought to admit, however, that my salutation was more automatic than reverential.

'Perhaps,' Sunjoy murmured, 'I ought to tell you now that I belong to the Kamli-Wallahs. I am a lay brother. Sister Myna, the Flame of the Forest, hopes you will kindly accept these beads as her message of welcome.'

X

'So that was that,' I said to myself as I got into the cabin retained for me by the lay brother of the Kamli-Wallahs, Sunjoy Dutt. 'Perhaps the Rajah of Luktam, too, belongs to the Kamli-Wallahs. And his niece, Myna? Myna must be something more than a mere lay sister.'

I swallowed a lump in my throat: my departure from Calcutta was so very different from what I had long visualized. In my day-dreams, how often had I not imagined for myself a lectureship in some remote and picturesque place like Bundi or Pushkar? I had fancied a grand farewell party in my honour and a send-off with bands and bouquets, gorgeous garlands and flowery speeches from those I had coached to pass their examinations. 'No pass, no fee' was my slogan, and I had to my credit that apart from the skinny girl of the Ultra-Modern Hindu Hotel, not one of my students had failed.... And now? I was running away like an outlaw, almost caught in the net spread by Ek Nambur.

It was getting bright outside, but I decided to stretch myself on my berth and to sleep off my fatigue. Ever since Charlie's arrival at Calcutta as my guest I had been leading the life of a homeless dog. With Charlie's departure came the Diwan's house-arrest. And then my own bother. All these happened at a time when I least expected them.

I was too exhausted to fall asleep immediately. So I kept on turning over in my mind the details of the events in their swift succession: my meeting Myna, my quarrels with Professor Foni Dhar, my working with the Diwan, my writing for *Life-in-Technikolor*, my entertaining Charlie, and finally my bidding adieu to Calcutta. For how long was I to stay away from Calcutta—the city I hated and loved at the same time? I did not know. 'Till the storm blows over,' was the time-limit suggested by Sunjoy Dutt.

What did I regret most at that moment? It may sound unbelievable, but it is God's truth, I sighed for Piram: I deeply regretted not bidding good-bye to that ferocious bulldog with bright eyes. Now I realized the bitter truth of Myna's casual remark: 'Many a man would rather have a good reputation with a dog than with the majority of his fellow men.' I fondled the 'silent' dog-whistle I had in my breast pocket; it was a cherished gift from a couple of Chinese boys who lived near Tu Fan's Chop Suey Shop.

What was the most amusing incident that came to my mind? My brief amorous interlude with Kusum, whose horrible cooking was tolerated by the inmates of my hostel not on account of my special pleadings on her behalf, but because they all had received, at one time or another, Kusum's favours. And I was foolish enough to think until recently that I was the only one to be so honoured! It was Charlie who had ferreted out this scandal and passed on the information to me, assuming that I was different from the rest. Thank God, I never revealed to him that I was the only one of the hostel to have made a pact with Kusum and received her invitation to stay whenever I wanted in her cottage at Midnapore; this privilege was mine because of the appreciative compliments I had showered on her generous bosom.

Kusum's prayer for the undoing of her one-time lover—the Bahurupi—came to my mind, and I chuckled:

> Lord! Make him remember my kisses:
> Let him but once whisper in tendress
> My name as he his mistress embraces.

It was equally entertaining to reflect on Charlie's marvellous gift of squeezing out unpalatable information from every possible source. The purity-drive was his chief distraction. Or was it a preoccupation?

What was my most soul-searing experience during my entire sojourn in Calcutta? The ordeal of entertaining Charlie. It was a privilege and a trial at the same time. If I were to write a full-dress biography of this remarkable Presbyterian, what should I do?

'Perhaps,' I mused, 'I shall call him a man of God, but a most difficult person to have as one's guest. A man who was anxious to identify himself with India's most outstanding men as well as with India's poverty-stricken masses. And at the same time he was ignorant of the Hindu mind!'

'Son, don't get me confused with your myths,' was his constant refrain. 'I know what I think. I am old enough to be your grandfather, and I have travelled from one end of India to the other. Now don't confuse me with your version of the legends and epics and myths. Max Muller's translations are good enough for me, and I don't like them.'

What about Myna? I should have loved to confront her with Charlie. Charlie would probably have called her 'Satan's snare' and refused to have anything to do with her. Would he have refused to hear her sing some of Padre Johan's favourite hymns?—'Laudato San Francesco, quel c'aparve en croce fixo como redemptore...'

I did tell Charlie about Myna, about her visions, about her

wanderings, about her absolute freedom from fear. 'Why does she gad about?' was his question. 'Can she not sit down somewhere and do some nursing or some such job? India has plenty of those singing women and nautch girls. If she had any intelligence she would settle down to do some practical work.'

Some practical work! It was this *practical work* that haunted Charlie like a demon. Like Ek Nambur he wanted India to be modernized, a rival to Russia and America. He did not understand the significance of Myna's statement to the photographer of *Life-in-Technikolor*: 'The life of the mind is of greater consequence than the mechanical aids for greater production. If we lose our sense of oneness with the other worlds in which lie the roots of our thoughts and feelings, we should be unhappy even in an earthly paradise—nay, we might even grow to hate it.'

'Just words!' This was Charlie's comment. 'Words, words, and words. Bengalis enjoy the concatenation of words.' There was nothing for me to do except shrug my shoulders.

Myna's very serenity was interpreted by Charlie to be a sure sign of her stupidity. I wonder if in this world of muddle-headed people he ever came across one so clear-thinking and cool-headed as Myna. It was perfectly true she was not concerned with bringing about any immediate reform for the material improvement of mankind as a whole. But she was intensely solicitous about the spiritual growth of such individuals as came across her path. She believed and practised the formula:

> The grief of another is our own
> Neither can we another's joy disown.

The world of the mind was her field—a field which Charlie as a theologian could not possibly ignore. But Charlie's theology and

Myna's were poles apart. How could I ever explain to him Myna's doctrine of *Prakriti*— the state of equipoise of goodness, passion, and darkness. 'To understand the nature of light,' she said, 'one must have knowledge of darkness and twilight, and thus alone will full perception of resplendence be possible.' Charlie always brushed aside these discussions with his usual formula: 'Son, don't confuse me with too many words.'

Certainly Charlie was a fearless man. He fought the Big Plantations over the issue of indentured labour at a time when it was tantamount to treason to breathe a word against this form of slavery. When the condition of factory workers in Calcutta was a shame to modern civilization, Charlie decided to court the disfavour of the Government and the all-too-powerful factory owners to bring about a radical change and betterment of the lot of the workers. Charlie was indeed great. His achievements proved beyond doubt that he was a man who might have walked cheerfully to the stake, so unshakable was his faith, yet in spite of his high thinking and great erudition he seemed to have lacked the simple common sense that is frequently the perquisite of less-gifted mortals.

He had lived for fifty years in India without learning a single word of any Indian language. In 1898 he had picked up one cabalistic phrase of Sanskrit from the then Boden Professor of Sanskrit at Oxford, and that was all:

Na nonanunno nunonno nana nananana nanu.

'No man is he who is undone by a low man...' A tongue-twister from Bharavi who lived in the middle of the sixth century. Charlie might as well have quoted '*Didon dina, dit-on, d'un dos de dindon* to prove that the French language was unworthy of a theologian's consideration, or, for that purpose, the English phrase, 'When one has not what one wants one must want what one has...'

Gradually I fell into a somnolent state, lulled by a nostalgic serenade—sung at that hour of the day—by a crazy Goan to a number of giggling girls in the next cabin. Its mongrel Indo-Portuguese words were banal: a farewell ditty addressed by a jilted swain to his false lady-love. Its simple air, however, was pathetic, with that peculiar pathos characteristic of the lyrical music of the Iberian Peninsula.

Adeos, adeos, adeos, adeos
Men coracao, Alma leva retratado
Para hoje en penar.

The departing serenader, I understood, was complaining of his soul being dejected and of his body being in pain.

Quantas vexes vos me destes
Vossa mao dejirea prata
Promet en do olhe que ser fermo
Come hoje sois engrato.

This, no doubt, referred to the hopes held out by the lady to the bard, and her subsequent ingratitude.

Ai demin triste coitado
Em que horaja nasceo,
Ja nasceo na huma planeta
Para boje penar.

The singer now bemoaned his hard fate and cursed the unlucky star under which he was born.

Tu tens olhas de matar
Sobran celhas de ferir
Tu tens boca de fallar
Coracao para sentir.

The false lady's eyes could kill, her eyebrows could pierce, her mouth could conquer, but her heart—her heart—made others feel...

I thought of my lady-love, and did not listen any more.

XI

A terrific crash as though a thousand china plates were being smashed against the sides of the steamer made me rush to the deck.

The steamer berthed at the jetty of Noa Gaon. The din was the music of welcome to greet the passengers—not all the passengers, only the pilgrims disembarking at Noa Gaon. There was some sort of a religious festival, and the landing-place was gaily decorated with flags and festoons. On the river bank itself a *jatra* show was in progress—a mystery play with songs and interludes of religious dancing. The orchestra of the *jatra* consisted mainly of cymbals, bells, gongs, and an infinite variety of drums.

The cymbal-crashers were mostly women, dressed in stiff costumes and wearing papier-mâché masks covering the upper part of their faces; they had elaborate headgear. All of them looked like the Javanese wayan-wayang puppets.

The sight was enough to make me forget my worries.

I asked the officer at the gangway if I could get off the boat for a while to stretch my legs? Of course I could, for the steamer was stopping at Noa Gaon for at least five hours. Now I understood why these boats took twenty-four hours to cover less than a hundred miles—the distance between Calcutta on the Hooghly and Luktam on the Rupnarayan.

Once Noa Gaon was Portuguese. It abounds in Portuguese relics. In fact, it was founded by them at the junction of the

Hooghly with the Rupnarayan on a fork of waste land; it is much nearer to the sea than the foundations of the other sea powers of bygone days: the French settlement at Chandernagore, the Dutch 'factory' at Chinsura, the Danish centre at Serampore, and the British foundation at Calcutta. Portugal's greatest poet, Camoens, spent some time here. The villagers even point out the exact spot where he used to sit and admire the shrine of Maha Manav—the Greater Man.

Naturally, it was the place for me to explore. I regretted not having a camera with me. I was suffering from *deformation professionelle* and still thinking of my photo-reportages for *Life-in-Technikolor.* Even with an ordinary camera I could have produced a wonderful article about the masked women beating the cymbals, and the stories—apocryphal or otherwise—concerning Camoens and his first vision of the Greater Man, Adamastor. The shrine of Maha Manav must have been the source of his Adamastor. The Hindu conception of the Greater Man was, of course, different from his. Camoens's Adamastor is a hideous phantom, while Maha Manav is a godlike being—the Greater Man yet to be.

I gave only a cursory glance at the *jatra* show. The masked actors and actresses were certainly from Shearikhela. One of the singers was extolling the mysterious nature of Krishna: the dark touchstone that tries gold, the source of all bliss; everything in the world is a manifestation of his many attributes...

Thou art the black bee ...
The grace of the coryphée,
The green bird with the red beak,
The sable cloud in whose breast sleep
The lightning, the seasons, and the sea.

'Won't you take a seat?' asked a little boy as he got up to make room for me. Evidently he was a local lad, for such politeness would be impossible from one coming from Calcutta.

'No. Thank you. I want to visit the shrine of Maha Manav—Adamastor.'

'You will see it,' said one of the masked cymbalists, 'only when the time is ripe. What's the hurry?'

'I beg your pardon,' I mumbled. I knew the masked dancers and mummers of Shearikhela were reputed to be touchy. Therefore I tried to explain that my eagerness to visit the shrine was not due to any lack of appreciation of the show. 'Only I am rather pressed for time.'

'Always in a hurry! Where's your sense of *matra?*' she asked as she raised her mask: she was Myna.

I gasped in surprise.

'Have you lost your head completely?' Myna went on. 'To be named after Balaram is a high privilege. And what are you doing about that privilege?'

What could I say? It was a most unexpected meeting. I told her that I had the impression that she was at Luktam. Anyway, she had read my mind aright: I was capable of getting off at the first halting place of my steamer.

'Have you forgotten,' she rated, 'Balaram went on ploughing his field even when a great battle was raging in his neighbourhood? The main thing is to cultivate your own field instead of meddling with many things—like improving the universe! Are you any different from Charlie?'

'I thought you were at Luktam,' I interrupted, 'at your uncle's place.'

'My poor Balaram! You do a lot of thinking. Far more thinking than is good for you. Let us have no arguments just now. I need a flautist. Please put on this mask while I get ready. Yes. You will get your flute in a minute.'

I protested that most of the musicians were women and I should be out of place among them. She simply refused to listen to me. I was told that there were among them men in women's clothes and I could do as they.

'The amount of wordly wisdom you have acquired,' Myna kept on, 'is simply frightening. You have outshone your hero, Kolej Huzoor, and made a perfect ass of yourself. Are you any happier for the pickle into which you have dragged yourself? Now, listen, it is high time that you should start learning other forms of wisdom. I want you to be my flautist from now on till I let you go. Maybe, in a year's time. Maybe, after a life-time. What do you say to it?'

'Give me the mask,' I said. I wanted some respite to think things over.

'That's right. Try it on, and listen to what I sing. You need not play on the flute if you don't want to. But you must pay heed to my songs.'

The exact words of Myna's songs escape my memory, because while she sang my mind kept on revolving round many things. She chanted about Krishna's messenger and the message being delivered by a simple touch.

'The touch,' I understood, 'comes in strange forms. Sometimes in the guise of a sound. Sometimes in the gesture of a hand. Sometimes in the roar of the thunder. Maybe in the quake of a landslide. Or in the caress of a kiss... And at that touch, even the mightiest rock shall crumble and moulder into lesser grains than the finest sand upon the strand. For a man is ground into dust before he is moulded anew into the greater man.... For such is the will of Krishna.'

~

By the time she came, back to rejoin me my mind was made up. 'Only a fool,' my inner self exhorted, 'will seek suffering to extend his range of experience.' And I felt no urge whatsoever to experience the agonies of a permanent interne in one of Ek Nambur's Re-education Camps for Political Recalcitrants. I decided rather to bide my time for hitting back, and reminded myself of the Penhari saying:

> Like a heron be, when 'tis your time for lying low:
> Like a heron be, when 'tis your turn to strike the blow.

Moreover, the life of a pilgrim visiting different shrines fascinated me. So I told Myna that to be a nameless wanderer in her company, to seek the world, would be a privilege: to hear her sing was a delectation. 'It is something to look forward to.' I spoke the truth: 'I am ready to accompany you anywhere as I am. I want to be a pilgrim.' At this she passed a rosary of one hundred and eight beads round my neck while I was made to repeat with her the acolyte's eight-syllabled prayer: the mystic formula of dedication. She then embraced me, and touched the middle of my forehead—in between the eyebrows—with the little finger of her right hand to make the *gopi-chandan* imprint as she murmured the benediction:

> May day by day all fair things thee befall,
> May loved Radha give her grace to all.